SHAKESPEARE

FOR SQUIRRELS

Also by Christopher Moore

CHRISTOPHER MOORE

Shakespeare for Squirrels

A NOVEL

WILLIAM MORROW
An Imprint of HarperCollins*Publishers*

SHAKESPEARE FOR SQUIRRELS. Copyright © 2020 by Christopher Moore. All rights reserved. Printed in the United States of America. No part of this book may be used or reproduced in any manner whatsoever without written permission except in the case of brief quotations embodied in critical articles and reviews. For information, address HarperCollins Publishers, 195 Broadway, New York, NY 10007.

HarperCollins books may be purchased for educational, business, or sales promotional use. For information, please email the Special Markets Department at SPsales@ harpercollins.com.

FIRST EDITION

Designed by Fritz Metsch
Title page image by Morphart Creation / Shutterstock
Endpaper art © Victoria and Albert Museum, London

Library of Congress Cataloging-in-Publication Data has been applied for.

ISBN 978-0-06-243402-9

20 21 22 23 24 LSC 10 9 8 7 6 5 4 3 2 1

For Chris Trimble,
a fine squirrel in his own right

The Cast

POCKET, *a fool*

DROOL, *a fool's apprentice*

JEFF, *a monkey*

PUCK/ROBIN GOODFELLOW,
   a fairy, jester to Oberon

RUMOUR, *a narrator*

DEMETRIUS, *suitor to Hermia*

HELENA, *smitten with Demetrius*

LYSANDER, *in love with Hermia*

HERMIA, *Egeus's daughter, in love
   with Lysander*

Fairies

COBWEB

PEASEBLOSSOM

FLUFFER-NUTTER

MUSTARDSEED

MOTH

The Rude Mechanicals

BURKE, *captain of the watch*

TOM SNOUT, *a tinker*

SNUG, *a joiner*

NICK BOTTOM, *a weaver*

FRANCIS FLUTE, *a bellows mender*

PETER QUINCE, *a carpenter*

ROBIN STARVELING, *a tailor*

GRITCH, *a goblin*

TALOS, *a goblin*

TITANIA, *queen of the fairies*

OBERON, *king of the goblins*

THESEUS, *Duke of Athens*

HIPPOLYTA, *queen of the Amazons*

EGEUS, *chamberlain to the duke,
   father of Hermia*

BLACKTOOTH, *man of the watch*

The Setting

The setting is a very mythical fourteenth-century Athens and the forest and mountains around it.

SHAKESPEARE

FOR SQUIRRELS

ACT I

The jaws of darkness do devour it up:
So quick bright things come to confusion.

—LYSANDER,
A Midsummer Night's Dream, 1:1

CHAPTER I

He Is Drowned and These Are Devils

WE'D BEEN adrift for eight days when the ninny tried to eat the monkey. I lay in the bow of the boat, under the moonlight, slowly expiring from thirst and heartbreak, while the great beef-brained boy, Drool, made bumbling snatches for the monkey, who was perched on the bowsprit behind my head, screeching and clawing at my jester's hat, and jingling his bells in a festive manner.

"Sit down, Drool, you'll capsize us."

"Just one wee lick," said the giant, grasping the air before him like an enormous baby reaching for his tiny monkey mother. The bow of the boat dove under Drool's weight. Seawater splashed the monkey's bottom; he shrieked and made as if to fling poo at the giant, but it had been eight days since any of us had eaten and he could birth no bum-babies for the flinging.

"There will be no monkey-licking as long as I draw breath."

"I'll just give him a bit of a squeeze, then?"

"No," said I. On the fourth day, after the water ran out, Drool had taken to squeezing Jeff (the monkey) as if he were a wineskin and drinking his wee, but now the monkey was dry and I feared the next squeeze would produce little but a sanguine monkey marmalade.

"I won't hurt him," said the oaf, so inept in the lie that he might as well have tied bells on the truth and chased it around the town square while beating a drum.

Drool dropped back onto the seat at his end of the dinghy, his weight sending the bow up so rapidly that Jeff was nearly launched into the drink. I caught the monkey and comforted him by slapping my coxcomb over his head and holding it fast until he stopped biting.

"But . . . ," said Drool, holding a great sausage of a finger aloft as he searched the night for a point.

"Shhhh, Drool. Listen." I heard something beyond the lap of waves and the growl of my gut.

"What?"

I stood in the boat, still hugging the monkey to my chest, and looked in the direction of the noise. A full moon puddled silver across the inky sea, but there, in the distance, lay a line of white. Surf.

"It's land, lad. Land. That way." I pointed. "Now paddle, you great dribbling ninny. Paddle, lest it be an island and we drift by."

"I will, Pocket," said Drool. "I am. Land's the dog's bollocks, ain't it?"

He showed less enthusiasm than the revelation should have engendered.

"Land, lad, where they keep food and drink."

"Oh, right. Land," he said, a spark finally striking in the vast, dark empty of his noggin.

The pirates had set us adrift without oars, but Drool's arms were long enough that if he lay down he could get enough of a hand in the water to paddle. By his sliding from one gunwale to the other, the little boat sloshed slowly forward. My arms would barely reach the water, and as it turned out, though the monkey could swim, even with a sturdy cord tied round his middle, Jeff was complete shit at towing a boat.

An hour or so later, what had been a calm sea began to rise up on rollers, and the blue-white lines I'd spotted churned into a briny boil. What had been the distant swish of surf now crashed like thunder before us.

"Pocket," said Drool, sitting up, his eyes wide and alight with fear. "I don't want to paddle no more. I wanna go back."

"Nonsense," said I, with enthusiasm I did not feel. "Once more unto the breach!"

And before I could turn to see where we were headed, a great wave lifted the boat and we were driven ahead on its face, racing as if on a sled down a never-ending slope. Drool let loose a long, terrified wail and gripped the rails as the stern was lifted, lifted— and then we were vertical on the face of the wave. I looked above me to see a great flailing nitwit flying in the night and a monkey tumbling with him. Then the wave crashed down upon us. I lost my hold on the boat and was awash in a confusion of salt and chill. Over and down and over until there was no up, nowhere to go for air, and no way to get there. Then a light. The moon. A tumble, and there again, the silver above, shining life. I kicked, hoping to find some purchase on sand, but there was nothing but water; then the moon, and a black specter diving out of the silver disc above— the boat. I tried to tuck my head but too late and then a shock and a flash in the eye as the boat struck me and all was dark. Oblivion.

*   *   *

THERE WERE flames dancing before me when I woke from the dead, which was not entirely unexpected. The devil was smaller and rather younger than I would have guessed. He danced barefoot around the fire as he stoked it in preparation for my torment. The fiend wore a tunic of rough linen, leaves and sticks clinging to it, and a bycocket hat with a single feather in the style of bow hunters back home in Blighty. Bit of a ginger fringe. Scrawny and pathetic, really, for the prince of bloody darkness.

As I stirred, the fiend made his way over to me and studied my face. He had wide eyes and high cheekbones, decidedly feminine, which gave him the look of a cat that has been surprised in the middle of his repast of a freshly killed rat—alert and fierce.

"He's awake," said the demon.

"Pocket!" I heard Drool say, at which point pretending to still be dead was a fool's errand.

I looked over to see the great oaf sitting splayed-legged on the other side of the fire, a massacre of nuts and berries in his lap, the smeared evidence of their fate already streaming down his chin in red rivulets. "Cobweb saved us," said the ninny. "She's the git's tits."

"She?" said I. "So not the devil?"

"'Fraid not," said the girl.

Of course, a girl. I looked over the figure crouched before me like some gamine gargoyle. Right tiny, and in need of a good scrubbing, but I supposed a girl she was. And not a child, neither, despite her size.

"I didn't do so much of the rescuing as your large friend," she said. "On the beach I jumped up and down on his back until he was breathing again. He carried you up here into the forest." She leaned into me to whisper. "Methinks he may have taken a blow to the head during the wreck. He seems a bit slow."

"Slow is his only speed, I'm afraid."

"You took quite a shot to the noggin yourself." She touched a spot above my forehead and I winced with the pain. "Covered in blood, you were. I cleaned you up."

I touched the tender lump on my head and bolts of pain shot across the corners of my vision, a deep ache throbbed behind my eyes. Only then did I notice I was lying on a bed of ferns and leaves, naked but for my hat, which had been draped modestly over my man bits.

"Your kit is drying still," said the girl. She shot a thumb over her shoulder to indicate my motley, propped on sticks before the fire, along with my jester's scepter, the puppet Jones. "You'll want to wash it proper in fresh water when you get a chance. Most of the blood came out in the sea, but not the salt."

"What about Jeff? Where's my monkey?"

"Weren't no monkey, sirrah. Just the big bloke and you." She held out a leather wineskin. "Here. Water. Slowly. Your friend drank it all in one draft and I had to fetch more at the stream."

"Had a wee chunder," said Drool.

I took the wineskin and thought I might swoon again as I drank the cool water and felt the fire in my throat abate.

"Enough for now," said the girl, taking back the wineskin. "There's food, too, if the big one's left anything."

"I saved you some, Pocket," said Drool, holding out my codpiece, which was spilling berries as he moved.

The girl returned and handed me the codpiece. "Wondered what these things was for."

"Thank you," said I. My cod was nearly full of berries and nut meats. I thought I might weep for a moment at her kindness and pinched the bridge of my nose as if chasing away a headache.

"Your friend says you are fools," she said, giving me shelter.

"I am a fool. Pocket of Dog Snogging upon Ouze, at your service." I tow a train of titles behind my name—royal fool, black fool, emissary to the queen, king of Britain and France—but I thought it ill mannered to be grandiose while lying on a litter of leaves with only a hat to cover my tackle *d'amore*. "Drool is my apprentice."

"We are fools *and* pirates," said Drool.

"We are not pirates," said I. "We were set adrift by pirates."

"But you were on a pirate ship?" she asked.

"For two years," said I. "There was a girl, a Venetian Jewess who fancied me. She wanted to be a pirate but became homesick. When she returned to Venice I was not welcomed to join her."

"So you stayed with the pirates?"

"For a while."

"And they set you adrift?"

"With no food and only enough water for three days, the scoundrels."

"But why?"

"They gave no rhyme nor reason," said I.

"It was because you're a shit, wasn't it?"

"No, why would you say that?"

"Because I only have known one fool, a fellow called Robin Goodfellow, and he, also, is a shit."

"I'm not a shit," said I. I am not, that she could prove.

"Did you insult them? Make sport of their efforts and appearances? Craft clever puns on their names? Play tricks on the naïve and the simple? Compose rhymes disparaging their naughty bits? Sing bawdy songs about their mothers and sisters?"

"Absolutely not. There was no way to know if they even *had* sisters."

"I think you were a shit, just like the Puck, so they set you adrift."

"I was not a shit. And who are you to say? Why, I am deft at being rescued by wenches of great beauty and character, one for whom my heart still currently breaks, and I'll not be abused by a waif, an urchin, a linty bit of stuff like you."

"Feeling stronger then?" she asked, thin, sharp eyebrows bouncing over her disturbingly wide green eyes.

"Possibly," said I.

A horn sounded in the distance, as if to call hounds to the hunt, and Cobweb leapt to her feet. "I have to go."

"Wait," said I.

The girl paused at the edge of the firelight. "What?"

"Where are we?"

"Look around, you're in the forest, you git."

"No, what land?"

"Greece."

"It doesn't look like Greece."

"Have you been to Greece before?"

"Well. No."

"This is what it looks like. I have to go. The night queen beckons."

"The night queen?"

"My mistress calls. Rest, fool. Your friend knows where the stream is and there are plenty of nuts and berries to eat. Stay clear of the captain of the watch. He's a shit, too. And not so playful as you and the Puck."

"Wait—" But she was gone like a spirit in the night.

"She were the dog's bollocks, was wee Cobweb," said Drool.

"She was not," said I. "And where is Jeff? Have you seen him?"

The ninny wiped a smear of berry gore from his lips. "No."

"Drool, Jeff is a friend and valued crew member. If you ate him, I shall be very cross with you. Very cross indeed."

CHAPTER II

Presenting the Mechanicals

TWO TICKS after Cobweb disappeared into the thicket, sunrise was on us like an angry red dog. I donned my dried and smoke-scented motley and fitted my three throwing daggers into the sheaths across my lower back under my jerkin, which was sewn and slotted to conceal them. My friend Montalvo had slipped the daggers and a calabash of water into the boat before we were set adrift. It was good Montalvo who had convinced the crew to spend the boat at all, rather than just cast us into the sea. For a pirate, he had been a gentleman.

Drool was learning the unpleasant lesson of how berries grow in proximity to thorns and I had to pick the pricks from his great paws before leading us further into the forest. Like me, Drool was an indoor fool and not suited for foraging. We would need to find a village or town from which to beg our supper, or we'd be little better off than we'd been a day before at sea. The forest was a primordial behemoth, with moss hanging from a canopy of trees with the girth of cottages, not the sun-bleached stone hills with the odd olive tree clinging to them that I'd been told composed the Greek countryside.

We drank deeply from the stream and then made our way in a general westerly direction, away from the sea, over which the sun rose, for no other reason than it was the direction Cobweb had fucked off to. If there *was* a queen in that direction, I reasoned, so would there be a town, and accommodations more suiting a brace of abused indoor fools.

We called for Jeff as we went along, with no response. I hoped that he had scampered into the great forest thinking he had happened upon monkey Valhalla, but as the hours passed, I began to suspect that he had perished in the sea, and while there was still a chance that Drool had eaten him, I wasn't about to dig through the nitwit's stool looking for monkey bones like some philosopher, so I took his word that nuts and berries had been his only fare.

When not calling, we listened for the jingling of Jeff's bells. He wore a tiny silver and black motley like my own, and while I had long ago traded my bell-toed jester's shoes for soft leather boots, and the pirate crew had trimmed the bells from my hat and puppet stick because they found them annoying, they had never been able to catch Jeff, and he had jingled in the rigging like a bright simian sprite.

I would grieve, when there was time. Jeff had been with me for years, through adventures and imprisonments, kidnappings and shipwrecks, but the gleam had seemed to be fading from his eyes of late. Maybe years pass more quickly for a monkey. There were white hairs on Jeff's little chin. Perhaps he was in his monkey way an old man, decrepit ancient, his senses going feeble, his mind dim, familiar faces becoming strangers in his monkey mind. That was my explanation, anyway, for why he spent our two years before the mast either frolicking in the rigging, flinging rhesus feces down upon the crew, or trying to shag the ship's cat. Jeff was a vile little creature, really, but still, he had been a friend. When my humors were restored, I would shed a tear.

When the sun was high overhead and our morning victuals of berries and ditch water had faded to a growling memory, we came to a clearing where five men were posing and orating in turn like a band of polite loonies—rehearsing a play, it appeared.

They were not gentlemen attired in togas, prosecuting a republic, and having each other up the bum, like proper Greeks, but hard-handed men, in leather and wool, each composed of wire and gristle into such sharp-jawed countenance as is shaped by hard work and lean diet. One roared like a lion and I pushed Drool behind a bush and bade him stay so as not to frighten the players.

"Hark!" said I, stepping into the clearing and waving my puppet stick in a grand flourish. "What pathetic creature cries out for mercy to end its consumptive suffering?" The five turned to regard me.

"It is I," said a tall fellow of perhaps thirty summers like myself. "Snug, the joiner. I play a lion."

"Who are you?" said a younger fellow, just coming into his beard, who, strangely enough, wore a woman's veil with his tradesman's togs.

"I am Pocket of Dog Snogging," said I, with great pomp. "Called the black fool."

"He's tiny," said a balding fellow on the end.

"I think he is an elf," said the director of the troupe, a sturdy fellow with a headful of curls going gray. I noted his position because he carried a scroll.

"But it is daytime," said a third, a curly-haired fellow a few years my senior, dressed as roughly as the others except for a finely woven waistcoat. "The people of the wood are not about in the day."

"The Puck goes about in the day," said Snug, who would be a lion.

"Speak there, traveler," said a fourth fellow, tall, thin, and long of foot, wearing a hat of poorly tanned doeskin so that the earflaps, meant to be tied under the chin, jutted into the air like the ears of a confused hare. "Are you wood folk or town folk?"

"Throw him a sock, Francis," said the director. "I heard that elfs can't resist picking up a sock."

The young bloke in the veil quickly pulled off a shoe and tossed a dirty sock at my feet. "There you go."

"Not an elf," said I.

"But he's so tiny," said the bald fellow, who was unwittingly close to having his brains scrambled by a sharp blow from a puppet stick.

It is fair, I suppose, to say that I am not a large fellow. In fact, while not actually tiny, I *am* fetchingly compact of structure. Not twisted of limb nor truncated of torso like some troll, but, in fact, composed with fearful symmetry—like the swiftest of horsemen—the very picture of perfection, if you imagine you are seeing me from farther away, and then there's a pleasant surprise when I arrive before you expected.

"Pardon my cohort, good sir," said the fellow in the fine waistcoat. "Clearly you are a gentleman of distinction and skill." He gestured frantically to the others at my motley and puppet stick. "A player."

"I am a fool by training," said I. Under normal circumstances I might have punctuated the announcement of my trade with a backflip or a bit of juggling, but I was still weak with hunger and light-headed from my injury.

"And I am Nick Bottom, the weaver," said he, explaining the fine waistcoat with a word. "We are players ourselves. A company newly formed to perform an amusement for the duke's wedding, four days hence."

"The Mechanicals!" announced the director. They all clicked their heels and bowed.

"So a bit of Greek drama, is it?" said the puppet Jones in a smaller version of my voice. "The old 'kill your da, shag your mum, and blind yourself before the final curtain'?"

"No," said Bottom. "We shall perform the most laughable tragedy and comic travesty of *Pyramus and Frisby*."

"Thisby," corrected the fellow with the scroll.

"*Pyramus and Thisby*," said Bottom. "Now, each man step forward as I call his name and present dignity and persona dramatic for this master lesbian, who can be identified as thus by his garments and puppet."

"Actually—" I began, but the players had lined up and Bottom proceeded.

"Peter Quince, the carpenter, step forward."

The graying fellow I thought the director stepped up with his scroll. "I present the chorus, a narrator and teller of prologues, epilogues, and assorted expositions; also the father of Pyramus." He bowed.

"Do not bow," said Bottom. "You have done nothing yet. Now, Snout."

The tall fellow with the ridiculous doeskin hat came forth. "Tom Snout, tinker. I present Thisby's mother. Also wall." He curtsied.

"Don't curtsy," said Bottom.

"No?" said Snout, an ersatz bunny ear raised in curiosity.

"Unprofessional," explained Peter Quince, the director and carpenter.

"Sorry," said Snout, who curtsied and backed away.

"Wall?" I asked.

Drawing figures in the air, Bottom said, "Pyramus, a brave and manly hero, and Thisby—"

"Most beautiful maid," said the young one, tittering behind his veil. "I am Francis Flute, bellows mender." He curtsied.

"Pyramus and Thisby are lovers," said Bottom. "Most unapproved lovers of two feuding families, whose houses share a wall. Forbidden to see each other, the lovers perpetrate their romance through a cranny in a wall."

"Presenting wall," said Stupid Hat, with a curtsy. He held out his fingers in a loop to present the aforementioned cranny in the wall. "Presenting cranny."

"So the lovers have each other off through a chink in the wall?" I inquired.

"A fanciful romance to be sure," said Bottom, "but more suited to Snout's talents than a dragon, which was the other story we had. But the lovers will but whisper and fling soft woo through the chink."

"Well that won't do, they'll need to chip the cranny out a bit wider, and do a bit of balancing on chairs," said I. "But once done, a dramatic and credible wall bonking will surely make the show."

"Oh, bravo!" said Peter Quince. And they all clapped politely.

"Oh, good sir," said Bottom. "I knew as soon as I saw your fool's motley you would bring skill and grand disaster to our play."

"Indeed," said I. "I will lend thee my mastery of stagecraft and verse when my strength returns." I looked about for any sign of food and spied a pile of rucksacks by a large boulder. "I will need the help of my apprentice, and as we have been traveling, any food and drink you might have."

"Yes," said Peter Quince. "Right here." He waved toward the rucksacks.

"Drool," I called. "Come out, please, and meet—"

"Hello," said the dim giant as he trudged out of the brush. The Mechanicals were awed. Stupid Hat gasped at Drool's sheer taurine enormity. Drool approximated the size of two well-fed men-at-arms stuffed haphazardly into a single skin without leaving room for a full serving of brains.

"Zounds," said the bald one. "He's fucking huge."

"Well observed," said I.

"Well, why then are you so small?" said the shiny-pated toss-bobbin.

"You *are* an elf, aren't you?" said Peter Quince. "Francis, throw him another sock."

"I don't have another sock," said the boy with the veil.

Quince winced. "You only wore one sock?"

"I didn't know there was going to be a bloody elf test," said the lad.

"I have a sock," said Snug the lion, revealing a vacant grin as he held up a tattered woolen sock.

Bottom said, "Snug, why is your sock not in your shoe with your foot?"

"I was afraid I was going to be late. I thought I would put it on when I got here."

I turned to address my apprentice. "Drool, we have at last found your tribe. Gentlemen, this is Drool, apprentice fool and onetime minister of wank to the lands of England, France, Burgundy, Brittany, Belgium, and sometimes Spain."

"Charmed," said Drool, reaching down the front of his canvas sailor's trousers to give a demonstration.

"Perhaps just a bow, lad," I instructed.

"Pleased to be of your acquaintance," said Drool, offering his hand to the bald fellow.

"Robin Starveling," said baldy as he backed away, hiding his own hand behind his back. "Tailor."

"Well," said I. "Now that we are all mates in the service of the stage, why don't you show us to the food, and while Drool and I refresh ourselves, you gents can run through your lines and I will give keen and critical review? Drool can load a great battery of gas he can set alight at intermission."

"I'm not giving up my lunch to another thieving elf," said Robin Starveling.

"Still not an elf," said I.

"Aye, can't trust an elf far as you can throw them," said Snout (Stupid Hat) the tinker. "Rascals every one."

"The last one stole my best hat and touched up my wife by the millpond," said Snug the joiner. "She's been useless for wifely duties ever since."

"Begging pardon, sirrah," said Bottom, doffing his hat. "Some in our troupe have been much abused by one of the wood folk, a jester as well, called Robin Goodfellow."

"The Puck," said Quince. "Said he'd teach us a fashionable dance to do for the duke. Took our coin, then buggered off to who-knows-where, leaving us fuck-all for our trouble."

"The rascal," said I. I exchanged a look of flabbergast with the puppet Jones. Truth told, until that moment, I had thought I, too, might bugger off to parts unknown, leaving them with fuck-all for their trouble, but now I felt honor-bound to mend the reputation of my fellow fool and rascal. There are so few of us, after all, subject as we are to being hanged by humorless royals. "That's in violation of the fool's code. I shall make good on the Puck's promise and teach you all a jaunty dance. After lunch."

"We don't need a dance now," said Francis Flute, *au falsetto* behind his veil. "We've Thisby and Pyramus to carry the day."

"Gentlemen," said Bottom, as he rifled through the rucksacks, drawing out bread, fruit, cheese, and various basketed jugs as he went and placing them on a shawl he'd spread out on the ground. "Let us allow our professors to regain their strength. I fear the romantic bombast of my Pyramus may otherwise overwhelm their sensibilities."

"Proceed, gentlemen," I said, as Drool and I fell upon the Mechanicals' lunch like wolves on the fold.

Peter Quince, carpenter and director, stepped forward. "Now am I the chorus."

"Pray continue," I said around a mouthful of coarse brown bread.

Quince unrolled his scroll. *"Two households, both alike in dignity—"*

"Rawr," said Snug, the tall fellow.

"Now is not the time to roar," said Quince. "I have not yet warned the ladies not to be afraid."

"Rawr," repeated Snug.

"No one will be afraid," said I.

"I shall wear a mane made of straw, and paint my jaws with the blood," said Snug.

"Do it again," said I, snatching a plum from our hoard and skipping to the lion's side.

"Rawr," said Snug.

"Pathetic. You have to summon the full wind and throat of the beast, lad, not simply say 'rawr.' Call up an echo from your memory, then let it roar from time's ear to today's lips. Hear the beast, be the beast."

"Hear the beast, be the beast," said Drool, note for note in my voice, which is the ninny's peculiar talent. It's bloody unsettling at times.

The Mechanicals stared in wide wonder at Drool.

"Like that," said I. "Make the sound you have heard a lion make."

"I've never seen a lion," said Snug.

"Well, extrapolate your roar from such fierce creatures as you *have* seen."

"I've seen a chicken," said Snug.

The knot on my brow suddenly began to throb and I pushed my coxcomb back to relieve the pressure.

"I believe I could improvise the most terrifying of chicken roars," said Nick Bottom. "If I may have a go."

"No!" said I. "There will be no roaring chickens. What ferociousness-deprived land is this? Have you no bears, no wolves, the odd fox with a cough—no wild beast from which to draw your inspiration?"

"We might," said Snug, "but they aren't about in daytime, and none of the town folk go into the forest at night, only the wood folk."

"That is true," said Bottom.

"Oh fuckstockings!" said I. Why had I not offered a song for our meal, perhaps a threat? I looked to Drool, who had laid waste to much of the tradesmen's lunch. We could dash now, I supposed, and leave them to their roaring chickens and wall shagging.

"I have seen a goat as well," said Snug, with more pride than goat-spotting generally merits. "Many goats."

"Perhaps a different approach." I reached up to Snug to bring him into my confidence, thought to put my arm around his shoulders, but he was so tree-fuckingly tall I ended up accidentally clouting him on the back of the head, knocking his cap to the ground.

"Hey!" said the hapless joiner.

"There you have it," said I. "If you have not heard a ferocious creature you must summon it in yourself. Now, think of when that rascal Puck had his way with your wife."

"He only just touched her up, he—"

"Roar, player! He ruined her forever! Used her like a common tramp while the whole village watched."

"But—"

"Roar!" I clouted him on the back of the head again for good measure.

"RAWR!" roared Snug, with great improvement, surprising himself and startling Drool so that he aspirated a bit of the sweet wine he was quaffing.

"Oh, well done," said Bottom. "Bravo, good Snug." He clapped politely and the rest of the Mechanicals joined in.

Snug smiled shyly and bowed his head. "If I *were* a lion I would bite the neck of that rascal Puck."

"Your ire serves you well," said I. "Gentlemen, shall we progress to actual lines from the text?"

"Who roars there?" came a voice from the edge of the clearing. I looked to see a large, scruffy fellow dressed in leather armor and trailing a sword at his waist, followed by a smaller bloke in black aiming a crossbow, loaded and drawn, upon poor Snug.

"Blacktooth," whispered Bottom. "Captain of the watch."

CHAPTER III

The Watch

THE CAPTAIN of the watch, Blacktooth, was the sort of beetle-browed brute I'd encountered my whole life at the fringes of royal courts: large men whose talent for violence and incapacity for original thought carried them into middling positions as enforcers, jailers, and executioners. There had been a dozen or so of that stripe on the pirate ship, and if not for my own wary quickness with a blade or fear of Captain Jessica's vengeance (she'd once dirked a fellow pirate in the dick for touching her bottom sans consent) I'm sure I would have been pummeled and cast broken into the sea long before we were set adrift. 'Tis best to proceed with caution when confronted by such slow-witted, quick-tempered creatures, particularly when they are backed by a ferrety second with a cocked crossbow.

"Bow to your betters, thou chicken-witted catch-farts!" exclaimed the puppet Jones, much to my surprise, because I had not thrown my voice nor worked the ring and string that move his mouth, which, generally, is how the puppet makes his point.

The ferrety watchman raised his crossbow and aimed at my chest. I dropped Jones and dove behind the thespians as I drew one of the daggers from the small of my back. Once I heard the bolt fly I might close enough distance between myself and the watchmen to send a dagger at the big one before his sword could clear its scabbard. There'd be an instant while the smaller one tried to reload, and I could send a second dagger to his throat. The big one would still be staggering, my slim blade a bloody brooch in his breast, but with good fortune, Drool could help me bring them both to a swift finish. (I am not a fighter by nature, and spent much of my time during pirate raids in the rigging shouting encouragement to my mates and withering insults at the enemy, but Drool, if you caught him between wanks and snacks, could summon great strength and fury when the dashing of brains needed to be done.)

I came to my feet, leapt, then launched myself off the shoulders of Snout the bunny-hatted tinker—a vault I hoped would put me in knife-throwing range of the watchmen. But alas, no bolt was loosed, and as I somersaulted, I saw the captain pushing his cohort's crossbow down. I landed lightly, and light-headed, not twenty feet in front of them. I shook off my dizziness and went to one knee with a theatrical flourish, fitting my dagger back into its sheath as I bowed.

"Gentlemen!" said I. "Good day to you, and greetings from our humble troupe of players, the Mechanicals!"

"The Mechanicals!" repeated the players (may all the errant gods bless them). They bowed in a rough approximation of unison.

The captain scowled at the archer. "Burke, we of the watch do not shoot a man for sporting an impotent puppet."

"Impudent," corrected Burke.

Blacktooth then turned to us, doffed his bronze officer's helmet, which looked like it might have been used recently for boiling beans, and said, "Beggin' your pardon, gents, Burke is under training these two years and is yet a nematode in the ways of the watch."

"Neophyte," corrected Burke.

"Take the shot, ya scurvy coward," said the puppet Jones from his spot lying in the dirt. "Or haven't you the stones for a fight?"

How? It was my smaller voice but not from me. Drool, perhaps . . .
"Drool, stop that!" I called.

The great ninny opened his mouth and an avalanche of half-
chewed bread tumbled down his front. Not Drool. What trickery
was this?

Then four more watchmen with spears stepped out of the
wood and the notion of a fight or escape sizzled like a butterfly in
a firestorm.

"Halt!" said the captain. The watchmen stopped. Blacktooth
turned and stepped up to me—loomed, as it were.

The ferrety archer slung his crossbow onto his back by a leather
strap and scampered past me. "Show your passports, citizens," he
commanded.

Each of the Mechanicals produced a wooden chit from his
pocket or from a lanyard around his neck, each chit bearing a wax
seal and burnt inscription of some sort.

Burke read aloud from each chit before moving to the next.
"Peter Quince, Joiner's Guild. Nick Bottom, Weaver's Guild. Francis
Flute, Bellows Mender's Guild."

"You have enough broken bellows to support a guild of mend-
ers?" I asked Flute.

"There's just me and another fellow," said Flute from the mod-
esty of his veil.

"Where is your stamp, little one?" Blacktooth asked me. "It is
unlawful to be indignant in Athens."

"Indigent," said Burke. "Unlawful to be *indigent*."

Blacktooth glared at his second; turned back to me. "Art thou a
knave?"

I stood to meet his gaze and fell short only by a foot or so. "I am
no knave, sir, but I'm most certainly indignant, thou putrid toss-
toad, thou—"

"Master Pocket," said Nick Bottom, jumping between me and

Blacktooth just as I was about to launch into a crushing recitation of the captain's ancestry, beginning with the syphilitic rat that impregnated a dusty boot to produce his mother.

"Master Pocket," said Bottom, "is our new *maître du théâtre*."

"Sounds suspiciously fucking French," said the puppet Jones. "I say fillet the rascal."

Did they all hear the puppet speak, or was the puppety voice a phantom born of my fatigue and a blow to the head?

Blacktooth loosened his sword in its scabbard, which served to capture my attention.

"I am a traveling actor," said I, the very ideal of a penitent player. "Here to serve the king."

"The duke," corrected Burke with a growl.

"Indeed," said I. "The duke."

Blackfoot looked me up and down, shot a glance at my puppet stick, then looked back to me. "You wouldn't be Robin Goodfellow, would you?"

I sighed. "I am not."

"Yet you wear the motley of a fool . . ." Blacktooth bent over, put a finger under one eye to better examine me. "Are you sure? If you are, the duke has sent us to fetch you."

Burke raised his crossbow and trained it upon me. The four spearmen lowered their spears and stepped forward.

"We are fools," said Drool, climbing to his feet. And they all turned to look at the dim giant, who stepped up to the four spearmen, puffed his chest, and said in a voice borrowed from Blacktooth, "And pirates."

"Drool, no," I called.

"Bloody viscous pirates, ya scurvy dogs!" Drool continued in the borrowed voice.

"Vicious," corrected Burke, by habit. He swung his crossbow toward Drool and raised it to aim.

"I think fucking not," said I. In a single motion I pulled a dagger from the small of my back and flung it underhanded at Burke, where it buried its point a thumb's length into his bum cheek. The watchman screamed as he let fly his bolt, which sailed well over Drool's head into the forest.

Meanwhile, Blacktooth had drawn his sword and made a mighty swipe that would have relieved me of my head had I not leaned away. I could hear the blade whistle through the air as it passed by my nose. I scuttled away from Blacktooth, readying myself for a second dodge, but the captain held his sword fast at *en garde,* then looked around it, as if the blade might be blocking his vision.

"Where did he go?" He swung his sword harmlessly through the air in front of him as if searching for a spirit. Behind me, the Mechanicals cowered together in a huddle.

He looked to Drool, who stared at me, more gap jawed than normal, a bit of dribble spilling down his chin. "Pocket?"

"Seize him," said the captain, and the spearmen fell on Drool, wrestling him to the ground. Burke was limping in a circle, trying to get a grip on my dagger, which wagged in his bum like the tail of a friendly dog.

"Run, you bloody idiot," called the puppet Jones, from his place in the dirt. "Run!"

There was no helping Drool, the spearmen were clearly better fighters than their commander and already had the great git pinned, a man on each limb.

"Run!" screamed the puppet. "Into the forest. Run."

And so I did, leaving Blacktooth staring at the spot I'd just left. I snatched Jones up out of the dirt as I ran. Drool was wailing my name as I passed by but if I stopped now we'd both be killed. This way, perhaps a rescue.

"Don't fight, lad," I called over my shoulder. Then I vaulted a fallen tree nearly as thick as I was tall and landed in a pile. I climbed to my feet and glanced back over the tree at my pursuers. But there were none. All the watchmen, even those holding Drool, were looking at the spot where I had ducked under Blacktooth's sword. Not even an eye turned my way.

"Bloody bumbling knobs," I muttered to myself. "Can't even give proper chase."

"Well they wouldn't chase, would they?" said the puppet Jones. "What with you being dead and all."

I tossed the puppet stick away; it bounced and came to rest on a bed of moss.

"Don't be such a wilted willy about it," said the puppet. "You'd think you're the only one ever had his head chopped off."

"My head is not chopped off." I tugged at my coxcomb to confirm my point as I am often unreliable.

"Fine, call to your mates."

So I did. I shouted at Drool, at the Mechanicals, called to Blacktooth, "Over here, thou bee-brained cocksplat!" Not a head turned. Not an ear perked. No ire was sparked. Drool whimpered and wept as he was bound by the watchmen.

"Dead," said the puppet.

"But I am here."

"Talking to a puppet on a stick."

"That does seem a bit out of order."

"'Tis often said, there's always a bloody ghost, you know?"

"And I am he?"

"Indeed."

"Why can't I see my dead body?"

"Rules, I reckon."

"So I am slain."

"Sharp as a rolling road-apple, you are."

"Fuckstockings!"

✤   ✤   ✤

WELL, DEATH was a darkling dollop of dog wank. Neither paradise nor perdition as promised. No shining gates to welcome me into the bosom of those I had loved, nor pit to pull me onto the pikes of mine enemies. No angels sang me into sweet slumber, nor did a thousand barb-dicked devils bugger me senseless. Even of peace was I deprived, for as my spirit wandered in that poxy wood, worry still wrinkled my bruised brow over Drool, sadness over lost love still weighed heavy in my heart, even hunger still dug at my gut. Had I known hunger would follow me into the undiscovered country I would have taken more time for lunch before shuffling off this mortal coil.

And what an ignominious death it was! Death by dunderheaded official? I grieved for myself, for despite the most minor snag in character or smudge of misdeed, in life I had been fucking lovely.

I thought to rend my clothes in grief but halted as I had only the one outfit to serve me for a death that might go on for a dogfuckingly long time; instead I leapt onto the fallen tree trunk from behind which I had watched Drool and the Mechanicals being led away by the watch, and I cried out to the empty forest: "Woe! Agony! And Despair! I am slain! I am slain and I grieve for a barren, broken world deprived of my delight."

"Oh for fuck's sake, shut your festering gob, you wanker!" cried the puppet Jones, who had persisted in chattering on without my help.

Oh, I had before lusted for the grave, years ago when my sweet queen was murdered, even for a moment when the wave overturned our boat and the briny deep pulled me down, I felt an instant of relief—surrender to sweet oblivion, only to be yanked back to a confusion of quick bright things. But if this were truth, even *then* there would have been no rest, but penance to wander sodden and sullen to the jabbering cadence of a self-possessed puppet. At least poor Drool might have been spared capture, and would now be licking berry juice from thorn-pricked paws while pert and nimble Cobweb stood by with eyes like harvest moons full in amazement. Poor dribbling giant, beyond my reach or rescue, but not my concern.

"Why not just let me drift in the dark!" I shouted to any gods who might have been listening. "Let me be to un-be!"

"So," said a bloke's voice, close enough behind to startle me. "Newly dead, are you then?"

I nearly fell off the log turning toward the voice. There, in the hollow of the broken, moss-covered stump from which my own tree had fallen, sat a nearly naked fellow, as pale as the moon, his head a mop of black curls that he shook out of his eyes as he grinned.

"It would seem," said I.

"Won't be needing that jaunty jester's hat then, will you?"

I touched my hat, black and silver satin like my jerkin, three tentacles, each as long as my forearm, once tipped with gaily jingling bells, now denuded, bell-less, sad and silent. "I quite like this hat."

"It's smashing. And will be more so once it graces my melon." He jumped onto my tree and scampered to me, held out his hand. "I'll have it."

"You will not have it, thou unctuous little hedgehog," said I. He was shorter than me by a head but sturdy. He was barefoot and wore nothing but a loincloth belted at the waist with a vine. A doeskin pouch hung at his hip.

"Come on, hand it over. You can't use it, you're dead. No one can even see you."

"Well you can see me, can't you?"

"Right, but I've got special talents, don't I, a person of the forest.

Normal, city folk can't see you." He leaned in and I could smell the odor of moss or something green coming off him. He whispered, "Because you're dead. Dead, dead, dead. You are an expired fool. A ghost. Now, hand over the hat, I've some tricks to perform, and they will appear even more wonderful if I am wearing a proper hat."

I stepped away from him, looked him over. Besides being small and pale, and having disturbingly wide green eyes, he had ears that came to gentle points. I hadn't noticed them among his dark curls at first.

"The Puck, I presume?"

"Called Robin Goodfellow." He bowed deeply. "Jester to the shadow king."

"The shadow king?" The consort, I guessed, to Cobweb's mistress, the night queen.

"The shadow king, Oberon. I craft clever japes in his court, trick and transform and make good sport. Bring him laughs and hoots and smiles—provide sweet respite for a while. Take the form of winsome filly and beguile the stallion horse's willy. I can put a girdle round the Earth in forty minutes—fetch a flower from every land I visit. Take the form of a three-legged stool, when auntie sits, dump her bum-bruised like a fool. I am the merry wanderer Puck, a player of jest, a changer of luck."

"And plagued by rhyme, evidently," said I.

"And you are a meager ghost. No station nor skills."

I stepped up. "I know a thousand songs in seven languages and ten thousand bawdy jokes in a thousand voices. I can throw a dagger and pierce a plum thrown in the air, then spear two more before the first one lands. I can juggle bottles, plates, clubs, swords, mooring pins, and fire, in odds, evens, and all at once if need be. I can scale a rope to the height of the battlements without using my feet, and descend it headfirst without using my hands. I can leap to a man's shoulders and do a double somersault off them, backward, laid out, to land as soft as a cat. I can play a lute, lyre, drum, or pipe, compose a song extempore with a verse to every lord or lady at court. I can stand on a bareback horse at full gallop, while juggling and singing a song. I can pick any lock ever made, recite Homer in Greek, Petrarch in Latin, and throw my voice to a vase or puppet without moving my lips. I have bloody skills, Goodfellow."

"Well the puppet can do his own talking, can't he?" said Puck.

"He's got a point there," said the puppet Jones from his spot on the forest floor.

"So, just mortal tricks?" said Puck. "No real talents? Powers?"

"Waste of a good hat, really," said Jones.

Suddenly, it occurred to me why others had always found the puppet so annoying—with a will of his own he was a right prick-thorn. I jumped from the log, snatched Jones up, and shook him at the Puck.

Jones said, "Give the stick a bit of a buffing while you're at it, would you, mate?"

"How is this wooden-headed ninny speaking without aid?"

"Perhaps you have but slumbered here and this is all a dream."

"It's not a bloody dream, thou barking dongfish. What goes?"

"Magic, I reckon," said Puck. "Shame you never learned."

"There is no bloody magic!"

"Said the bloody ghost." Puck giggled.

"I am *not* a ghost." I tossed the puppet away. "If I am a ghost, why do I not see my deceased loved ones? How is it I can move objects corporeal?"

"Buggered if I know," said Puck. "Issues unresolved? Wrongs to be righted? Revenges to be taken? Perhaps you've a bit of haunting to do before you drift into the eternal never-again. I don't make the rules. The Puck deals in jests, japes, and magic."

"There *is* no magic," said I, my conviction somewhat drained by the sight of Puck's leaping from the log and descending slowly to the forest floor as if lowered by a crane. "Bollocks," I muttered.

"Even now I am sent by the shadow king to cast a spell on young lovers." He dug into the pouch at his hip and retrieved a funnel-shaped flower blossom and held it up to the light streaming down through the forest canopy as if trying to catch sight of a spirit hiding in there. "The potion, squeezed from this purple roofie flower collected in the west, if dropped upon the eyelid of a sleeper, shall cause them to fall deeply in love with the next creature they see."

"Bollocks," I repeated, with some incredulity.

Puck sniffed the funnel tip of the blossom, as if to test the aroma of the potion. "I have two, if you'd like to give it a go. Oh, but no one can see you . . . Oh, that won't do, will it? Sorry."

"Perhaps a drop or two on some unsuspecting victim for yourself?"

"Oh, I have no need of such potions, as I am an excellent lover. Of great renown. Very much in demand, is the Puck. What only today I have seen two queens, a joiner's wife, and a marmot shagged."

"A marmot?"

"Yes, rather like a large squirrel. Lovely creatures. Live in burrows."

"I know what a marmot is. You shagged a marmot?"

"Went right to the rodent without a proper 'well done, lad' for the other lot. That's just disrespectful of a fellow fool's work."

"A woodchuck, you shagged a woodchuck."

"Unfriendly," said Puck.

"Fine, well done with the two queens and the other tart."

"Better," said Puck. "Sure you don't want me to use a flower on you? Might help someone see past your sour aspect."

"Still a ghost."

"Oh, right. Sorry."

"But if you know a way I might help my apprentice . . ."

"You have an apprentice. I never had an apprentice. Want to trade for him? I have these smashing love potion flowers. I know a lovely marmot I could introduce you to."

"He's been taken by the captain of the watch."

"Oh, Blacktooth, there's a nasty bit of business. And his lef-tenant, Burke, twice as bad."

"Drool's a great empty-headed giant, but gentle, and loyal as a spaniel—he won't do well in a den of blackguards. Help me, good Robin."

"Would that I could," said Puck. He tipped the roofie flower as if toasting me with a tiny chalice. "Duty yet due to the shadow king. But I can send you the right way. I know where they'll take him."

"Where?"

"I'll have the hat." He stowed his magic flower and held out a hand.

It wasn't as if I would need it. Would I even last on this mortal plane long enough to help Drool? I pulled off my coxcomb and handed it to him.

He fitted it over his curls and began to march in a tight circle, singing:

> "Up and down, up and down,
> "I will lead them up and down,
> "I am fear'd in field and town,
> "Goblin, lead them up and down."

"Oh for fuck's sake, Puck!"

He stopped, pulled the hat off. "What?"

"Where do I find my apprentice?"

"I'll have one of them daggers at your back, too."

"In your arse, you will. I'm down one already." I snatched one of my daggers out of its sheath, flashed it by his nose.

"Fine," said the Puck. "Just I never had a knife before. They'll be taking your friend to the gendarmerie in the city. It's under the duke's palace. Go west with the sun. You'll not reach there by dusk, so it's another night in the forest for you, but keep west, you'll see the spires of the palace when first you break out of the wood, from there it's a piece of piss."

"You haven't any food, have you?" I asked.

"The forest is full of food," said the Puck. He pulled my hat back on and grinned. "Be dark soon, you best head west. I've lovers to find. Goodbye, stingy ghost."

With a giggle, he was gone. He didn't run off, or dance, or leap, he was simply gone, a bit of green dust settled where he had been standing.

"So, you waiting for your funeral procession or shall we be on our merry way?" said the puppet Jones from the spot where I had tossed him.

"I could have traded you for a marmot," said I. "At least I could have eaten the marmot. *You* won't even make a good fire."

"You don't frighten me," said the puppet. "You're a shit ghost, really."

I snatched up the puppet and smacked him smartly against a tree as I headed west, toward the dying light, a vengeful ghost on the march. Evidently.

"Tosser," said the puppet.

CHAPTER IV

There's Always a Bloody Ghost

WHAT PUCK and the puppet Jones didn't realize about my death, despite how clever and magical they thought themselves, was just how knob-twistingly lonely it was. If only I could hover ethereal over Jessica when she heard the news of how her cold rejection brought me to a violent end. Her tears would be like balm unto my soul, her regret like a lover's sweet whispers in my ear. My friends, my subjects, my lovers, my family—the bundle of nuns who raised me—my apprentice, my monkey, even my enemies, who were legion, and many deceased for their trouble: none were there to grieve, gloat, or glower at my passing. Dead and alone, was I, at the same time. They don't tell you that bit in the churches and temples.

And thus I trudged through fern and forest for hours before I heard weeping in the distance, another lost soul, perhaps, who had met her mortality. Whence it came I could not say, for the woods had gone batshaggingly dark, and while the full moon cast a tattered lace of silver through the canopy, it was only enough light to allow a lonesome fool a few quick steps before running into the next tree trunk. I followed the sound, however, for as the eye was deprived, the forest served the ear a feast of menacing sounds, most made by scurrying creatures that wished me harm.

There, ahead, in a pool of moonlight, on a large rock, sat a rather tall young woman. Her hair was dark, pinned up, her dress white and light as summer, high necked, the collar and cuffs embroidered with small pink roses. She hugged herself and rocked, as if each heartbreaking sob wrenched out a bit of her soul, then she refilled her bellows in broken gasps with the world's sorrow. The sound brought tears to my eyes and I would have embraced the poor creature, offered her comfort, had I been more than a spirit lost in the wood. Instead, weary, I sat down on the stone beside her.

She shrieked, high, shrill, and girlish, and jumped to her feet.

I shrieked, high, loud, and somewhat less girlish, and jumped to mine.

She wheeled on me, angry, her eyes still wet with tears. "Thou knave! Thou sneak! Back, villain!"

"You can see me?" said I.

"Of course I can bloody see you, despite your creeping up on me like some lurker in the dark!"

"I did not creep. I am a ghost, invisible to all but the magical forest people."

"Well I can see you, and I'm not a bloody forest person." She wiped her eyes and stepped back from me, looked me over in an overly personal way, as if trying to spot a burr snagged in my motley. "Say," said she, "you used to be a monkey, didn't you?"

"I did not. I was a fool. A charming, clever fool."

"Well earlier there was a monkey dressed in that same fool's outfit. Had his way with my hat and ran off. I've heard all manner of magical things happen in this wood. It would just be fitting that the only man who would deign to talk to me is a hat-shagging monkey." She leaned in closely. "You, sir, have the look of a hat shagger."

"I do not. But I know a monkey who is quite fond of hats. Called Jeff."

"Good you specified," said the puppet Jones. "Lest we blame some other monkey dressed in black and silver jester togs."

"Quiet," I told the puppet. *Jeff? Alive?* Why, I had barely had time to miss him.

"I'll have my hat back now," said the girl. "Or have you used it and cast it aside, too? You men are monsters, even those of you who used to be monkeys."

"I am neither a monster nor a monkey, I am but a sullen newborn ghost, and I only stopped because I heard you weeping and thought I might help."

"You may help, if you can lead me out of this sodding forest."

"Me? I was going to ask you. Is this not your country? How is it that you find yourself lost in the forest of your own familiarity?"

"I followed my love, my handsome Demetrius, into the forest."

"And he was eaten by a bear?"

"No, that's horrible. Why would you say such a thing?"

"He's not here, is he? And there you are, sobbing like you've been dirked in the dick by grief's dark dagger. *Ergo. Ursa. Arborem.* Therefore, bear in the forest."

"That means 'bear in a tree,' fool. And there was no sodding bear. Demetrius has run off after my used-to-be-friend Hermia, who is petite and beautiful, fair of hair, and sweet of voice. If you saw her you would love her too. All men do."

"I would not. I am soured on love. Also, deceased."

"Oh, you would dote upon her, make great cow eyes at her, and sing her your songs of woo."

"I would not. I do not make cow eyes, nor do I moo woo."

"You would. Just like Demetrius. Oh, he wooed me. Promised me future and family, but when Hermia's father showed him favor, he forgot me and had only eyes for her and her fortune. She does not love him. She loves Lysander, a boy she has loved since school, but her father detests Lysander, and so commanded her to marry

Demetrius on pain of death. The duke backed him but would condemn her to life as a nun, forever without the company of men. So she and Lysander ran off together to live under protection of Lysander's maiden aunt. I told Demetrius of their plans, thinking he would forget her and love me again, but he did not. He ran after them."

"And you after him?"

"Well, obviously. But he pushed me down and ran off, faster than I could follow. Skirts are shit for running in the woods." She waved to the skirt of her long white gown, the hem was stained green and brown, snagged with nettles and foxtails.

"Forget this Demetrius, he sounds to be an opportunist fuck-weasel," said I with a wave of dismissal I reserve for such creatures. "Look at you . . . What is your name?"

"Helena."

"Look at you, Helena, you are fairly fit and probably not entirely unpleasant when you are not shouting. You can do better."

"But Demetrius has touched my soul and fired my heart."

"Has anyone else touched your soul? I mean, if you've only had one soul-touch you might not be as on fire as you think. You might just need a raucous, all-night drunken soul-touching that leaves you a puddle of soggy embers in the morning. Then you'll forget all about him." I bounced my eyebrows at the prospect, then winced, as the bruise on my forehead was still tender and bright. I swooned a bit with the pain and sat again upon the rock.

"No," said Helena, sitting down beside me. "I shall become a nun, and forever eschew the company of men. Loneliness shall be my lot, and I shall dwell in quiet contemplation of my misery." And she began to weep again.

"Cheer up, lass," said the puppet Jones. "You'll probably starve to death in the forest first."

"Shut up, Jones!" said I.

"Or be eaten by elves . . . ," the puppet added.

"Oh woe!" the girl cried, and buried her face in my shoulder.

I wrapped a tentative arm around her shoulders. "I know, lamb, love is a besquished toad ripening in the sun. But despair not, life in the nunnery is not completely devoid of joy. I was raised by nuns. Once a week you'll be able to share a sumptuous raisin with your sisters, and then there's the perpetual flicking of the bean in the dark, for which you'll have ongoing guilt and repentance during the day, so you'll stay busy."

"But I don't want to be a nun, I want to go home. Take me home, fool, please. It's dark, and you know what happens when it gets dark in the forest?"

I had spent more than a few nights in the forests of Britain in my youth and I remembered little to fear in the forest dark beyond the cold and damp, which, to be fair, was often the case any place or time in Old Blighty. "Supper?" I ventured hopefully.

"Not supper! Creatures of the dark! Evil ravening creatures that rend the flesh from your bones and eat it while you watch. Some say it's the forest people themselves, transformed into night beasts. They are demons, sir. No one who has seen them has lived to tell the tale." She flinched, startled by a noise in the bushes. She dug her nails into my arm and pulled me tight, as if to use me as a shield against the stirring. "Alas, it is too late. They are upon us."

"Unhand her, you rogue," said a male voice from the bushes, and then an entirely unremarkable yellow-haired bloke stepped out of the bushes. He was dressed in a belted jerkin, leggings, and tall boots, so not at all how I had been led to believe proper Greeks dressed from the vases I'd seen, which was a nappy and a sword.

"Demetrius!" said Helena. She moved to rise but I held her fast.

"Oh, that scoundrel," said I. "Shall I purple up his eyes, milady? Shall I relieve him of his teeth so he may send his stuttered lies through broken bleeding lips? Give the command, milady."

"You can't say that," said Demetrius. "She is . . . I am . . . You are . . . Helena followed *me* into the forest."

"And you did not want her. Used her. Spurned her. Pushed her down and ran after another."

"Well, yes, but I don't want anyone else to have her."

"And you have come back to me," said Helena. She stood and rushed to him, her arms wide to receive his embrace. He stepped aside and she tumbled headlong into the shrubbery.

"I'm lost," said Demetrius. "I heard voices and ended up here."

Helena climbed out of the bushes. Her hair had shed some of its pins and hung in tendrils in her face. She spat out a leaf. "And you returned to rescue me," she said with entirely too much hope.

"I was hoping someone would know the way back to town," said Demetrius, ignoring the girl.

"You don't know the way to Athens and you're not wearing your nappy and sword. You are a shit Greek, Demetrius."

"Sir, count yourself lucky that I have left my bow and sword at home, for on my honor, if I were armed, I would make you pay for your words."

"A shit Greek, I say. Everyone knows that you always go about with a sword, maybe even a shield if you're out walking your three-headed dog." I have read the classics. "I, too, am unarmed, but just as well, that I might box your ears until you beg for mercy, then slay you later at my own convenience."

Of course I lied about being unarmed. I'm not mad, the Greek was a foot taller than I, two stone heavier, and had probably eaten more than a handful of nuts and berries over the last week.

"Lay on, thou piss-haired spunk-whistle!" I should probably have stood up at that point, but truth be told, I was feeling weak and thought if I stood up quickly I might faint.

The Greek looked confused. He had stumbled into a fight he

did not want over a girl he did not fancy, and even in the moonlight I could see his eyes darting around in search of an exit like flies buzzing in a jar. And an exit was granted, as from the other side of the clearing a great roar sounded out of the bushes, and a figure rose tall in the darkness, thrashing in the undergrowth as it charged.

"Bear!" cried the puppet Jones.

"Did that puppet just talk?" asked Demetrius.

"Run," said Helena, grabbing Demetrius's hand and dragging him off into the forest, both of their voices rising in high terror as they went.

I stood, then, and reached into the small of my back for a dagger, which I drew and held before me, but I swooned and fell back onto my bottom on the rock. "Oh balls," said I as the moonlight-laced clearing began to spin. As I dropped my dagger and as I sank into the darkness I heard high, happy giggling.

"Haw, haw," sang Cobweb. "They thought I was a bear!" She danced a jig before me, hopping from foot to foot, as if some piper were trilling a shanty only she could hear. "Haw, haw. Cobweb the scary bear. Did I scare you?"

I shook my head, more to clear the haze in my vision than as an answer. "Most excellent bear, Cobweb. And well done on the timing, as well."

She giggled, clapped, and hopped, delighted with herself. "I saw you was going to fight that straw-haired bloke and you didn't look up to the task."

"Well, I was murdered at lunchtime, so I'm not at my best."

"Where's your big friend?" She picked up my dagger and handed it to me. When she bent before me I got a good look at her right ear, which tapered to a gentle point, like the Puck's. So.

"Taken by the watch," I said, sheathing the dagger. "And the blackguard captain who killed me. I reckon I am doomed to walk among the living until I rescue the great ninny, and only then will I find eternal rest."

Cobweb tilted her head as if examining a spot between my eyes, like a cat might consider a dragonfly before dashing it to bits with a quick claw. "You're daft and you stink of rotting fish. You didn't wash your clothes in the stream like I told you, did you?"

"It was on the agenda, but then I was murdered."

"No you weren't. Now shed your shabby husks and I'll give them a slosh while you eat." She turned and marched to the edge of the clearing.

My stomach lurched at the mention of eating. "Where are you going?"

"To build you a nest to lie in so you don't fall against the rock and dash out what's left of your brains. Now off with your kit, fool."

"I'm fine," I said, standing up to show I was, but stumbled a bit to catch my balance. "Bit dead, but for a ghost, fine."

"Pocket!" she said, using my name for the first time, wheeling on a heel. She strode back across the clearing and stepped up to me until her nose near touched my chin. "You are not dead. You *may* be a bloody loon, but you are *not* dead."

"I am. Slain this very day by Blacktooth."

"Are you hungry?" she inquired, stepping again so close she might have rung the bells on my toes if the pirates had not stolen them.

"Yes," I replied.

"Are you thirsty?"

"Well, yes."

"Does this hurt?" And at that she viciously pinched and twisted my starboard nipple.

"Ouch!" I pushed her away, resisting the urge to return a twist of the tit, as I am a fucking gentleman. "That is no proof—"

"Does it hurt?" she snapped.

"Yes! Yes it hurts, thou venomous mouse."

"Then you're not bloody dead, are you?"

I rubbed my offended man-pap and considered her thesis. The eternal sleep did seem rather uncomfortable, itchy even, although not so much as to constitute hellish torment. "Well, I *was* dead. Blacktooth and the guard could not see me, even as I passed not an arm's length before them. Explain that."

"Trickery," said the puppet Jones. "Or more likely you're bloody barking and you imagined the whole thing."

"That's quite clever," said Cobweb, looking at Jones, who leaned against the stone. "I didn't even see your mouth move."

"I didn't do it. Since I died this wooden-headed ninny has been babbling away on his own."

"Then I'd have to agree with him," said Cobweb. "You're barking."

She skipped to the edge of the clearing, where she began collecting leaves and branches and arranging them in a circle with practiced alacrity. She gamboled in the forest like a purposeful butterfly, barely stirring a stem or making a sound. In no time she had constructed a nest of soft ferns with pine boughs woven over it. "Here you go," she said, patting a bed of silvery leaves. "Hop in and get your kit off. I'll fetch some nuts and berries."

I thought to argue, but it was an excellent nest, so I climbed defiantly under the entry boughs, plopped down, and removed my boots without another word. Cobweb was laying a fire not six feet away from the nest. I got a good glimpse of her ears again as she struck steel on flint. I rolled up one of my stockings and tossed it so it passed in front of her.

"What's that?" she said, looking at me as if I might be daft.

"Nothing," said I. "Thought you wanted my clothes. For washing."

"Right," she said.

I rolled up the other stocking and tossed it by her.

"No elves," she said, without looking from her labors.

"Sorry?"

"There are no bloody elves here, so stop throwing your socks at me."

"'The stockings of the dead run far,' we say in England." I stripped off the rest of my kit and handed it through the arch of branches, keeping my sheath of daggers in my lap to cover my man bits, and I settled into the nest. The leaves lining the floor were as soft as lambs' ears against my bare bottom.

"I'll wager no one in England or anywhere else has ever said that. And you're not bloody dead. Do I have to prove that again?" She made a pincher movement with her fingers and grinned malevolently.

"Translated from the French," I added for flavor. "Smashing nest though."

"They're usually built up a tree, out of reach of bears, but I can't have you falling on your head again, can I?" She gathered my kit into a bundle.

"Bears?" I inquired.

"I'm off to wash these and gather some food." She unslung a water skin from her shoulder and tossed it into the nest. Drool had been arrested with the previous one she'd given me. "Do try not to be eaten while I'm gone."

"Bears?" I inquired further.

"No, the fire will keep bears away." And with that she was gone into the night.

"Bloody elfs," said the puppet Jones.

I sat, I drank water, and being again among the quick, I had a wee at the edge of the firelight and contemplated my resurrection and responsibility. At some point I curled into a ball on the leaves and dozed off.

✢ ✢ ✢

I AWOKE to a wet whisper in my ear and a warm body pressed to my back.

"There's food, when it suits you," she said.

I moaned, stubborn to stay drifting among my dreams. "In the morning," I said.

She snuggled against me, her fingertips danced over my brow, down my back, over my ribs, as soft as a sigh. I felt I might melt into the touch, so long had it been since I'd been touched without anger or utility. A delicate hand slid over my hip and down over my manhood.

I rolled away, wide awake. Her eyes were black with orange specters in the dim firelight, surprised but not alarmed. "Friends?" she said, with a bit of a pout.

"Knackered," I replied. "Perhaps just a cuddle, for warmth. And put your frock back on, love. A fresh young thing like yourself, defenseless before my wisdom and charm, well, I would not take advantage, it would be unseemly."

"I am nine hundred years old, sprout."

"You are not."

"I am."

"Elf!" cried the puppet Jones.

"You said there were no elves here," said I.

"There *are* no elves," she said.

"Liar!" said the puppet Jones.

"Fuckload of fairies," she said, "but no elves."

"You're a fairy?"

"Aye, since the blossom first opened to reveal me curled inside it."

"A fucking fairy?"

"Well no need to be a knob about it, one can't control the calamity of birth. Do I disparage your people for their dribbling giants and twatty talking puppets?"

"And you're nine hundred years old?"

"And thus well prepared for your wisdom and charm," she said with a grin, reaching for my man tackle.

"Thou lecherous crone!" I rolled away from her, pointing my bits toward the night and fire. "I've barely a score and a half of summers on my back and yet you would use me like a public boot scraper by the church door."

"That's a completely shit metaphor. I shall use you like the cheese-stinking man-tart that you are."

"I do not stink of cheese."

"You are a cheese eater. All your people stink of cheese."

"And your people don't eat cheese?"

"My people are of the forest. Where in the forest would we get milk?"

"I don't know, badgers?"

"Aye, that'd be why there are so few of us. We've been undone by milking accidents in pursuit of our insatiable taste for bloody badger cheese."

"Possibly, fairies are not my *milieu*," I said, thinking to baffle her with a bit of fucking French. "You are my first."

"Second," said she. "Or did you think you were invisible and your puppet is talking on his own because of your magical wisdom and charm?"

"The Puck?" I ventured.

"*The Puck?*" she mocked, making me sound simple and slow to grasp the obvious. "Go to sleep, fool." She lifted her frock above her head and let it fall over her. "In the forest, it is only common courtesy, you know, to share a friendly tumble with a kind soul who brings you supper."

I said, *"Take heartfelt thanks from this fool true and humble, / But dinner free-given comes not with a tumble."*

"Did you just rhyme at me?"

"Did you like it?"

"No."

She settled into a spot on her side of the nest. "Sodding cheese eater."

What fresh curse was this fierce, feral creature of wit?

"Good night, sweet hag."

CHAPTER V

I Am Slain!

W HEN I awoke Cobweb was gone. A pile of nut meats and
berries big enough to fill a yeoman's helmet waited by the
opening of the nest on a trencher fashioned from a large leaf. I re-
sisted the urge to curse the fickle fucking fairy for abandoning me,
for she *had* left breakfast and I was ravenous. She'd left me another
waterskin as well and I drank deeply until the chill shuddered
down my belly and made a shy turtle of my willy. My boots and
motley stood propped on sticks before the smoldering bones of the
fire, the salt stains and much of the soil and grit washed away, no
doubt in the same stream where she'd filled the waterskin.

I dressed and sat down by the fire to eat my breakfast and plan
my next move. On to the city, to be sure, but now that I was not
dead, nor invisible, I would need to be careful. Blacktooth and
his watch would be looking for me, and my having dirked his leftenant in the ham would not help in making my case for Drool's
release. No, I would have to find my way to the gendarmerie and
see if I might free Drool by way of stealth, trickery, and cunning,
the tools I'd learned as a cutpurse, and, failing those, subterfuge,
guile, and duplicity, the skills I'd acquired at court.

I finished the fairy's fare. What forest magic she had employed
to shell so many nuts in the night without waking me, I could not
say, but for the first time in a week my gut unknotted and I could
turn my attention to other tasks undistracted. But which way was

west and the city? The sun lay well below the forest's canopy, and I could not remember which side of a tree moss was supposed to grow on, nor why moss was supposed to have a better sense of direction than I in the first place. Then I spotted it, three straight sticks laid out upon the ground in the pattern of an arrow. Good Cobweb, called by her night queen's horn, had thought to leave me directions. Perhaps I had been too harsh with the haglet for simply succumbing to my prodigious charm.

I slung the waterskin around my shoulder, hitched up my cod, and set off in the direction in which the arrow pointed. I set a stuttering pace, picking my way through the ferns and deadfall until, perhaps after an hour, I encountered a path, where I, at last, felt my sea legs slip away and marched steady and fast until I heard a squirrel-startling scream from ahead.

"Help!"

Wisdom would suggest the best route would have been away from the shout, but having been only recently rescued from the sea by a stranger, the spirit of human charity bubbled high in my heart, so I ran toward the call. (Which also happened to be the direction in which I was headed, anyway.) I broke out of the trees and came onto a grotto with a shallow stream running by it, and there, not twenty yards away, at the water's edge, by an enormous boulder shaped like a turtle, stood the fairy trickster Puck, clutching desperately at a sapling, as if he could not catch his breath.

"Puck," said I.

"Oh, alack, alack, alack, good Prince Pocket of Soggy Dog, I am slain! I am slain!"

"You are not," said I. He was standing right there, wearing my hat, decidedly un-fucking-slain.

Then the Puck loosed his grip on the sapling, gasped, and turned as he slid to the ground, facedown. I could see the shaft and fletching of an arrow jutting from his ribs just below his right arm. Blood coursed down his side with each beat of his heart. By the time I splashed my way to him, the coursing had slowed to oozing. I crouched and rolled the Puck onto his side as best I could, careful not to disturb the arrow, but my concern was for naught, the fairy was quite dead. I held his head in my lap and scanned the banks of the stream for the archer—listened for kicked rocks or rustled brush, but heard none. The blood trail in the sand ran only a few steps back. The Puck had fallen nearly where he'd been when the bolt struck, which meant that I, in the open streambed, would make an easy target for the next bolt. Hairs bristled on my neck with the thought of the murderer taking aim.

"Rest in peace," said I, pulling back his hat and crossing the fairy's forehead with a quick drawing in his own heart's blood. I had not been on speaking terms with the god of my nunnery in many years (in my defense, he started it) but the passing of this Puck, this magical, perhaps ancient, magnificently annoying creature, deserved some reverent observance, even if done only to irony, the god of all fools. That done, I leapt to my feet and sprinted for the cover of a stand of bushes in the direction from which I'd just come, bracing for a bolt between the shoulder blades that might come any instant. I scrambled under the bushes and peeked out at Puck's body, one of my throwing daggers already in hand. Not a movement in the trees, not a sound but the gentle jingle of the brook. The only direction I knew not to contain the killer was the one from which I had come, so after a quick three-count, I was on my feet, running back down the path with urgent stealth, only a squirrel chittering away above betraying my presence. Yes, it was away from the direction in which I thought the gendarmerie and Drool to lie, but I could trace a wide arc to my destination later if it meant avoiding a murderer now. This wasn't the work of a random cutthroat or highwayman. The Puck's name had been on the lips of every person I'd met since landing here, a favorite of kings and court, and who knew how old he might have been, how many half-marmot sons he might have fathered who would be seeking vengeance? No, the death of Robin Goodfellow would not go unnoticed, and whoever had done it would think nothing of murdering a charming wisp of a fool to cover his crime. And then . . .

"Fuckstockings," I said to the trees, to the sky, to the sodding squirrels. "My hat."

And I turned and padded back again toward the stream and the scene of murder most foul, to retrieve my coxcomb. My hat, which had been made to match my motley. My hat, which had graced my noggin in the company of nearly every random Greek I'd met. My hat, which now rested like a pillow beneath the head of the dead Puck.

Puck looked like a sleeping child, lying there on his side against the turtle rock, his feet in the water. From the spot behind my shrubbery, I scanned the streambed up and down, and, seeing no one, made my way to the body.

"Sorry, mate," I said as I retrieved my hat from under the Puck's head. Poor creature, not even a hat to his name. The fairy's feet, washed clean by the brook, still lay in the water. Perhaps having been so recently a dead fool myself, I could not leave him thus, his feet to be eaten by prawns and snails and whatever other watery creatures lived in a Grecian stream. I arranged the Puck's arms over his head so as not to disturb the arrow in his side and dragged him a few feet away from the water. Perhaps his people would find him before the woodland creatures made their supper of him. I saw now the arrow in his side was not an arrow at all, but a bolt from a crossbow, some heavy black wood, perhaps even metal, composed its shaft, the fletching made from stiffened leather, not feathers. Just so, the arrow from a proper English longbow would have been three times the length. This one appeared to have pierced the Puck to his heart or nearby, only a handbreadth protruded from his ribs.

"Halt!" came a voice from behind me.

I looked over my shoulder to see a watchman stepping out of the forest behind me. I dropped the Puck's arms and turned to run.

"Hold there, or die on the spot," said a different voice. I glanced over my other shoulder to see Burke, leftenant of the watch, lowering a cocked crossbow at me. I stopped. Three watchmen at his flanks lowered their spears, then Blacktooth stepped from behind a tree.

"Oh, good captain," I said. "Look, I've found the Puck for you. I trust there will be a reward."

*　　*　　*

"POCKET! MY friend. My friend," called Drool through an iron grate in a heavy cell door as we entered a wide, round antechamber lined with cells. I was slung by my bound hands and feet from a pole being carried by two watchmen, which was how I'd made my way through the forest and then the walled city into the tunnels of the gendarmerie—Blacktooth feeling that was the safest mode of transport after my previous disappearance into thin air. Likewise, the dead Puck was slung from a similar pole between two other watchmen. At the stream, Burke had argued that dispatching me on the spot would ensure my secure delivery to the city, but Blacktooth countered that my continued presence among the quick might mitigate to the duke their colossal cock-up in retrieving the Puck.

"Hi-ho, lad," I called to Drool. "How fare thee?"

"Had a wee beating at first," said the ninny. "But they gived me a drink of water what was lovely."

"The beast yanked two watchmen's shoulders out of socket when we untied him," growled one of my bearers. "Took six of us to get him in the cell."

"Just out of socket? Well, the lad hasn't had a proper meal in a week. Off his game, I reckon. Normally he'd pluck the arms from spearmen like petals from a daisy."

The spearman shuddered and signaled his mate to lower me to the ground.

"Leave him bound," said Burke. "In the cell like that."

They slid the pole out from between my limbs and dragged me into a small cell across from Drool's, this one with an open barred door. One of the spearmen threw my coxcomb in after me, then bolted the door. The two watchmen carrying Puck's body dropped him on the floor in the antechamber.

Blacktooth, who had watched the transfer from a heavy chair by the antechamber entrance, was picking his teeth with one of my daggers. "Burke, tell the chamberlain to tell the minister to tell the duke that we have retrieved the jester, Robin Goodfellow as previously festooned, and have further disinterred ourselves to our duties by also ingratiating his murderer."

"Should I report that the Puck is dead?"

"It is implied in the subtaint."

"Subtext," corrected Burke.

"Aye, go."

"Aye, sir," said Burke, and off he went.

"I didn't kill him," I shouted.

Blacktooth climbed out of his chair, returned my knife to the sheath with its two brothers, which he threw to the floor next to the chair, then came to the door of my cell.

"Here is the case as it permits itself," said the captain, counting on his fingers. "First, motive: thou art a known blackguard, having dirked Burke in the leg by magic."

"That wasn't magic, I threw the bloody knife."

"Guilty, as confessed," said Blacktooth. "Third, opportunity, you knew the diseased, and his name was said before you escaped."

"I'd never seen him."

"Sixth and finally," said Blacktooth, "method, as you were going about with arms, which is forbidden to all citizens except soldiers, men of the watch, and criminals."

"I had knives. He was killed with a bloody crossbow."

"And second," said Blacktooth, who had mysteriously run out of fingers to count on, despite having left several unused, and so was making his point by counting one of the bars on my cell door, "you were found *au gratin* with the victim when he was first defenestrated by the stream, as witnessed by various members of the watch. *Non. Compos. Mentis.*" He dusted off his hands as if he'd made a point.

Idiot.

*   *   *

A MOMENT before lightning strikes, a charge fills the air, the hairs on your arms stand up, a general unsettledness comes over you, and holding a thought is like grasping at smoke, as if power and heat and blinding fucking light are about to reduce you to a cinder of memory, and so was the air in the gendarmerie when she entered. Even curled in the corner of my cell, hands and feet still bound, I could feel it. Watchmen who had been talking, laughing, or playing dice a moment before fell silent, as if the rude ribs of the castle had collapsed, dropping the mountain upon them.

I slid myself up the wall and hopped to the door of my cell. (Yes, I could have easily untied my hands and feet now that I was no longer slung under a pole, but as I was able to move and eat and even have a wee in the bucket in the corner while thusly trussed, I felt no need to put my captors on alert to my ability to free myself.) Blacktooth stood at attention by perhaps a dozen watchmen as Burke led her through the arch in the antechamber opposite from the one through which I'd been carried.

She was a woman in full, perhaps thirty years old, a head taller than Burke, although not so tall as Blacktooth. Her dark hair was woven into plaits with golden cord and tied back so that it fell to the middle of her back. She wore a long white gown with a plunging neck and back, the first garment I'd seen that looked like something a proper Greek would wear when modeling for pottery, except under it she wore a chemise of fine chain mail that looked to be fashioned from gold. Her arms were burnished by the sun, slim, strong, and lined with a net of fine white scars, bare but for a single silver armlet on her right arm with the head of a snake-haired Gorgon cast upon it. On her left arm was a patch of pale skin where she had worn another armlet, but the hair-fine scars stopped at the edges, as if the armlet had shielded her for many battles. This was not the look of a royal in any court I had attended.

"Ma'am!" said Blackfoot, coming to attention. The watchmen all came to some version of what they thought to be attention, although there was no uniformity to their motion.

She nodded to Blackfoot but looked at me. "Is this prisoner the one you found by the body of Robin Goodfellow?"

"Aye, Your Magnificence. We first encountered the knave yesterday, perspiring with a group of crude mechanicals, and he did fling a dagger into the bullocks of my consort Leftenant Burke, causing gracious injury, before disappearing by use of majiks."

Burke stepped up and presented the bandage around his thigh with a flourish, then bowed and backed away a few shuffling steps.

"Begging your pardon, Your Municipal," continued Blacktooth, "but we—not the royal 'we' as in *your* we, but the 'we' as in 'us,' meaning Burke and I and the men, being the 'we' collective, but not the 'we' as in the wee that me and the men have been known to take—"

"Oh for fuck's sake!" said I. "Spit it out, you addlepated ninny."

"Ahoy!" called Drool through the little portal in his cell door at the mention of a ninny.

"Yes, do go on, captain," she said.

"Aye, Your Radiance. The following day, that being today, while searching for the Puck at the behest of the duke, may the gods smile upon your union and the fruit of your looms, we came upon this scoundrel dragging the fresh corpse of the previously apportioned Robin Goodfellow, who was freshly expired by an arrow to the antiquated chest."

"Anterior chest," corrected Burke.

She looked to me. I smiled, removed my coxcomb, and bowed. "Your Grace," said I.

She did not return the smile. "I would see the body," she said.

Blacktooth led her to the next cell, where they had carried the Puck's body. The watchmen shuffled in their ranks, none with the slightest idea what he should be doing. I had the distinct impression they were not accustomed to a royal presence in their cellar. In two ticks she stormed out of the cellar, a bloody crossbow bolt in hand.

"So this scrawny rascal is the killer?" She pointed to me with the bolt.

I stood as tall as my form permitted and thrust my codpiece forward so it arched through the bars and she might see my hidden potential. Scrawny, indeed?

"We heard the Puck scream, ma'am," said Blacktooth. "And not three shakes of a lamb's pail later, we came out of the wood to find him over the body. This fiend is most certainly the percolator."

"Perpetrator," corrected Burke.

"And where is his crossbow?"

"We did not find it," said Blacktooth. "Only a brace of daggers strapped to his back. We had a third which he'd left in Burke's nethers."

"Your Grace," I ventured, with a bit of a bow, "perhaps a more obvious killer presents . . ." I pointed through the bars to the crossbow slung across Burke's back.

Burke's eyes went wide and he swung the weapon around. "No, ma'am. The bolt's too short. Would sail off the rail or hit the bow itself." He drew one of his own bolts from a quiver at his hip and held it next to the bolt that had killed the Puck. Burke's was nearly twice as long. "That one came from a smaller bow, ma'am. Carried by a smaller bloke, no doubt." The scoundrel nodded furiously my way.

She flung the bolt against the wall and stepped before my cell. "Did you kill the Puck?"

"I did not, Your Grace. I am but a simple fool, set adrift by pirates to crash upon your shores but two days ago with my apprentice, Drool."

"Oi," said the dim giant through his window grate. "It were sad. We almost eated Jeff."

"We've barely had time for a proper meal, let alone to make enemies—other than these scrofulous merkins." I gestured in the general direction of Blacktooth and Burke.

"Tell me the truth, fool, or the watchmen will hold you while I cut a hole in you with your own dagger and slowly walk a trail of your entrails around the room while you watch."

"Oh, you wicked little vixen," I said with a grin. "This is not your first dungeon, is it?"

If she was going to kill me, better it not be dragged out, so to speak. If she wasn't, and was indeed as fierce as her aspect and the reaction of the watch implied, she might be amused. This was not *my* first dungeon either.

She laughed. "All of you, out. Leave me to talk to this fool alone."

The watchmen scrambled through the arch leading to the outside, weapons and armor rattling like pans on a tinker's wagon.

Blacktooth and Burke stood in the archway, arms folded, looking not defiant but embarrassed.

"Well?" she said. "Out! Out! Out!"

"We can't, ma'am," said Blacktooth.

"Weapons, ma'am," said Burke. He nodded to a rack of spears and halberds against a wall.

"Your people are not permitted weapons, ma'am," said Blacktooth, staring now at his shoes. "Even Your Most Superfluous Radiance."

"I see," she said. "And yet I am a queen and will be duchess of all of Athens in but three days?"

"'Tis so, ma'am."

"And, good captain, if I commanded thee to kill all your men and then yourself, would you do it?"

"I would be duty-bound to do so, yes, Your Magnetized."

"Majesty," corrected Burke.

"So you see the burden of the crown. My only way to speak to this prisoner in private is to command you to put everyone to death, then fall on your sword. Does that seem about right?"

"Spot-on there, Your Municipal. Spot-on. I would be duty-bound to do it."

"Or," she said, "I could spare you and your men and instead command you to fuck off for a few minutes, and then call you back and you could go on with your miserable lives. Unless you think I can smuggle a halberd or a spear out under this gown?" She took a step so her bare leg emerged from her gown up to her hip.

Blacktooth looked to his scruffy leftenant, Burke to his commander. Both nodded enthusiastically with the bloody obviousness of it all.

"Well," she said, "do fuck off, then. Please."

"As you command, ma'am," said Blacktooth, bowing his way out of the chamber. Burke curtsied and limped after his captain.

She turned to me. "Now, on your life, fool, the truth. Did you kill Robin Goodfellow?"

"Why would I kill him? He was smaller than me. A rare pleasure. One so misses having someone to look down upon besides children and monkeys."

"Did you see who killed him?"

"I did not. I heard him scream and ran to the stream to help. By the time I reached him, his heart's blood was pumping out onto the stones."

"Did you see either of those two idiots take anything from the Puck's body?"

"No, ma'am. The Puck had nothing."

"He spoke to you? What did he say?"

She seemed rather more disturbed than would a queen be by the death of a simple fool. Then I remembered the Puck had bragged of having shagged two queens that very day. I gentled my tone, for perhaps her fierceness was covering grief.

"He said to remember his love to the queen, that is you, I presume." A kind lie, what could it hurt?

"It is. I am Hippolyta, queen of the Amazons."

"Well, that's a wiggly wagonload of wench wank," said I. "Amazons are mythology, fantasies penned by poets. What game are you about, madam?" Although, her chain mail and scars were not the usual decorations for a coddled class—

"Why would I lie to a prisoner with only a tick left on the clock of his life? Believe me, fool."

"Lady, I am not like your watch captain, some dribbling fuckwit, although I do travel with one for emergencies."

"'Ello," said Drool, his face in the window grate across the chamber. He had begun a rhythmic thumping on the door, and a great goofy grin painted his features in the window.

"Drool, are you having a wank?"

"Just a wee one," said the oaf. "She are right fit, Pocket."

I grinned at Hippolyta. "Compliment, really, innit?"

She waved off the distraction. "We'll kill him later. Now, you, fool, what else did the Puck say?"

"Just to remember him to the queen. Although I had seen him the day before and he was talking about putting a spell on some lovers for the shadow king. Did you know the Puck could turn a bloke invisible?"

"Fairy," she explained. She shrugged, then turned, strode to the rack of weapons, and snatched up a halberd. "And you, fool, you were two nights in the forest?"

"I was."

She carried the halberd before her as if advancing on an enemy and I hopped away from the bars. This had gone pear-shaped rather quickly.

"So you are not afraid to be in the forest at night?"

"I am, generally, an indoor fool, but no, I am not afraid of the forest."

"The killer will be found in the forest."

"How do you know? There were watchmen and tradesmen from town there as well."

"The size of the bolt. It had to be a fairy. Wretched creatures."

She thrust the blade of the halberd through the bars. "Come here. I'll cut your bonds."

"Fine, I have been dead twice in as many days, so I am well rehearsed and ready to hit my mark, milady." I hopped forward, reticent, but truly, if she wanted to kill me there was no reason to do it herself, nor to be subtle about it. She sawed through the ropes on my hands and then my feet.

"Thank you," I said, shaking the blood back into my extremities.

"You owe no fealty to king or country, then?" she asked.

"No, milady. All my kings and queens reign only over worms. I am a free lance."

"You'll have to do, then. I'll have a passport made to give you safe passage among the watch and townsfolk. You are mine now—" She paused, leaned on the halberd. "You are called . . . ?"

"Pocket, ma'am. Pocket of Dog Snogging upon Ouze, all-licensed fool to Lear of Britain, consort and king to Cordelia of Britain, France, Burgundy—"

"Enough," she said.

"He are a smashing pirate, too," said Drool, who had finished his dread business. "Pocket are the dog's bollocks."

I bowed at the flattery.

"You are mine now, Pocket," said Hippolyta. "You must return to the forest. I need to know where the Puck was, who he spoke to, what he said, what happened to what he was carrying, and yes, who killed him if that comes up."

"The Puck said he could put a girdle around the Earth in forty minutes. It may take me some time to retrace his path."

"You have three days. You must return before the third watch on the night of my wedding, three days hence. Come directly here, to the gendarmerie. Tell Blacktooth, and have him come only to me, not the duke."

"Blacktooth? Ma'am, if discretion is required . . ."

"Quite right. Blacktooth is much too much the crashing ox for subterfuge and guile. Burke then."

"I'll need my daggers," said I. "Over there on the floor, by the chair."

She fetched my daggers and grabbed a great iron key from a hook on the wall by a rack of halberds. She tossed my bundled daggers through the bars. This daft tart was actually going to let me go. As I strapped on my daggers she turned the key in the lock. "I'll need to take along my apprentice, as well," I said.

She threw the door open and stepped aside. "Three days or the giant dies."

I might have run then, bolted down the tunnel and out into the city, but she had, quite deftly, drawn one of my daggers from its sheath and put the point under my chin.

"I will cut your throat where you stand," she said. "Harken, fool, I do not trust the duke's men or the watch. My warriors are confined to the castle, and the townsfolk are afraid to go into the forest at night. You are the only one who can do this, and not because I have any reason to trust you, but because I trust you know that I will kill both you and your great simple friend, slowly and painfully, if you do not do as I command. And if you think to turn to your dark magic, remember this mercy I extend to you now, your life."

"You fancy me, don't you?"

She grabbed me by the jerkin and threw me across the chamber into the rack of spears. They rattled down over me. I climbed out from under the weaponry.

"A little bit?"

CHAPTER VI

Once a Hero

As I made my way out of the gendarmerie I stepped lightly and sang a little song called "Blacktooth the Goat Blower," which I composed as I went, my spirits lifted for the first time since my pirate wench had abandoned me to suffer among the salty dogs. I suppose it is a testament to my rebellious nature that I do not feel alive unless I am under threat of death by some poxy royal. I am a bit of a calamity whore, I figure, but with Hippolyta's sword hanging o'er my head, I was absolutely giddy with the prospect of my task. I even encouraged the young, spot-faced watchman who escorted me out to join in on the "Goat Blower" chorus, but alas, he was too earnest in his duty.

I made note of my path—locks, gates, and portals—as I went, should I need to return in stealth to extricate an enormous ninny and sneak him by a half-dozen watchmen and as many guards. (Drool's forlorn farewells had shaken me as I left the dungeon, and I had promised him I would return.) At last the labyrinth opened into the bright, cobbled street bustling with peddlers, beggars, and bawds. I caught the aroma of peaches wafting from a basket on a passing merchant's back, a perfume so sweet as to roil a starving fool's stomach. But alas, I had no coin.

"Buy us a peach, lad," I said to Spot Face.

Spot Face snatched a peach off the top of the basket and tossed it to me. "Watchmen don't have to pay," he said.

"Wanker," the merchant grumbled as he ambled away.

I bit into the peach with such abandon that I nearly chipped a tooth on the pit, and as the juice streamed down my chin I thought I might swoon—I closed my eyes and sank into the sweet peachy oblivion of it—but before I could take a second bite I was caught up and lifted roughly by the armpits, and my peach, my gentle fuzzy friend, was dashed on the cobbles.

"Duke wants to see you," said Blacktooth, who had hooked me under my right arm.

"Thought you were away, eh, wee pirate?" said Burke, who had me under the left arm.

I made as if to struggle and when the watchmen braced against my efforts I swung my feet forward, then back over my head into a somersault, and slipped out of their grip, landing in a crouch in front of Spot Face with a dagger in each hand. Before Blacktooth and Burke had turned I was behind Spot Face with one dagger at his throat. The other I flipped and held by the blade, and held ready to send it to a happy home in Blacktooth's eye.

"Back! Another step and I'll cut his throat."

Blacktooth looked to Burke, Burke to Blacktooth with a shrug, then to me said, "Go on then."

"I will," said I. "I'll spill his lifeblood out onto the cobbles."

"Get on with it, then," said Blacktooth. "Then we're off to see the duke."

I found it odd that neither drew a weapon. Burke's crossbow remained slung across his back, Blacktooth's sword in its scabbard.

"Look there," said I, nodding toward my fallen peach, "you've ruined a perfectly lovely peach and this lad will pay for it with his life." Spot Face squirmed in my grip and I pressed the tip of my dagger into his neck to still him.

"Oh, all right," said Blacktooth. He ambled to where my peach had fallen, took a small knife from his belt and trimmed off the bit where I'd taken a bite, then spat on the fuzzy bit and wiped it on his sleeve. He held the peach out to me. "Here you be."

"Aye, slay the lad, take your peach, and we'll be on our way," said Burke. "The duke is waiting."

"Oh bugger," said I. "I'm not going to kill this pup for the loss of a peach." I shoved Spot Face away and sheathed one of my daggers. In the same motion I pulled a chit of wood from my belt, a royal seal was impressed upon it in sealing wax. "But I've this passport from Hippolyta, and I'll wager if you cross her, she'll decorate her bedposts with your heads merely for the music of the night wind whistling through your eye holes."

"Come along," said Blacktooth. "Put up that pig sticker and follow us. You're not a prisoner. Duke just wants a word."

"Fine," said I.

"Fine," said Burke.

"Fine!" said Spot Face, his voice breaking with impotent outrage. "Take your bloody puppet stick, then." He pulled the puppet Jones from his belt and tossed him at me. "I hope the duke spears your liver." He looked to his superiors as if to add them to his curse but stopped himself and stormed back into the tunnel.

"Fine," said Blacktooth, who, to my surprise, turned to lead us around the wall of the castle, rather than back into the gendarmerie.

The duke's castle was not the gleaming marble edifice with gobs of columns that I'd been led to expect from Greek etchings and pots, but a squat and sturdy fortress atop a plateau (the stone hill into which the dungeon and gendarmerie had been carved). Along the battlements stood a guard every two yards, and even as we passed through the halls a pair of guards stood outside every doorway—a heavy martial presence for a kingdom at peace. In the great hall—a soaring, well-windowed, Gothic chamber, built later than the thick outer walls and other buildings in the bailey—I saw the reason for so much military. Fighting men wearing the duke's crest stood around the walls of the chamber and on the six balconies above, numbering perhaps fifty in all, but between each man-at-arms stood another warrior, a woman, and these soldiers, decked in leather, mail, and plate, as muscled and scarred as their male cohorts, were unarmed. Amazons. Hippolyta's soldiers.

"We'll have them daggers," said Burke. "Just while you're seeing the duke. You'll get them back."

What damage they thought a speck of a fool could do with throwing daggers when surrounded by a hundred soldiers, I could not figure, so I unstrapped the harness from under my jerkin and handed it to Burke.

"Only two? Where's the other blade, fool?"

"Left it behind," said I. "Needed the spot in the sheath for that bolt, there. Orders of Queen Hippolyta." And indeed, the harness held only two of my knives, for in the third slot was snuggled the black bolt taken from the Puck's ribs. Burke nodded as if he understood, not considering there might be an errant dagger wandering around his jail.

They led me past a dais upon which sat a simple throne, to a door at the back of the chamber. A guard thumped the shaft of his spear on the floor twice. Burke shoved me through the door into a vaulted antechamber containing a long wooden table, at the head of which stood a rather road-worn chap of perhaps sixty hard summers, wearing an extravagant robe trimmed in gold and a thin golden crown fitted over iron-gray curls: Theseus, Duke of Athens.

Blacktooth and Burke immediately took a knee and bowed their heads. The guards, spaced about the room, Amazon and Athenian alternating, a dozen in all, clicked their heels. Theseus sat, arms folded, as if waiting for something, then a tall old fellow in a silk robe and hat scampered out from behind an arras and unrolled a scroll.

"Egeus," whispered Blacktooth.

"Lord high steward," whispered Burke.

"Toady," said I, *sotto voce*.

Egeus, his head thrown back as if trying to stanch a nosebleed, read from the scroll: "His Grace, Theseus, beloved High Duke of Athens, who defeated Sinis, the pine bender, vanquished Procrustes of the tortuous bed, dispatched the fire-breathing bull of Marathon, slew the Minotaur of the Cretan labyrinth, who defeated Hippolyta, queen of the Amazons, and did bring her kingdom under the loving protection of Attica."

"Well that's a bubbly basin of bull bollocks," said the puppet Jones.

There were various gasps from around the chamber, even from Blacktooth and Burke. One of the Amazons behind Theseus giggled, then caught herself and looked stern. A scribe, sitting by Theseus with quill and parchment, paused in his scratching as if considering whether he should write down puppet-speak.

I looked askance at Jones and shook him on his stick. "Beg pardon, Your Grace, the puppet's been enchanted since yesterday." It was I working Jones this time, because someone had to speak truth to power—and it *was* bollocks. *The* Theseus of legend, who had defeated the Minotaur, would have had to be a thousand years old now—but better the puppet lose his head than I, should Theseus prove less feeble than he appeared.

"The fool and pirate Pocket of Dog Snogging," announced Burke, pushing me forward so I stood at the end of the table opposite Theseus.

"Enchanted?" asked Theseus.

"Aye," said I. The scribe scribbled and looked up, distressed.

The duke said, "The captain of the watch tells me that Hippolyta gave you audience this morning. Of what did you speak?"

"This and that, Your Grace. It is not my place to say, but if you ask the lady, I trust she will tell you."

"You will tell me. If you lie, your life is forfeit."

I drove a quick, sharp boot heel into Blacktooth's shin. "You said he just wanted to chat!" Burke made as if to restrain me and I smacked him sharply on the bottom on the spot where I'd sent a dagger a day before. He yowled and limped in a tight circle.

"Enough," said the duke. "Answer me, fool."

I shrugged. "Your lady wished to know if I knew who killed the Puck and if I had spoken to him before he was murdered."

"Aha!" said the duke, as if he'd caught a pie thief in the kitchen.

"Aha!" repeated Blacktooth, dropping a heavy hand on my shoulder. "Do you prefer the fool hanged or broken on the rack, Your Eminents?"

"Or both," added Burke, grabbing me by my bicep.

"We found him standing over the Puck, Your Disgrace," said Blacktooth.

"Your Grace," corrected Burke. "We encountered the fool on the previous day, as well, conspiring with a group of rude mechanicals, with no passport upon him, and would have arrested him on the spot, but he vanished."

"Vanished?" Theseus seemed to lose his breath for a moment.

"Not even a puff of smoke," said Blacktooth. "Just chucked a knife in Burke's bum and vanished."

"Did you kill the Puck?" asked the duke.

"Did you?" I replied.

"No, not that I—I sent the watch into the forest to find him."

"To what end, if I may ask, Your Grace?"

"Well, I . . ." Theseus was not used to answering questions.

"Perhaps you were going to have the Puck entertain at your wedding, Your Grace," said Egeus.

"Yes," said Theseus. "That's it—"

"Not that he was hammering your queen like a blacksmith setting rivets?" said Jones. I pounded the puppet on the table.

"Manners, you wooden-headed ninny," said I. "Sorry, duke. Do go on."

The great Greek hero Theseus fluttered his fingers like a flustered dowager feeling dog breath on her naughty bits. "Oh my, no," said the duke. "My Hippolyta is a most chaste and modest lady."

"She's the queen of a race of bloody warrior women who keep men as pets, bonk them for offspring, then make coin purses from their scrotums."

The tall, blond Amazon behind Theseus who had giggled earlier held up a small brown coin purse and grinned. I shuddered.

"Everyone out!" commanded the duke. "I would speak to this fool alone."

The guards and watchmen headed for the door.

"Wait," said the high steward. "Your Grace, the fool could be the assassin. Your safety."

"Fine. You lot"—the duke waved to the cohort of guards behind his chair—"stay and see that I am not attacked by this flea turd of a fool."

"Bit harsh," said I.

All but the four guards, two armed Athenians and two Amazons, scurried out of the room.

"Sit here." Theseus patted the arm of a chair where the scribe had been sitting. I made my way to his side and sat. "Tell me now, fool, are you of a kind with the Puck?"

"In that he was a fool, possessed of many talents, as am I, yes. But as I am much more handsome and wear proper motley rather than run around the forest dressed in leaves like a savage, no."

"I see," said the duke, stroking his short beard.

Theseus, ruler of Athens, slayer of monsters, seemed less sure of himself than I, a half-starving flotsam fool. I knew not why the royals held Robin Goodfellow in such regard, but I would have been foolish indeed not to take shelter in the Puck's reputation.

A moment passed, the duke glanced over his shoulder at his guards, then motioned for them to move to the far end of the long chamber. When they were in place, he whispered.

"Do you know, did the Puck seduce my Hippolyta?"

"I think not, Your Grace. The puppet was merely making a jest at your expense." It was not a lie, really. I did not know for a fact that Puck had been bonking the warrior queen. Speaking truth to power is a noble endeavor but of limited utility if one's head is in a basket.

"Good, good. I took her as a spoil of war, but since the battle she has fired a passion in me I have never before known."

"Well, she's a flinty bit of fluff to be sure, and I've been well used by a brace of warrior wenches myself in the past. But for the rattling armor and random bossiness, they were quite lovely."

"So you know? I would possess her, not as a prisoner, but as her lord."

"A distinction without a difference, to be sure. How may I be of service?"

"Blacktooth tells me you go about the forest at night, is that true?"

"It is." City of cowering wallies, was Athens, all afraid of the dark.

"Then I would have you find out if the Puck completed a task I sent him on. It can only be done at night."

"You sent Puck on an errand?"

"He was my jester and servant. I sent him to take a message and fetch a trifling thing from the fairy queen Titania. The fairies can only be found at night."

That explained Cobweb's disappearance each dawn. "I'm your man," said I. "Messages and fetching are well within my wheelhouse. What's the message? I can compose it into a bawdy limerick if you prefer. *There was a young fellow called Bucket—*"

"No, you don't need to know the message, just whether Titania received it. And she will know the thing you are to fetch and give it to you if she sees fit. Tell her the Puck did not have it with him."

"Honored to be of service," said I. "I will need my apprentice to accompany me, of course. He is held in your dungeon and I will need him for navigation and protection."

"I think not," said the duke. "Blacktooth has told me of your simple giant. He will stay here to assure your return."

"Oh balls!" said I, somewhat disappointed.

"I'll have the scribe make you a passport with my seal. It will give you my protection in the city, and with Titania's servants, but I cannot guarantee your protection from other forest dwellers. Return here before my wedding, three days hence. If you accomplish your task, bring me what I require, you shall be the royal jester and your friend will be set free."

"I will be honored to put my awesome and terrible powers in your service, Your Grace. But I'll need money, for food and provisions. I've not had a decent meal for days."

"Very well, give him money for food," Theseus said to the guards. "Egeus will reimburse you. And call the scribe."

The tall, blond Amazon grinned as she pulled a silver coin from her nut-sack and threw it to me across the table. The scribe was summoned and he constructed a passport on a thin shingle of wood and applied to it the duke's seal in hard wax. I tucked it in my belt with its brother. I was dismissed and Egeus, the high steward, restored my daggers to me and led me out of the castle.

"So you will go to the forest?" asked the steward.

"Aye," said I. "Secret quest and whatnot."

Egeus leaned down to me. "My daughter, Hermia, ran away into the forest two nights ago. If you bring her back with you I will see that you are richly rewarded. I am a wealthy man."

"And she will come willingly, will she? I am but a speck of a fool and not suited for taking prisoners."

"Tell her all is forgiven and I will allow no harm to come to her. You will find her with a young rascal called Lysander. If you kill him in the process there will be a bonus in it for you."

"Just like that? Kill the lad, fetch the girl, gold and glory in the castle?"

"Yes."

"Shall I bring you the lad's head?"

"No, that might upset Hermia. She is mistakenly in love with him. Just bring a swath of his shirt stained in blood. That and my daughter's tears will be proof enough."

"Lovely," said I, strapping on my daggers. "Now point me toward the city gate, toady, and give me a route that takes me by a market, I'll need a hearty meal if I'm to spend the evening murdering and kidnapping."

ACT II

And that distilled by magic sleights
Shall raise such artificial sprites
As by the strength of their illusion
Shall draw him on to his confusion.

—HECATE,
Macbeth, 3:5

CHAPTER VII

The Slow and the Quick

"R AWR!"

"Shut up!"

"RAWR!"

"Shut up!"

"RAWR!"

"Snug, if you roar one more time I shall lop off your knob while you sleep."

"Rrrrr, rrrrrr—"

"Snug!" I called to the joiner, who was outside of his shop on the edge of Athens, having a discussion with his wife. She was a round and sunny woman, in contrast to her husband's gangly dimness.

"Master Pocket," said Snug. "We thought you were killed in the forest." He turned to his wife. "This is him, Bess, the master of theater I told you about. High jester of Dog Tosser, he was. Tell her, Master Pocket, how I got to rehearse so I can be a proper fierce lion."

Snug made as if he was going to roar again and his wife put a hand in his face for silence as she rolled by him to look me over.

I bowed extravagantly, hat in hand for the flourish. "*Enchanté*, Madam Snug," I said in perfect fucking French.

"He's right tiny," she said, inspecting me from head to toe, pausing a moment to regard my codpiece. "Say, you ain't an elf, are you?" She winked at me hard enough to approximate a seizure, with all the subtlety of a head wound.

"It's not real," said Snug. "And he ain't an elf. And don't you think about it again. Go make us some lunch, woman."

"I thought you was having lunch with your mates in the forest."

"Go," said Snug, a stern finger pointed to the shop doorway.

Madam Snug rumbled off into the shop. Snug turned to me, affecting the aspect of a whipped dog. "Apologies. She's been like that since that rascal Puck touched her up by the millpond. Ruined, she is. You'll have lunch with us, I hope. Just bread and cold mutton."

At the market I'd purchased a loaf and some cheese and a skin of wine, which I had slung over my back in a flour sack, but before I set out into the forest on a quest to find a killer and buy release of Drool, perhaps a chat with one of the only people I knew in this land who did not wish to imprison or murder me was in order—even if he was bone simple and possessed of a wandering wife.

"We was supposed to rehearse at lunchtime in the forest, but Bottom never came home yesterday. I reckon he's dead."

"Dead?"

"Aye, overnight in the forest. Probably kilt by elfs or lions. You wouldn't want to play Pyramus for the duke's wedding, would you?"

"Aren't you even going to look for him?"

"Not me. If the elfs got Bottom, clever as he is, I got no chance at all."

"I'm heading into the forest," said I. "I'll keep out a look for him."

"Right decent of you. Maybe bring back his waistcoat or a toe so his wife's got something to bury. Otherwise she'll worry, you know. Come along, lunch."

I followed Snug into his shop. A large window of waxed parchment panels lit the space with golden light like a wall of candles.

Various tools of his trade hung on a side wall: saws, planes, hatchets, hammers, and spokeshaves. The carpenter at the White Tower, where once I jested for King Lear, had befriended me, and while he worked we often had long conversations about theology, carpentry, or the nocturnal benevolence of various wenches about the castle, so I at once felt at ease in the shop. The smell of newly milled lumber hung in the air and put me in mind of my long-ago home.

Snug led me past his workbench, where a wooden-jawed vise held his current work in progress, a yard-long piece of oak he had been shaping with a spokeshave. Curled ribbons of wood littered the floor below the bench. Above the bench hung a half-dozen other oak constructions, the finished versions of the piece in the vise. They looked quite familiar.

"Good Snug, these pieces you're working, are these crossbows?"

"Aye, they are. Just the stocks. I makes 'em for the duke's men."

"I thought only soldiers and the watch were permitted weapons."

"These ain't weapons, just bits of weapons. I makes the stocks, then they goes to the smith, who makes the trigger and what-not. Another chap makes the bows, gluing up layers of horn and wood, and Jim the fletcher makes the bolts. Tom Snout the tinker puts them all together before they go off to the armory. You remember Snout from rehearsal. Bloke with the fine deerskin hat."

"So you never have a finished crossbow?"

"They gived me one to make me patterns and jigs from."

"Do you still have it?"

"Aye, around here somewhere. I'll find it for you after lunch."

"So all of the tradesmen you named, they each had a finished crossbow to work from?"

"Not all of 'em. Some just got the part they was to make. Me and Snout got one though, because he had to put them together and because I am slow of study and could not do my work without seeing what the finished one looked like."

"So, because you're thick as pig shit, they gave you a working weapon?"

Snug thought for a second, looking at the row of crossbow stocks as if they might have the answer inscribed in the wood. "Aye, that sounds about right," he said.

He led me through a low doorway into a narrow chamber where he and his wife lived: a cozy hovel of a home, with two small waxed-parchment windows, a bed, a stove, and a small table with two chairs. A loaf of rough brown bread and a tin pitcher of ale sat on the table next to a joint of smoked mutton that had been worn at with a knife.

"You take the chair," said Snug. "Bess can sit on the upended bucket."

"You can put the upended bucket on your empty head," said Madam Snug.

I sat down and dug in, my manners drowned long ago in a sea of pirates, nitwits, and monkeys. As I ate, the Snugs sniped at one another. Robin Goodfellow's name was batted back and forth in quite unflattering terms. In denying her liaisons with the Puck, Mrs. Snug did not paint the fairy fool in endearing colors, and Snug was far from forgiving the fairy or his wife's transgressions.

"Why, I wouldn't let that rascal touch me if he was the last idiot in the village. A right trickster and a liar, he is, and tiny to boot." She turned to me. "Nothing wrong with being tiny, mind you, if a fellow is true and knows his way about a lady's bits, just as long as he's not a lying scoundrel like that Puck." She winked extravagantly again and hitched her bosoms up in her frock in my direction.

I looked to Snug as if I had not heard her. "Have you ever

made a smaller crossbow? One, say, made for someone my size or smaller? One, say, that would fire a bolt like this?" I drew the black bolt from the sheath across my back and put it on the table.

Snug set his ale down, then picked up and examined the bolt. "Made out of some heavy wood. Ironwood or something that don't grow around here. Tip is forged black iron and tied on with sinew. This ain't a bolt like what Jim the fletcher makes. But it don't speak to the size of the crossbow. You could shoot this out of one of the ones I make if you wanted to."

"Balls," I spat under my breath. "So this bolt could be shot by any crossbow carried by the watch, or the duke's guards or soldiers?"

"Aye, as long as it ain't too big around to fit in the arrow shelf, that groove on top of the stock, and it ain't. But heavy as it is, you wouldn't have range like with a longer bolt. Three score yards shot flat, I reckon."

"So plenty for the forest?"

"Aye. But that bolt ain't for hunting. Would have a wider head to bleed the animal. That one's for poking through armor."

The whole time Snug and I had talked about the weaponry, Madam Snug had chewed the same mouthful of bread, her gaze captured from the moment I'd drawn the crossbow bolt. I resheathed the bolt, drained my cup of ale, and stood.

"A fine repast, Madam Snug." I bowed and tipped my hat in thanks. "But I must go; errand for the duke. Before I go, Snug, might I have a look at that finished crossbow of yours?"

"Aye," he said. He let go a roaring belch, stood, and led the way into his shop. I waited by the front door, while he rifled through every beam and scrap on and under every table, only to come up with a shrug. "Sorry, Master Pocket, I can't seem to find it. Perhaps the missus took it."

"I didn't touch your sodding crossbow," said Bess, who had watched from the hovel doorway during the search. "What would I do with a crossbow?"

"You might have given it to your wee lover-man, Robin Goodfellow."

"No I didn't. I wouldn't give that two-faced scalawag the dust off my shoe."

"Little chance of that, good Snug," I told the joiner. Dead obvious, then, that news of the Puck's demise had not yet reached the realm of the Mechanicals. I made my way out of the shop into the street. "Thank you for lunch, but I must be off. You sure you won't join me? Perhaps you can look for your friend Bottom." I confess, I am accustomed to traveling in the company of my own personal nitwit, and until Drool was liberated I thought Snug might suffice. An attending idiot can be a whetstone for the wit, and, in the event of bears or other beasts, a fine distraction while a quick and agile fool makes his escape.

"No, I gots work, but if Bottom's alive, please to tell him how splendid and frightening my lion is. RAWR!"

"Shut up!" said Madam Snug, who appeared in the doorway. "You can tell your elfin friends they can stop here if they need a rest from forest life. Always happy to help a weary traveler."

"Oh my," said the puppet Jones (under my control), "the Puck made a right deep impression on you, didn't he?"

"Did not. He was a crooked little tomcat, he was. You be on your way, now, puppet."

"And a fond farewell to you, madam," said I as I tucked Jones down the back of my jerkin and scampered away.

Was, she had said. He *was* a crooked little tomcat. I pondered it as I made my way over the fields and orchards that surrounded the city and into the forest. The ninny's wife? A missing crossbow? The weaver Bottom not returned from the forest overnight?

Everyone in the city terrified of the forest people, yet the young lovers two nights away and Egeus sending me, a stranger, out to murder his daughter's suitor without so much as a glance at my CV? A duke and a queen overly curious about what the Puck had been doing in the forest before he was killed, and neither overly concerned with who had done the killing. Peradventure, I was not the first assassin sent into the woods this wedding week.

*   *   *

I THOUGHT it best to begin my search where the Puck had fallen, so I made my way to the path on which Blacktooth and the watch had carried me into town. It was easy going for a bit, a wide path under a canopy of massive trees, so I took time to note the annoying and uncomfortable things that filled the forest, ferns and thorns, all the time keeping watch for any wolves, bears, or dragons that might find a winsome fool delicious. I moved as nimble and spry as in my youth, although I could not say from where this vigor sprung, for I was still less than two days from starved and drowned. But upon my spirit I felt a dull ache, a hunger—no, a hollowness. Had it been so long since I had been on my own that a mere hour alone was making a shell of me?

"More of a bellend," said the puppet Jones. (Yes, I was working him, but I pretended it was magic.)

"What would you know?" said I. "Nothing more than an empty head on a stick, you are."

"In that we are of a kind. And both move at the whim of cruel masters."

"That's it, isn't it?"

"Aye, you're not lonesome, you git, you're craving your freedom."

I'd had no master but love for my two years with the pirates, and now, once again, I was doing the bidding of a pair of scheming royals, under threat of death.

"Oh balls," I said to Jones, choking him somewhat to make sure I had his attention. "I am a fool."

ENTER RUMOUR, PAINTED FULL OF TONGUES

"And with that, the bloody obvious rose like a viper to bite the fool on his bottom."

"Ahhhh!" said I, jumping straight up perhaps a yard and controlling my fluids only just. He was an annoyingly tall fellow, thin and pale, wrapped in a robe and wearing a hat, both quilted with what appeared to be human tongues that moved even as he stood, his long scone of a nose so turned up I might have, with better light, seen his brain writhing in its den. Whether he had stepped out from behind a tree or fallen out of one, I did not know, for there was no crunch of leaves or brush of branch, he was just bloody *there*. "Who are you?"

"I am Rumour, planner of plots, seer of schemes, teller of tales, a humble narrator, at your service."

"I smell a device," said I. The tongues on Rumour's robe waggled at me and I jumped away, holding Jones *en garde*. "Back, thou skulking loony."

"Loony? Moi?" he said in barely passable fucking French. *"You were the one talking to a puppet."*

"I thought I was alone. And besides, conversation frightens off bears."

"No, it doesn't. And you aren't alone, silly fool."

"Well not now, but before you crept up like some tongue-covered spider . . ."

"Not me. You've been followed this last hour by a squirrel." Without looking, Rumour pointed a long finger up to a tree behind him. Indeed, a red, horn-eared squirrel peered down from a branch. It chirped and scrambled to the far side of the tree. *"See?"*

"You saw it there just now and you're trying to be clever. That is a coincidental squirrel."

"*No, it has been over you since you entered the forest. You probably would have heard it had you not been nattering on to your puppet while you stumbled along aimlessly.*"

"I have not been stumbling, and my stumbling has not been aimless. I am on a mission." I produced my passport and waved it under Rumour's prodigious nose. "From the duke."

"*You're going the wrong way. You'll find no clue to the Puck's movements in that direction.*"

"How do you know I've any interest in the Puck at all?"

"*Rumour knows all, sees all. I am the agent of outrageous fortune and twisted narrative.*"

"Well, that's a bumptious barrel of bear wank."

"*Pardon?*"

"You're lying."

"*I do not lie, although I am notoriously unreliable. A hundred yards ahead the path will fork. You will want to take the branch to the right. That will lead you to a clue of what the Puck was doing in his last hours.*"

"And you know what he was doing?"

"*I do.*"

"So you could just fucking tell me and save me the hike?"

"*And deprive you of the adventure of a mystery and the joy of discovery? Never.*"

I drew a dagger from the small of my back and held it low. "Or I could just start carving bits out of you until you tell me." He was a thin and willowy fellow, even if tediously tall, and I am quick as a cat and well practiced with a knife—if it came to a fight, things would not go well for him.

"*Oh, thou daft spoon,*" said Rumour. "*You'll never catch me.*"

"We shall see," said I. And with that I flipped the dagger, caught it by the blade, and sent it a half turn toward skewering him in the foot. I didn't actually mean to injure him but aimed so, at worst, I might nick a toe, and, at best, tack his soft shoe to the forest floor, but in a blink, he was ten feet to my right, giggling among the ferns.

"*Ha! Too slow. The quick and the dead,*" he said. "*I am, at your service, the quick.*"

"That is not what that means," said I, retrieving my dagger from the loam, where it had buried itself to the hilt. He was frightfully fast, but the miss was mine. I was not a bully born—I am shit at forceful coercion.

"*Yes it does. Nothing exceeds the speed of Rumour. 'Twas I taught the Puck to put a girdle round the globe in forty minutes.*"

"I do not care." I thought then to cast a devastating insult, a weapon more suited to my skills, but then thought a softer tack might be preferred. I bowed my head. "Good Rumour, I apologize for my temper, but I am desperate. If I don't find out the Puck's movement and who ended him the royals are going to kill my apprentice. He's a dimwitted ox of a lad, but gentle, and my only friend. Have pity on a poor fool."

"*And tell me, when you tell the royals what they want to know, what is to keep them from killing you both?*"

"Honor?" I ventured, realizing at once how weak it sounded.

"*It seems to me you won't know what each of them will do until you know what it was the Puck was doing, what it was that he knew that they are so eager to find out.*"

"And then they'll kill us?"

"*Not if you can find the favor of one over the other. They each sent you separately, did they not?*"

"That's true."

"*And did either Theseus or Hippolyta seem eager to have the other find out about the other's intent?*"

"No, there appears to be no love nor trust between the two. The Amazon's warriors are allowed no weapons. She is a caged bird, and he a captor afraid of his captive."

"*There you have it, then, you'll have to find out the Puck's intent and hope you can leverage that information of one of them against the other.*"

"And if I can't?"

"*Then I'd say you're right fucked.*"

"I am not. What do you know? You've tongues all over your robe and cap."

"*Said the fellow dressed head to foot in black and silver argyle. You look like a sock with a single toe sticking through.*"

"Touché," said I, in perfect fucking French. I tipped my hat in salute.

"*The lovers are the key to your quest, fool. When the path forks ahead, go right, it will lead you to what you seek.*"

"Or you could just tell me."

"*No fun there,*" said Rumour. "*Adieu, fool.*" And with a whirlwind of leaves he was gone.

"I am not fucked!" I called after him.

I was fucked.

The red squirrel chittered above.

CHAPTER VIII

The Course of True Love

I TOOK THE right fucking fork in the path and as night lowered o'er the forest, I came upon a hollow of great mossy rocks where four young Athenians flirted and fought like loquacious kittens.

Two youths, the straw-haired wank stain I'd seen before, called Demetrius, and another fellow, more fit than the first, with a dark, closely trimmed, pointy beard, were on their knees on either side of the tall girl, Helena, flinging woo at her like Jeff flinging monkey spunk on a day out at the hat shop. A second girl, petite and auburn haired, looked on, quite unhappy with the entire scene.

"Oh, good forest elf," Helena called. "Help me, for these three conspire to make cruel sport of me for being unloved and unlovable."

"Not an elf," said I.

"Unloved?" said Demetrius. "She is anything but unloved. I adore her, I dote on her in idolatry."

"Not so much as do I," said Dark Beard. "Here, good Helena, put your foot upon my head, so you will know I am your servant, your spaniel—for I would be the soil upon your shoe if it means I may be that close to you."

And with that, Dark Beard put his head upon the ground by Helena's foot, and was quickly joined by the straw-haired Demetrius, who put his ear to the ground by her other foot. "Lady, my goddess, tread upon *my* face, and if perchance your small toe should enter my nose hole, so will I breathe in your essence and never exhale, ere I explode with your love. Both small toes, in my nose, I beseech thee!"

I looked to the auburn-haired girl, who seemed the only one viewing this spectacle with the appropriate amount of horror. "Lunatics?" I inquired.

"Bloody enchanted," she said. "Both were in love with me yesterday, although I love only Lysander." She pointed to Dark Beard, who had Helena by the ankle and was trying to put her foot on his head by force.

"Don't believe her," said Helena. "Hermia is part of this cruel joke. She delights in my humiliation."

"Hermia?" I inquired to the auburn-haired girl.

"Yes, Hermia, daughter of Egeus," said she, unable to stop herself from making a polite curtsy.

"Charmed," said I, bowing over her hand. "Pocket of Dog Snogging, at your service."

She said, "Last night, while we all slept, separate and chaste, the Puck placed some drops in their eyes. He thought I slept, but I saw him. When they awoke they were both in love with Helena and have nothing but scorn for me."

"Wretched cow," called Demetrius, rubbing his face into some leaves.

"Shut your fetid cakehole, thou festering canker blossom," Hermia shouted at the piss-haired Athenian. To me, she said, "See? Enchanted."

"Well cursed, lass," I said.

"Don't trust her," shouted Helena, who was trying to stop Lysander from licking her shin. "She was a vixen when she went to school, and though she be but little, she is fierce."

"Little, is it?" said Hermia. "I will show you little, thou lumbering maypole. I shall decorate your inconstant lovers with your splattered brains." She snatched up a heavy branch from the ground and made for her friend. I caught her by the sleeve as she passed by, swung her around, and relieved her of her weapon. She looked at me wide eyed, both surprised and offended.

I slapped her cheek ever so lightly to bring her attention to the fore. "The Puck, you say?"

"Hit her again," shouted Lysander. "She distracts me from my love. I loathe her."

"I loathe her more," added Demetrius.

She made to grab for her club and I cautioned her by waving the stick in her face.

"Tut tut, love. Your father promised me good recompense for slaying Lysander and once my blade is bloodied it will be no trouble to cut all your throats." I am shit as a fighter, being ratshaggingly small and all, but I am the very mutt's nuts when it comes to crafting a threat.

"Do your worst on her," said Lysander. "I love her not and would not stand in your way."

"Neither I," said Demetrius. "I wouldn't have her if she were naked and carrying her weight in gold, annoying dwarf that she is."

"Fine," I said. I handed Hermia back her club. "Brain them, love. I'll wait."

"Please, good Hermia," said Helena, hopping from one foot to the other to stay out of the affectionate grasps of her suitors, "let your mercy be as sweet as our friendship was once: kill only Lysander and leave Demetrius to me."

Hermia stomped up to her friends, menaced them all with her stick, then screamed in frustration and cast the club into the rocky hollow. "If I were going to kill anyone it would be that rascal Puck. He's at fault for this—this disgusting display." She waved at the two grovelers. "This is not a natural allure, but some trifling elvish magic. And *you* know it, Helena."

Helena's face went slack as anger gave way to revelation. "They're not having me on?"

"No, friend," said Hermia.

"And they don't really fancy me, either?"

"You saw the Puck in the night."

"You jesters!" Helena kicked Demetrius and Lysander until they scuttled away a few feet and sulked like scolded puppies. "You buffoons, you have been duped by the Puck."

"No, lady," said Lysander, "if I thought the Puck had but put the taint of insincerity on my love for you I would puncture his liver most mortally."

"And I his other liver!" said Demetrius.

"What are these knobs on about?" said Cobweb, who was suddenly standing at my shoulder without the courtesy of a cough or crunching leaf to announce her presence. I leapt a foot or so into the air and yelped a bit, as a courtesy, so as not to deprive her of the satisfaction of thinking she'd surprised me.

"Where have you been?" I inquired.

"Tending to the night queen, as is my duty."

"You didn't even say goodbye."

"I left breakfast for you. There was frolicking to be done. You look better. Didn't find your giant friend, then?"

"Oh, I found him. He's locked in the dungeon under Theseus's castle, and if I don't return within three days with the answers Hippolyta and Theseus want, they'll kill him."

"Fuck's sake, Pocket, trouble follows you like a fluffy tail. What kind of answers do the mortal royals think you can give them?"

"Like who killed the Puck and what he was doing up until the time he died."

Cobweb snorted. "Killed the Puck! Haw-haw. What fools these mortals be. Robin Goodfellow is forever, he can't be killed."

"No, Robin Goodfellow was slain this morning, in this forest.

I found him myself, his heart's blood spilling out a hole in his ribs made by this." I drew the black bolt from the sheath at my back and held it before Cobweb, whose wide eyes were filling with tears. She took the bolt from me and sniffed it, touched her tongue to the iron tip, then dropped it to the forest floor.

Her eyes rolled back and she began to fall. I caught her around the waist and held her up, pressing her head against my chest until I could feel her will return.

"Rather I would kiss a dog's arse than Hermia's bubbling lips," said Lysander.

"You had no trouble with these bubbly lips last evening," said Hermia.

"I was a fool. The scales have fallen from my eyes and I see now Helena's radiance."

"I, too, was a fool, a bigger fool," said Demetrius. "When I wooed you for fortune and position I saw not how truly hideous you were in comparison to glorious Helena."

"Mock me, cruel rogues," said Helena. "I am deserved of it, for I am as ugly as a bear."

"You are not," said Hermia. "But these two, enchanted or not, are as stupid as chickens."

Cobweb pushed away from me and looked up, blinking the tears out of her eyes. "Circe's balls, they're annoying." She looked over her shoulder at the lovers. "With their tallness and their painted faces and their—their shoes."

"Agreed, but they saw the Puck last night. The duke tasked me with finding the Puck's killer and I am yet to ask them about the encounter."

"I'll do it." She snatched up the crossbow bolt and charged the lovers. "Shut up, you shiny-haired fuckwits!"

Everyone grieves in his own way. Evidently the fairy way was violent and armed.

The lovers hadn't even noticed the fairy's arrival, but they noticed now, as she marched up to them, her jaw jutting hard and sharp like the ramming prow of a tiny warship.

"Look," said Helena. "An elf! She's even tinier than you, Hermia."

"Not an elf," I said to no one, as that is who was listening. The lovers, forgetting their own self-made calamity, had lined up in a semicircle around Cobweb and were examining her as if she'd been presented to them for purchase.

"Look at her little ears," said Helena. "They're pointed."

"There are sticks in her hair," said Hermia. "We should keep her. Have her groomed and show her off at the duke's wedding."

"I've never seen an elf before," said Lysander. "Is this why no one will go into the forest at night? Seems silly now, when you see this wisp of a girl."

"You've seen the Puck," said Hermia. "And you might have seen him again last night if you hadn't been so knackered from trying to shag me all night."

"So you say," said Lysander. "That seems but a dream to me now."

"Well if I saw him fiddling with people's feelings," said Demetrius, "I'd make him sorry indeed."

"By sticking him with this!" said Cobweb, and as she spoke she swung the crossbow bolt up from behind her back. I think she may have intended to present it before Demetrius's face—confront him with the instrument of his dread-dickery—but whether she was moved by anger or her vision was obscured by her tears, she misjudged somewhat and stabbed the Athenian quite smartly in the tip of his chin.

Demetrius screamed and went over backward, clutching his chin, which spurted blood no little. Cobweb leapt on him and knelt on his chest, the bolt raised over her head. "Did you kill him, you great yellow-haired twat? Tell me or I'll make a Cyclops of you with the next plunge."

"No, no, no, I didn't even see him."

Cobweb jumped off Demetrius and landed before Lysander, who cowered against the mossy rocks. "How about you? Did you kill the Puck?"

"No, no, madam, I did not see him."

Cobweb leapt to a spot between Helena and Hermia. "You? Did you kill him?" She raised the arrow over Helena's breast. "I will pop your black, broken heart from your chest and eat it while you watch, shoe whore!"

"I don't even know what that means," said Helena, shaking.

"Did you kill him?"

"No." Helena turned and hid her face in her hands, preferring to take the fairy's killing blow in the bum, evidently.

"You!" Cobweb said to Hermia, who was small enough that the fairy could menace her eye to eye. "Tell me, did you kill the Puck or do I pin your tits together like bloody apples on a spit?"

"No. No! I saw him put the drops in the boys' eyes. That is all. I didn't even speak to him."

"RAWR!" Cobweb roared in Hermia's face, and the ingénue burst into tears and turned away.

Cobweb spun on a heel to face me. "They didn't kill him." She trotted back to me and handed me the bolt. I replaced it in the sheath at my back. "These well-kept types don't do their own killing, though. They would have hired an assassin."

"And they might be lying," said I.

"Oi, are you lying?" Cobweb called to the lovers. They all shook their heads ardently, even Demetrius, who held his bloody chin and grimaced in pain with the movement. "See?"

"Sweet Cobweb," said I, "you are the very vicar's knickers when it comes to nest building and rescuing seafarers, but you are shit at interrogation."

"*You're* shit at it," she said. "What's a vicar?"

"Are you all right, love?" I asked her.

She regarded me with recrimination.

Over by the lovers, Lysander said, "I told you I should have brought my crossbow."

"Wait," said I. "What? You have a crossbow?"

"As do I," said Demetrius.

"Ladies are only allowed longbows," said Hermia, "but I am quite a proficient archer myself."

"And she is ever so pretty, with her arrows quivering," said Helena, "while I lumber like a great ox spraying bolts about the green, willy-nilly."

"Oh, stop it," said Hermia. "If you are going to feel sorry for yourself at least wait until you don't have two suitors hanging on your skirt hem."

I was about to inquire whether everyone in this bloody country was armed, when from behind the rocks there came a great raucous caterwaul that set my various sphincters on high tension, even as I reached behind my back for a dagger.

"Bear!" said Cobweb.

The lovers, who had huddled together at the first call, bolted, led by Demetrius and followed by Lysander, who herded the girls ahead of him, all of them letting out horrified yowls as they ran. I thought to follow, but then I saw Cobweb was laughing, nearly doubled over with her private joke.

The caterwauling sounded again, closer now. It was definitely not a bear.

"That's not a bear," said I, the very herald of the obvious. We'd had a trained bear for a while at the French court and it made no sound like this bellowing in the forest. Did she ever tire of frightening people with possible bears?

The bushes by the trail parted and a great horse-headed creature stepped into view.

"Holy rancid fuckcheese!" said I. "A centaur." The thing had the body of a man—fully dressed in trousers, a shirt, and a fine woven waistcoat—and the head of some equine creature. It let loose another bellow, a bray, really, illuminating its species as a donkey, not a horse. I suppose the long ears might have given it away, but rather than committing the time to study, I was considering fight and flight, and would have done one of those, I'm sure, had Cobweb not exclaimed, "Bottom, what are you doing here? The night queen will be furious if she wakes to find you gone."

"Bottom?" I said, to myself more than the world. The waistcoat did look familiar.

"Oh, Master Cobweb, that is just the trouble," said Bottom. "I awoke in Titania's bower utterly alone, the lady had abandoned me. I was desperately in need of breakfast. I see you know Master Pocket. So good to see you, maestro."

Cobweb turned to me and grinned. "Master Bottom was an honored guest in the queen's bower last night. Very honored guest." She made a vulgar thrusting gesture while rolling her eyes and lolling her tongue.

"Bottom," said I. "Thou art transmogrified. How happened this change?"

"It were a revelation, maestro, for I was using the very method you taught our troupe of players. When last evening the queen wished that I have the personage of a donkey, I conjured the memory of when in the past I had sensed myself to be an ass, thus your coaching transformed me."

"Good Bottom, that is a fluttering firkin of fairy wank. I invented that *method* on the spot because Snug was so bloody stupid he crafted a lion's roar from chicken sounds."

"Nevertheless, here you see the result," brayed Bottom. "Your method and magic have enchanted me."

"The Puck," Cobweb whispered in my ear.

"The Puck? You saw the Puck last night? Why didn't you say so?"

"You were busy chatting up your fancy Athenian shoe tarts," said Cobweb. "The Puck often keeps company with the night queen, as she employs him for spying and other services."

"I thought Puck was the jester for the shadow king."

"Do you not have spies in the mortal world? Dual loyalties are rather their speciality."

"Well, we need to see the night queen, then," said I.

"And have her command me to imagine myself a weaver again," said Bottom. "Mrs. Bottom will be very cross if I return in this form."

"You may be surprised," said Cobweb, giving an encouraging pat to the prodigious bulge snaking its way down the inside of Bottom's trouser leg.

"Oh my," said Bottom, letting loose a laugh that degraded into a string of wheezing whinnies.

"Come on then," said Cobweb. "The queen will need tending to." And she led us off down a path opposite from the direction in which the lovers had run.

As we walked, Bottom said, "The lads must be beside themselves. This will be the second rehearsal I've missed. I fear the part of Pyramus may be more of a challenge than before, unless you may work another spell on me, perhaps sharpening my jaw and giving me the steely-eyed aspect of a hero."

"Bottom, I do not have magical—"

"Shush!" said Cobweb, spinning around and shaking her head in a stern and angry manner, followed by a less-than-subtle wink, which wasn't lost even on Bottom.

"But I myself saw you disappear in front of the watch, and this . . ." He gestured to his ears and muzzle.

Cobweb growled a threat, a sound as if she might be concealing a small dog under her frock.

"Quite right," said I. "Magical. We shall see about the magic in a bit. But, good Bottom, I've just encountered several young Athenians, all of whom said that they owned bows or crossbows. Is everyone in this bloody country armed?"

"Just the toffs," said Bottom. "Working folk aren't allowed."

"But Snug the joiner told me that only the watch and soldiers were permitted to carry weapons."

"Well Snug is a ninny, isn't he?" said Bottom.

"There you have it," said Cobweb. "Right from the horse's mouth. Come on, you, the night queen will shit a hedgehog if she finds her donkey boy gone. And you'll want to have a chat with her, Pocket."

Cobweb went ahead, leading us down a forest path that was all but invisible to me, but the fairy moved in the moonlight as sure as under the noonday sun, so Bottom and I kept in sight of her pale frock as we navigated the dark forest at a quick pace. We'd gone perhaps a half mile—hard to say with the meandering and whatnot—when a banshee scream sounded out of the dark above us and three slight figures dropped out of a tree, nearly landing on Bottom. Before I could draw a dagger or shimmy up a tree they were on him, tugging and tickling and generally making a ruckus. Three fairies, no bigger than Cobweb, swarmed the donkey-headed man, who brayed with delight as they tugged his ears, rubbed his muzzle, and dry-humped various parts of him, none designed for such purpose.

"Oi! Oi! Oi! You lot, get off of him," cried Cobweb, and the fairies turned their attention on her, leaping and tackling her, trying to pull her frock over her head, wetly and loudly kissing her ears, and generally shaping themselves into a giggling pile.

"Stop!" Cobweb shouted. "We got fucking guests, you twats. To see the queen."

The fairies fell into a rough approximation of a line while

Cobweb crawled to her feet. "This here is Pocket of—of the Far Away, and he's a king's fool." With that, the fairies came to attention. Three of them, two female, one male, the latter wearing black military trousers and no shirt. They stared at me in bloody awe, I reckon, all of their eyes as disturbingly wide as Cobweb's.

"That's right," said Cobweb. "Like the Puck, so don't give him no trouble or he'll change you to a toad quick as you please."

"Sorry," said one of the girls. "We was looking for Bottom and was excited to find him."

"And I am most abundantly found," said Bottom.

"These here are my mates," said Cobweb. "That there is Moth." The first girl in the line curtsied and grinned. She had hair the color of an eggshell, short, like Cobweb's, and wore a similar rough linen frock, in mossy green, that hung to just above her knees, although there were fewer burrs and sticks tangled in hers. "That there is Peaseblossom, she's dead simple." Peaseblossom, with light brown locks, rounder and a bit shorter than Cobweb and Moth, curtsied and nodded in agreement. "And that rascal there is Mustardseed."

"I am also simple," said the boy. Well, not boy, really, just a small, slight man, with pointed ears and short black hair, cut in the same manner as the others', which was, from appearances, with a knife, in the dark, by someone who was angry. He bowed. "At your service, good sir."

"Fancy a frolic, Master Pocket?" said Peaseblossom.

"Oh, that would be lovely," said Mustardseed, jumping on his toes.

"Yes!" said Moth.

"Master Pocket don't frolic," said Cobweb. "Now, we need to get Master Bottom back to the queen's bower or she'll roast our dicks on a stick. Go on."

Mustardseed and Peaseblossom took Bottom, each by a hand,

and led him further into the forest. Moth hung back and held her hand as if for me to take it.

"Go on," said Cobweb. "Follow the others. I got this one. Go, and no fucking frolicking along the way." She waved Moth on and fell back beside me, letting the others get far enough ahead that all I could see was Moth's white hair bobbing in the dark like, well, a moth.

"Don't say nothing about the Puck being killed. Not yet," Cobweb whispered as we went along. "And you can't let on you haven't magic like him. Do some tricks with your puppet stick there, and juggle and sing and hint that you have fearsome powers."

"You think that will work?"

"It must. Show the queen your passport from the duke, too."

"How do you know about that? I didn't show you that."

"And she's going to try to shag you, so be ready."

"I am no stranger to deflecting the attention of lascivious queens. My aspect is fair, but I have a particular charm that keeps them at bay."

"I know, you are a shit. But the queen has a *particular* taste and you'll want to stow that cracking big codpiece or you'll never be rid of her."

"Perhaps you could wear it as a lovely elven hat," said I.

She rolled her eyes at me in the manner of a priest surrendering my filthy soul to hell, which is an expression I had seen more than once, and called, "Oi! Mustard! You want to wear the fool's stupid codpiece?"

"Is it magical?" Mustardseed called back.

I nodded furiously.

"No," said Cobweb, "but it'll be cracking for carrying your nuts and berries."

Mustardseed made his way back to us. I untied my codpiece and handed it over.

"This will be smashing with some black kit the Puck give me," said Mustardseed. "Trousers, a jerkin, and now a codpiece. I'll be fancier than a mortal watchman."

Cobweb whispered, "And I still don't believe the Puck's dead."

"I'm sorry, lamb, he is. I held his chill form in my arms."

"You don't know how tricky he can be," Cobweb said.

CHAPTER IX

Queen of Tarts

BOTTOM LED us into an open space in the forest canopy where, bathed by moonlight, a multitude of fairies were lashing saplings together into great Gothic archways and weaving a cupola of willow over the lot, tying branches with vines and strips of bark, until it appeared that a great green cathedral was rising out of the forest floor as fairies scurried up, down, and around the branches and beams, fitting in new pieces with industrious fury.

"The night queen's palace," announced Moth.

I looked to Cobweb. "It's just a great bundle of sticks."

"Don't let the queen hear you say that," said Cobweb.

"How many fairies attend her?" I asked.

"I don't know. Seven?"

"Seven? There are at least a hundred I can see."

"I don't know," said Cobweb.

"We're not good at counting," said Moth.

A team of four fairies dashed around the edges of the construction snatching fireflies out of the brush and tossing them into lanterns constructed of gold-flecked mica, until each lantern glowed brighter and softer than any oil lamp. Then one would climb into the growing dome and place it among the arches.

"We build it every night," said Mustardseed.

"The queen is ever so particular that it's suitable for entertaining," said Peaseblossom.

"She's been right cranky since Oberon chucked her out the Night Palace," said Moth.

"How long ago was that?" I inquired.

Moth shrugged. "Many." She danced into the fray and began helping another fairy to lash branches to the dome.

The fairies were all as slim and tattered as Cobweb but dressed in many colors and styles, as if they'd found their kit on a beach, the flotsam of a shipwreck. None wore shoes or any jewelry, although some had striped their limbs with clay or dye. Meanwhile, Mustardseed was strutting around the perimeter wearing my codpiece, thrusting it at anyone who dared look up from their work.

A flaxen-haired girl fairy called from atop the dome, "Mustard! What you got there?"

"It's my new kit," said Mustardseed. He thrust it at her. "Fancy a frolic?"

The blond fairy ran down one of the ribs of the dome, as sure-footed as if she were on flat ground, and, while still five yards above the ground, leapt off the edifice, landed with a roll, and came up onto her feet in front of Mustardseed, where she honked his codpiece. "It's lovely," she said. She grinned around our group, her hand still on the cod, her gaze coming to rest on me. "Who are you, sir?"

"He's a fool," said Cobweb. "Like the Puck. Pocket of the Far Away. Pocket, this here's Fluffer-Nutter."

Fluffer-Nutter curtsied and averted her gaze to the ground. "Beg pardon, sir."

"*Enchanté*," said I, in perfect fucking French.

"Is he fucking French?" Fluffer-Nutter whispered to Mustardseed.

He shrugged. "Don't know. Mayfly, I reckon."

Dismissing it all with a wave, Fluffer-Nutter looked back to the ribs of the great growing dome. "We'd best get to work. We're behind and the queen will be steaming if we don't finish before she arrives." With that she turned and ran back up a sapling making up one of the arched openings, as quick and agile as Jeff the monkey might have been. Mustardseed, Moth, and Peaseblossom followed her up with the grace of dancers. I am an accomplished acrobat myself, having been trained as a boy to be a second-story man for a thief, and later as an entertainer to the king, so I could climb and tumble as well as anyone I'd ever seen, but these fairies moved about the green rigging of their cathedral like they were born to the trees.

A tattoo of drumming sounded from out of the clearing and a cohort of perhaps fifty fairies marched out of the forest bearing a covered litter festooned with flowers upon their shoulders, followed by a line of fairies carrying trays of fruits, others carrying earthenware amphorae, presumably filled with wine, or maybe, since these were fucking fairies, some kind of nectar.

"That's her," said Bottom. "And if past is prologue, I am to be most grievously and jauntily used—used like a—like a—"

Bottom snuffled his muzzle against my shoulder and his long ears batted about the tentacles of my coxcomb as if trying to make friends.

"Like a beast of burden?" I suggested.

"Aye," said the ass-man. "Like a beast." He hid his eyes against me and let loose a wheezing whinny.

With that, the diaphanous curtain of the litter was swept aside and Titania, queen of the night, stepped out onto the green. She was no taller nor rounder than the other fairies, and, but for garlands of flowers draped across her hips and breasts, quite naked. Her skin was as pale as the moon, so pale it seemed that she might be composed of moonlight herself. Her cape of curls was woven with flowers and fragrants so numerous that a moment passed before I could discern that her hair was the same light brown as Peaseblossom's. Her eyes were emerald green and so wide it seemed she was in a perpetual state of surprise, or perhaps excitement, but definitely—as they darted around like minnows in a bucket—undeniably, as mad as a fucking bedbug.

"Oh, sing again, my glorious mortal, thy song is as beautiful as thy shape." She danced, tiny steps, across the forest floor until she stood by Bottom, where she stroked his long ears with delicate fingers. "Oh, sing again, my love. Sing again."

The fairies around the green bowed or averted their eyes. Those who had been working in the ribs of the growing dome clung close to their branches as if trying to become unseen, and while all attention was upon the fairy queen, all pretended to attend to other quiet occupations to create a privacy in the midst of a crowd. I had seen such behavior before, in the mobs about the pagan henges, when the Druids searched for the suitable sacrifice. *Fear.* Even cheeky Cobweb had folded herself into a stand of tall ferns and grabbed only furtive glances at her fairy queen through the parted fronds.

"Help," Bottom whispered, but alas, no plan of action came to mind. I was here to see the queen and it appeared that I was doing quite well at it.

Titania moaned softly as she stroked Bottom's ears, her eyes closed, head thrown back as if in an ecstatic trance, running one hand up his ear, the other down the leg of his trousers, her cheek to his bristly muzzle, even as he nuzzled tighter against my shoulder to escape her. The queen pressed her breasts against Bottom's arm as he pulled closer to me. She took a long ear in each hand and pulled herself hard against Bottom's leg; he turned to keep the great growing donkey dong snaking down his trousers away from her, me trying to escape both, which resulted in the three of us doing a rather slow turn in the middle of the forest, until Titania, in renewing her grip upon Bottom's ear, caught one of the tentacles of my hat, yanking it off my head, at which time she ceased moaning, opened her eyes, and looked at the black and silver hat in her hand, half expecting, I suppose, to find a severed donkey ear, but alas, no. She slid down Bottom's leg to her feet and peeked around the cringing ass-man's head to look me in the eye.

"Hello," said I.

"Who are you?"

"Pocket of Dog Snogging," I said. "Royal fool, onetime king, and current emissary of Theseus of Athens." As Cobweb had suggested, I pulled Theseus's passport from my belt and held it out so she could see the seal. "I have been sent," said I. I bowed, as much as I could with Bottom clinging to me.

She looked at the seal, looked at me, looked at the seal, looked at Bottom, cowering against my shoulder, shook her head in what appeared to be disgust, looked at me again, then turned and walked through one of the arches into the makeshift palace. Over her shoulder, she called, "Wash the cheese stink off of him and bring him to me."

A rather small boy of perhaps eight, naked, brown, and scrawny, peeked out of Titania's litter, then, seeing that the path was clear, padded after her into the green palace.

✣　✣　✣

THE FAIRY queen reclined in a raised nest under the domed chamber lit by lamps full of fireflies and a portal in the ceiling open to the moon. I stood before her, naked but for my puppet stick and a vine-belted loincloth the fairies had wrapped me in, and, except for my face and hands, nearly as pale as the fairy queen herself (no one wins the war of the wan against a sun-starved son of England), if a bit pink from the sand scrubbing the fairies had given me at the stream to remove the odor of cheese. (And I had shared my sack of victuals with them to boot, ungrateful, dog-eared vermin.) Cobweb and Moth attended Titania in her nest, weaving fresh blossoms into her hair. Bottom cowered in the far side of the nest, where Peaseblossom scratched his ears with a forked green stick. The other fairies I knew had blended back into the multitude. Some busied themselves with trussing up the last few branches on the dome, others slowly crept away into the forest. It had been no different in the stone castles and palaces where I'd lived and attended; one served as quickly as possible and left the court to their own dirty dealings, except Titania had no court, no clerks or guards. When the scene settled, there were only the servants who waited on her, fewer than a dozen, none armed. Somewhere out of sight, someone played softly on a pan flute.

"So, fool," said Titania, "what is the message you have brought me from Theseus?"

"Not so much a message as questions, ma'am. First, when was the last you saw the Puck?"

Titania sat up and waved Cobweb and Moth away. Cobweb was shaking her head furiously at me as she retreated to the back of the nest with Bottom, Peaseblossom, and the small brown boy, who was curled into a ball as if trying to disappear up his own bum. "Just that?" said the queen. "Theseus wants to know when I last saw the Puck? Just that?"

"No, there are others, ma'am, but I'm not to ask them until you answer the first."

"I am the queen of the night, fool. Ruler of all the fields, forests, and fairies. Only with the dances of my fairies do the grains ripen, the apple trees blossom, the clouds bring life-giving rain. Only by my command do tides turn and the moon bless the fertile fruit of babies to be born. You stand before me, in my palace, and dare to ask trifling questions? You would hold messages from a king hostage under condition of my answers? In my palace?"

"So, last evening, I'm told, was when last you saw the Puck?"

The night queen leapt to her feet, leaving her garlands in a pile, and although I was still heartbroken and not attuned to such tastes, she was right fit for an ancient fucking fairy, and if Cobweb was right, and the queen was to have her way with me, I would try to savor my suffering.

"Insolent fool, on your life now, deliver Theseus's message or suffer my wrath."

"Will you be especially wrathful, then?" I inquired.

"I will." She seemed less sure than when she'd first spoken. "Probably."

"Well then, I should get to it. Theseus wondered if you received the message he sent by way of the Puck."

"I did," said the night queen.

"Aha!" said I, storming up to the very edge of her nest, which was built upon some small tree, higher than my head, so I backed up a bit so I could look the queen in the eye. "Aha!" I repeated. "So you did see the Puck last evening?"

"Yes, I just saw no reason to tell you."

"And what was that message?"

"Theseus sent you, and Theseus knows, does he not?"

"He forgot, so I was to ask again."

"He did not forget, fool. Must I have you seized and scrubbed again?"

Truth be told, I hadn't been so much *seized* as the fairies had asked me to come along, and they were so enthusiastic and annoying that I accompanied them to the stream and submitted to their scrubbing on the condition that my kit was kept close at hand, except for my codpiece, of course, with which Mustardseed had absconded into the wood. Still, if Titania felt a good sand scrubbing was a viable threat, who was I to disabuse her of the notion?

"Oh no, ma'am, not that. But the duke was expecting you to send something to him with the Puck and he wonders if you sent it."

"He does not know?"

"Well, no, since nothing was found with the Puck when they found his body."

And everything paused, as if everyone in earshot were gathering a breath for a song.

"Oh for fuck's sake, Pocket!" said Cobweb, which came out rather louder than I think she expected. Titania and all the fairies turned to regard Cobweb, and the girl fairy slid her bycocket hat down over her face and attempted to hide behind Bottom, who had folded his long ears down over his eyes and was pretending to sleep.

"Which you knew because you killed him," said the puppet Jones, in my voice, as I was working his string. And suddenly everyone's attention turned from Cobweb to the puppet, as had been my intent.

"Apologies, ma'am," said I. "Your fairies gave the puppet a good scrubbing as well and he's surly when he's damp."

"Aye," said the puppet Jones. "Cross as a cat when wet, I am."

"Aye," said I.

"Aye," said Jones.

Titania's mad green eyes went wider. "What sorcery is this?"

"Simple fool craft, ma'am. Nothing any extraordinarily talented jester could not do."

"Like the Puck?" she said.

Behind the queen Cobweb had peeked out from behind Bottom and was nodding at me hard enough to shake her eyeballs free of their sockets.

"Aye, ma'am. Just like the Puck, who is, if I had not made it clear, quite dead."

"Dead?" said she.

"Quite."

Whispering commenced in the ferns and shadows—fairy voices

trying to hush alarm and disbelief. Heart-shaped faces peeked out from the branches above, one fairy, who must have been hiding in the green dome, lost his grip and plummeted into the middle of Titania's nest, then, before anyone could react, jumped to his feet and swung out the far side of the nest and out of sight. The odd sob and sniffle sounded out of the dark. The pan flute ceased.

"Murdered, ma'am," said I. "With—" I looked for my clothes and weapons. "Where's my kit?" I called to the gallery.

Mustardseed popped up out of a stand of ferns and strutted forward, codpiece on his prow rigged for ramming, carrying a bundle of my clothes, the harness with my daggers draped over the top. He set the bundle at my feet and stepped back, grinning like a loony, first at me, then at the queen, then at me again.

"Thank you. Well done," said I. "Fuck off, then."

Mustardseed proceeded to fuck off back to his hiding place, but Titania called him back. "Wait, you."

Mustardseed waited, turned, grinned, basked in the attention of his queen.

"What is your name?" asked Titania.

"Mustardseed, ma'am," said the prong-donged fairy.

"Mustardseed, join my personal attendants tonight." She beckoned him up into the nest, then shooed him to the back with Bottom and the others. She turned to me. "So, the Puck is slain?"

"Yes, Your Grace. Murdered last morning with this." I held up the black crossbow bolt.

"He was a . . ." Titania seemed to be searching for a tribute to the fallen jester, searched the air before her as if it might be written in fireflies, then sighed and gave up. "And who did this dread deed?"

"That is what I am to find out." I tried my thumb on the point of the bolt. "By Theseus's order. So, Your Grace, if I may, did you give something to the Puck?"

"I did. A potion, a flower really. But I haven't another. They grow it in a faraway land, and the Puck was the only one who could fetch it and return before it lost its power. Unless you would like to fetch another for your master, Theseus."

Cobweb peeked out again from behind Bottom and gave me a stern look I took to mean, "If you give up the game now, you jabbering jizzwhistle, I will murder you in your sleep." A look I had learned to recognize over my many years of dealing with the more delicate sex.

"Oh, I could shag a brace of queens and put a girdle around the Earth in thirty minutes, if I so desired, but Theseus seemed rather determined I find out who killed the Puck. However, if you are the killer, I'll have my answer and can fetch your flower and perform whatever other Puckish duties you require."

She did seem rather unmoved by the demise of a fellow she'd bonked only the day before—if the Puck was to be believed—but royals can be fickle fucks in affairs of the heart, or that has been my experience.

"Me? Of course not. Robin Goodfellow was in my service, I would not harm any in my charge, for I love them as my own children. I see to the change of tides and the warm winds that bring fertile fruit to the valleys. I command the moon and—"

"Right, right, right, you can roll road apples into gold, and I would be in slack-jawed awe at your power and splendor if you didn't live up a fucking tree, so, if I may, where were you at dawn today, and was there anyone with you at the time?"

"I was here, in my nest, until late morning, watching the sweet creatures of the forest lick the morning dew from the leaves."

"You weren't here when I woke up," brayed Bottom. He'd climbed to his feet and come to the fore of the nest. "I looked everywhere for you. Was still looking for you when I ran into this lot in the evening."

Titania's face hid a storm full of clouds as anger, and fear, and confusion passed over her.

"Tits are flushing, ma'am," said I. Well they were! If she was going to run around in the altogether, she needed to get control over her bubbly bits or she'd never master proper royal subterfuge and guile. "Bit of a tell, love, the pinkening of the knockers, on someone as fair as thou."

"Oberon!" she blurted out. "The shadow king killed the Puck, or he will know who did. That arrow is from his people."

"Don't you have the same people?"

"No, I am queen of the fairies, he, well, his is a darker lot."

"Goblins," said Bottom.

"How do you fucking know?" I said. "Yesterday you thought I was a bloody elf."

"It has been a strange day's night. I have seen things. Horrible things."

Titania glared at the ass-man and he retreated to the back of the nest with Cobweb, Peaseblossom, and the brown boy. Evidently the queen's infatuation with Bottom had come to an end.

"So, goblins?" I prompted Titania.

"Oberon's goblins have such weapons," she said. "You'll find your answer at the Night Palace."

Her knockers had gone snowy again, so I presumed she was not lying.

"And why, lady, do you not reside with the shadow king? He is your consort, I presume."

"Oberon and I are quarreling. He wished to take my young charge as a squire and I will not have it. I was ejected from the palace and he has forbidden my fairies from dancing until I relent, which shall be forevermore, for I will not surrender my boy."

"You split the kingdom over a slave?"

"The boy is not a slave. Come here, young master. Come, Raj."
She waved for the boy to come forward. He scurried to her side
and hugged her hip as she tousled his hair. "His mother was a
priestess of my order in India. And in the spiced Indian air, often
she gossiped by my side. She would sit with me on Neptune's yellow sands and we would laugh to see the sails conceive and grow
big bellied with the wanton wind; even as my lady did grow big
bellied with my squire. But being mortal, she did die of the boy,
and for her sake do I rear him up, and for her sake I will not part
with him. She was my friend."

"Well, children are a fucking blessing, aren't they?" said I. "Especially if you get them when they're grown and not so damp and
leaky all the time. True joy. So, the potion you had the Puck fetch,
what was it for?"

She looked to the side, suddenly coy. "A little love potion. You
drop the liquor from a small purple flower into the intended's eyes,
and upon awaking, they fall in love with the first creature they lay
eyes on, be it man, woman, or beast."

"And who did he intend to use this potion upon?"

"I know not. Perhaps, as he is your master, you should ask him.
Perhaps if you find who wanted to stop the Puck from delivering
it, you will find who it was for. Ask Oberon."

"That I will," said I.

"Then away to the Night Palace with you, fool." She turned to
her retinue. "Fairies, prepare me a bath."

The fairies, including Cobweb, Peaseblossom, and Mustardseed,
scrambled upon her order.

"Your Grace," I called. "While I am the very model of the magical fucking fool, in this strange land I do not have my finding
spells sorted, so if I may borrow one of your fairies to lead me to
the Night Palace? A Mistress Cobweb who led me here was quite
a competent navigator, and she is indifferent to my cheese odor."

"Poor thing," said the queen. "Very well, Cobweb, go with this fool. Lead him to Oberon's castle."

Cobweb scrambled out from behind the nesting tree, came to my side, and wetly whispered, "Get the others," in my ear.

"And, ma'am," said I, "for some of my magics I will require others to attend, mainly to gather my scattered bits if something goes wrong. Might I borrow Peaseblossom, Moth, and Mustardseed as well?" The queen's mad eyes were darting at the request, so I quickly added, "You'll want as many fairy eyes in the Night Palace as possible, if the shadow king has taken to murder, don't you think? I've played in a multitude of courts, and once the killing has started it seldom stops until everyone is dead. It would be wise to be informed of conditions."

"Very well." She called the three fairies, and they scampered from various parts of the green cathedral and joined Cobweb and me, except Mustardseed, whom the queen called back. "Not you. I'll need you to attend me in my bath."

Mustardseed winked at me, honked his codpiece (for certainly it was his now, as he was about to earn it), and swung himself back up into the nest.

"You'll need a passport, beyond that of Theseus's, or Oberon's goblins may slay you while you're still in the wood." She reached into her hair and plucked a small white flower. "Raj?" Without looking back the little Indian boy came forward, took the flower from her, leapt to the ground, and gave it to me.

"It's a flower," said I.

"Yes, Oberon and his people will know it is mine and that you are under my protection."

"But it's a flower. A tender one at that. It will wilt."

"Then you had better hurry, hadn't you? And when you are finished, before you return to Theseus, return here and tell me what you found. Take note of any mortals in the Night Palace."

I bowed. "As you wish, ma'am."

Cobweb was already headed into the woods, the other fairies right behind her. I picked up my kit, tucked Titania's passport flower in my hat, and started to follow.

"Master Pocket!" called Bottom. "Please, I am transformed and we have a play to do and I must get home or Mrs. Bottom will be very cross."

I shrugged. I knew not how I could pry the weaver-turned-ass away from the fairy queen. "Can you help him, ma'am? When you are no longer in need of his services, that is. He is expected to perform at the duke's wedding."

"Take him. I am finished with him," she said. "Go, creature. Go with him."

"And could you turn him back to Nick Bottom the weaver, so as not to detract from his performance?"

"Oh, that is up to you, good fool, for he was turned by the Puck, and only the Puck may turn him back, or someone with his powers."

"Come then," I said to Bottom, who had begun to weep in great honking sobs.

CHAPTER X

Fancy a Frolic?

THE FAIRIES led us on a path wide enough that moonlight could find the forest floor and it was easy going. Moth and Peaseblossom were in the front, each holding one of Bottom's hands, leading him as he wept and whined all along the way. Cobweb and I brought up the rear, some twenty paces behind the others.

"Well you got a set of bollocks on you, I'll say that," said Cobweb. "Just told her, 'if you didn't live up a fucking tree,' like she was some common wood wench. I thought you were done for."

"Gentle fairy, when I was young I was jester to a feeble old man who called himself the Dragon of Britain. He raged day and night about the fury of his wrath, the sum of which was bluster and betrayal. Since then, I have seen a real sodding dragon—a more fearsome creature than has ever walked upright on two legs—and yet I survived. For most of my life in service, my pillow has been the headman's block, the axe always a royal whim away, and yet I learned to sleep, and now, with the loves of my life in the tomb or gone on a pirate wind, I simply do not care. I am not afraid. It affords me some license."

"Good on you, then. Don't know when I've seen her so rattled."

"I am somewhat disturbed that she didn't try to shag me as you predicted."

"That's because I saved you—threw Mustardseed to her as a sacrifice, didn't I?" She winked, did a little skip of a dance step.

"Heartless way to treat a mate, especially one who is a bit simple."

"I have seen how you treat your mate, who is a bit simple, if 'a bit' is a bull-sized barrel of bloody simple."

"Drool is not my mate, he is my apprentice," said I. "And I do try to do my best by the great ninny."

"As I did for Mustardseed. He'll get to shag the queen, do you think he's not willing? If he survives he'll never stop talking about it."

"You may have saved Bottom as well. She was quite cross with him, and if she's dangerous—"

"She is dangerous enough," said Cobweb. "But she doesn't kill her lovers. Although they do disappear from time to time. I think they might be hiding."

"She has a lot of lovers?"

"Like a cup at the public well she is—well used and always ready for the next thirsty bloke. It was forbidden, for a long, long time—shag a goddess, burst into flame and all that—but when she went mad, it was game on."

"And the shadow king does not object?"

"Has his own appetites, I hear. Haven't seen much of him for a while."

"What about Puck? He said he'd shagged two queens in one day."

"She used to meet with the Puck all the time. Made like it was some affair of court. Secret and all. Wouldn't let any of us follow. Or watch."

I counted on my fingers as we walked. "So, Puck was shagging Hippolyta, *and* Titania, but also working for Theseus, and he's jester to Oberon. And he was taking a love potion to Theseus, for Titania. Which only he could fetch. What did Titania get out of it?"

"Roll in the hay with Long Ears, there." Cobweb pointed ahead at Bottom. "That's the Puck's trickery if I ever seen it, and I seen it."

"And she said so," said I.

"Aye, and you can bet Puck gave her a sample of that love potion. Should have seen her doting on Bottom while you was getting scrubbed up. Like he hung the moon for her, two ticks later she wouldn't piss on him if he was afire."

"She had herself enchanted to love Bottom? For the night? Why?"

"Love-sweetened bonk, methinks," said Cobweb. "It gentles her bitterness over Oberon."

We'd entered a bit of the forest where the canopy obscured the moon and walked a bit in silence, just the soft padding of our feet, and once, the distant hoot of an owl, at which the fairies jumped. Poor primitives, probably some omen of doom for them. I, on the other hand, had spent years among the ravens that dwelt above my quarters in the barbican at the White Tower, and I had befriended Hunter, the falconer at the castle, and sometimes passed afternoons watching his raptors rend rats into tasty strips, so birds held no menace for me. I felt, as we moved along, part of the forest. Perhaps I was not an indoor fool after all, but a more rugged creature, suited for these great green environs.

I was about to mention my leafy epiphany to Cobweb when I caught the toe of my boot upon something in the dark, a root I suppose, and I tumbled bum over eyebrows into a patch of nettles.

"Pocket," said Cobweb, who came to my aid and began testing my limbs for breaks. "What happened?"

"Well it's dark as the devil's dirty dick hole out here, isn't it?"

"Are you all right?"

"Trees! Bloody buggering branchy bastards! The Druids had

the right idea: burn the whole lot to the ground and have a cele-bratory bonk by the light of the fire."

Bottom and the other fairies had heard my call and tracked back to join us.

"He all right?" asked Moth.

"Took a tumble," said Cobweb. "Nest up, shall we? Before the mayflies surrender their ghosts due to bloody darkness."

"Mayflies?" inquired Bottom.

"What we call mortals," said Moth.

"On account of you lot dying at the touch of a slight breeze," said Peaseblossom.

"Hardly worth learning your names, really," said Moth.

"Mates!" called Cobweb. "You'll want to make a nest for Long Ears if you fancy a frolic before dawn."

In a blink Moth and Peaseblossom were in the branches of a small oak, weaving together the platform for a nest.

"Come on then," said Cobweb, offering a hand up. "We've a nest to build."

I let her pull me to my feet and dust me off while I surveyed the branches above. "What's a suitable tree?" I asked.

"Methinks a nice nest safe on the ground is best for you. I'll build it. If you still have your flint and steel we could use a fire."

ENTER RUMOUR, PAINTED FULL OF TONGUES

"And so, the clumsy and awkward fool, alive only by the grace and kindness of the dimwitted fairies, was no closer to solving the mystery of the Puck's murder, even as his apprentice languished in the dungeon, the executioner's blade poised above his brutish neck."

"Oh do fuck off," said I. Rumour had just appeared, it seemed, on the trail, an uncanny and annoying light shone around him.

"Whosat?" asked Moth, looking down from her prospective nest tree.

"And who you calling dimwitted?" said Cobweb. "I'll have your nuts in a knot, tosser."

"Though she be but little, she is fierce," quoted the puppet Jones. I had drawn the puppet from down my back as a misdirection. I was not so nonplussed as I had been upon my first encounter with the unctuous chorus, and despite his blazing speed, I thought to gain an advantage, perhaps compel him to tell me his secrets, or at least visit a soupçon of humility on him by way of a calming wallop to the noggin.

"This loony's got tongues all over his frock," said Peaseblossom. She'd dropped out of her tree and was twiddling the tongues on Rumour's cloak.

"So he does," said Moth, who dropped to the other side of the narrator and began twiddling the tongues on that side. "On his hat, too. Bend down, love, let us have a wee squeeze."

"Fancy a frolic?" said Peaseblossom, snuggling against Rumour's leg, at which point Cobweb giggled in a tone much more high and girlish than her nine hundred years would have suggested.

"*Stop that,*" said Rumour.

Moth grasped one of the tongues and held it tight between her fingers. "Say something now. See if you can."

Rumour snatched his cloak away from the fairies and in an instant was three yards down the path, leaving Moth and Pease-blossom grasping at empty air. "*Enough!*"

"I believe I'm stuck up here," said Bottom, wedged between branches of the nest tree.

Startled, Rumour looked up and squeaked a girlish scream himself. "*A horse!*"

"Ass-man, we call him," said I. "I thought you were seer of schemes, teller of tales, planner—what was it?"

"*Planner of plots,*" said Rumour. "*But that fellow has the head of a donkey.*"

"A future you didn't see coming, I'll wager," said I. It appeared that I was relieved of the need to conk Rumour in the head to bring him down a notch. "Why are you here?"

"To correct your path, to point out your errors before you completely cock up the narrative." Rumour swiped at the fairies, who had resumed twiddling his tongues. *"Stop it."*

"Well get on with it," said I. "We're knackered and the ladies need to finish their nest building so they can frolic the bloody daylights out of old Bottom here."

"Thank you, good sir," said Moth with a curtsy.

"Pocket is a fucking gent, he is," said Peaseblossom.

"Why are you glowing?" asked Cobweb, approaching Rumour now. "Are you having a self-frolic under that frock?"

"Does it have tongues on the inside, too?" asked Moth excitedly.

"May I wear it?" asked Peaseblossom.

Moth pulled open Rumour's robe to reveal nothing at all—not even legs or feet, just empty space. She pulled his robe shut as quickly as if slamming the door in the face of a menacing dragon. "Well that's bloody disturbing," she said.

"This geezer's magical," said Cobweb.

"Magically dried up my nethers like salt on a slug," said Peaseblossom, unhanding Rumour's tongues.

"Stop talking about me as if I'm not here," said Rumour.

"They do that," said Bottom.

"It is our way," said Moth.

"We are simple," said Peaseblossom.

"Just her," said Cobweb. "She's the simple one."

"That's right," said Peaseblossom. "Sorry, I forgot. I'm—"

"We know!" said I. "Rumour, state your purpose, or do fuck off."

"The key to the mystery is the lovers," said Rumour.

"You said that before, and I've seen the lovers, and they're useless and silly."

"At the same time," said Cobweb, nodding gravely. "They didn't kill the Puck. I asked them myself."

"Well you've missed the clue they bore. Examine them again. And there are three simple words that will reveal the Puck's purpose, and thereby his killer. Three simple words."

"The Puck would say that, about the three words," said Cobweb, "when the night queen was displeased with him. 'I could fix this in three words,' he'd say."

"What are the words?" I asked.

"That you must discover for yourself or your apprentice shall perish," said Rumour.

"I have already discovered the Puck's message and what he was carrying to Theseus. And there is no shortage of credible rascals I could blame for his murder."

"And what of the potion he was to deliver? Was that not part of your task?"

I looked to Cobweb, she to me. "Fuckstockings," said I.

"And so, the doomed, dull-witted drudge, the soon-to-be-dead Pocket, realized his own futility, and—"

"Wait, you're the one who said you taught Puck to circle the globe in forty minutes. *You* could fetch the flower for me," said I. "You could save Drool."

"I am for drama, I am for intrigue, I am for misdirection and mystery. I serve only the story. Why would I do that?"

"To get your hat back," said Moth. With that the towheaded fairy leapt to nearly twice her height, spritely even for a sprite, and snatched the hat of tongues off Rumour's head, then landed as soft as a cat and rolled, coming to her feet with the hat held high. "Ha!"

The rest of us stood, mouths agape, for what we thought would be Rumour's head was, indeed, nothing at all. Where his forehead ended was just nothing down to his neck in the back, so it appeared that his ears were simply escorting a long-nosed tragedy mask through the air, and tragedy was his expression, even as he let loose with a long, high-pitched, horrified scream. With a whoosh, in a streak of light, he was gone, taking his annoying glow with him, leaving the call of *"The passion of the Puck lies with the prince,"* hanging in the air behind him.

"Ha," said Moth. "New hat." She fitted it on her head and commenced to nest building without further comment, the tongues on the hat wagging as she went.

"Told you he was magic," said Cobweb. "He's right about you getting back to Theseus without the flower."

"Not to worry, lamb," said I. "I, the all-licensed fool, shall fetch the flower before I return to Theseus."

"You know that I know that you don't have Puck's magical powers, don't you?"

"I'll make a fire," said I, choosing to overlook Cobweb's stubbornness. "Peradventure, the shadow king will help us."

"Probably not," said the fairy.

"I know," said I.

*   *   *

WHEN THE nests were built, and our bellies were full of nuts, berries, and the last of the bread I'd bought in Athens, I curled into the nest Cobweb had built on the ground and laid my head on my coxcomb folded over, facing the fire's embers. Cobweb crawled in behind me and ruthlessly spooned me, snaking a delicate hand under my jerkin to rub my shoulders.

"How's the bump on your noggin?" she asked.

"Sore, but only to the touch."

"In the morning it will be just you and Bottom. Stay on the path north. This far into the forest, the path is used by both the fairies and the goblins, even the occasional mortal, so it's well worn and will be easy to follow."

"You'll return to Titania?"

"Not to worry, we'll find you at dusk. You just keep on the trail. We'll be to the Night Palace by tomorrow midnight."

"Shouldn't we keep going tonight, then? I'll only have two days to save Drool."

"We need to rest. *You* need to rest. You won't want to go before Oberon without your wits at their sharpest and you the full and right rascal you can be."

"I am not a rascal."

"It was a compliment."

"How far from the Night Palace to Athens?"

"Less than a night's march. We have time."

"Good night then, good Cobweb."

"Fancy a cuddle then?"

"No, lamb, I'm sad and knackered."

She slid over on me and kissed my ear. "I don't think you are. You say you are, but since you came back from Athens, you haven't been sad at all. You were right jolly when sparring with the night queen and that Rumour bloke."

"No. I am heartbroken."

"I am also sad," said Nick Bottom, from the nest perhaps ten feet above us. "And Mrs. Bottom frowns upon me frolicking with strangers."

"Well we ain't strangers and no one was going to frolic with you, anyway," said Peaseblossom. "Was just having a bit of a cuddle. And now I seen that thing awake, I don't want nothing to do with it."

"Huge, innit?" said Moth.

"I am sad and my knob is huge," cried Bottom, with an asinine whimper.

"Blossom, you should have a sit on this hat of tongues," said Moth. "Oh my, this is lovely."

"Give it," said Peaseblossom.

"Sad and huge," said Bottom.

"Bottom, do stop whinging about your enormous dong," said I. "We are trying to sleep."

"I miss Titania," said Bottom.

"Last you saw her you were terrified of her," I said.

"Absence makes the fond grow harder," whispered Cobweb.

"Shhhh," I shushed. It appeared that among the fairies, or at least this small cohort, I had at last found my lost tribe, and they were a herd of tiny hopeless horn-beasts. And so, with equine nickers susurrating into snores on the breeze and the hushed yips of a pair of fairies sharing a hat of many tongues, with the dying fire warm on my face, and with gentle Cobweb kneading the cares of the day from my shoulders and back, I slipped softly into slumber.

When I awoke she was on me, urgent, naked, and wet—an irresistible force—sliding into my shirt with me, her face against mine, her lips on mine, her breath on my cheek, her voice in my ear saying something in a language I did not know. No jape or objection rose in my throat, no thought of repelling an ancient forest sprite or quick-witted girl, nothing feeling so far away as another being at all; I was for her, as she was for me, and that was that. I don't know how long, but when I finally looked away from her, the fire was out, and when I looked back I could see her pulling her frock on and a dark star reflecting in her eye. I heard her smile more than I could see it. She put her hand on my cheek and kissed me on the eyebrow. "Sleep, fool." Then one quick kiss on the lips. "I'll find you on the morrow."

I heard her pad off into the forest and a few seconds later, two more sets of footsteps followed her.

Time passed, I dozed, then above me I heard a rustling, and before I could get my wits about me to look out from under the willow canopy Cobweb had built over the nest, Nick Bottom crashed through it, flying in the manner of all non-winged equines, reducing the lot to a brush pile with a charming fool at its core.

"Bottom, thou flea-brained numpty, get off of me."

"So sorry, maestro. I spotted a glowing in the distance and I stretched out of the nest to see better."

I crawled out of the compost and pulled my kit out piece by piece. The moon was straight overhead so I was able to see a bit better than when we'd struck camp. And while Bottom's plunge had done dire damage to the nest, he seemed to have missed my person, if only by a handbreadth.

Bottom crawled out of the pile and tested his limbs, apparently finding them in working order. "That way, maestro. You can just see the glow." I followed his gaze, and indeed there was a bluish glow off in the forest, unfortunately not the way of the path.

"That's the way Moth and Peaseblossom went. You can see it better from above."

"I'll take your word for it," said I as I pulled on my leggings.

"We should go see," said Bottom, dashing off into the dark forest like some horse-headed loony.

"Wait," I called, but off he went, probably to his death, and as soon as I'd pulled on my boots and tucked my leggings in them, I gathered up the rest of my kit and took off after him, probably to my death, because sod all, I'd found my tribe of tiny tarts and I was duty-bound to do something mind-bogglingly stupid on their behalf. Evidently.

When I caught up to Bottom he was crouched behind a great fallen tree at the edge of a clearing from which the bright blue glow was emanating. He pulled me down beside him and bade me be quiet by putting a finger to his lips and blowing a damp raspberry of donkey spit over me.

"Fuck's sake, Bottom," said I, wiping the spray out of my face.

"Shhhh," said Bottom, "look." He gestured for me to peek over the fallen tree trunk.

I did, and there in the clearing, a space as wide as a country church nave, danced Cobweb, Moth, and Peaseblossom, their bodies glowing blue in the mist, their skin sparkling as if containing the dust of stars. In my time as a pirate we once captured a treasure from a merchant ship in the Black Sea that contained stones called opals, which shone in many colors, as if they had whole worlds of moonlight trapped within them, and now, the fairies put me in mind of those stones, but with their light emanating from within. The dance was free of form, like butterflies flitting on invisible breezes, the fairies moving light in leaps, with spins, even somersaults, but without the weight of whatever stuff we mortals carry.

"Frolicking," whispered Bottom.

"But I thought—"

"So did I," said the ass-man, "but what you were doing with Cobweb is not a frolic. Peaseblossom so explained to me, swearing me to secrecy."

Even as we watched, the fairies lifted in the air until their feet were only brushing the tips of the ferns and they were, indeed, floating. The ferns and other low plants took on spectral highlights around them, as if embers of glowing ice were floating out from the circle the fairies formed.

"How do you know what I did with Cobweb?" I said. From what I could tell, it had been a private and quiet thing, and I was aggrieved that anyone had even a bit of it beyond us two. Also, Cobweb had placed a delicate hand upon my mouth and gently bade me to shut the fuck up when passion rose to voice.

"Not to worry," said Bottom. "Yours were not the rutting wails of the bawdy house, more like the sound of suckling puppies. Sweet and lovely, really."

"It *was* lovely," said I, rather more defensively than was called for. Had I suddenly become shy in my dotage?

As I watched Cobweb and the others dance I felt something brush my knee and I nearly leapt out of my boots. Bottom steadied me and reprised his horse-spittle shush, spraying me once again. He pointed to the ferns around our feet, which were unfurling new fronds as we watched, even small blossoms of white and violet pushed their way out of the forest floor below.

"Remember what Titania said about how only with the dance of the fairies do the grains ripen, the fruit trees blossom? This!"

"Well bang on keeping the secret," said I.

"I thought Cobweb would have told you."

The dance went on, I know not how long, for I was mesmerized with the light and life of it, the grace of it, and even as I felt myself a low and loathsome thing by contrast, there, too, was a joy, a delight in it. These were magical creatures, divine creatures. In all my life I had never seen nor felt anything like it, except perhaps for moments that very night making love with Cobweb.

Then, as I was carried on the seeming dream of it, I heard the call of a songbird, then another, signaling the coming dawn. The blue light in the clearing began to fade, then recede to the center, where the three fairies floated, hand in hand, to the ground, even as the light emanating from them faded and once again they appeared to be flesh, three naked nymphs standing in the forest (I had not even noticed that they were not wearing their rough linen frocks). In the next second, as the first light of dawn broke through the trees, the three receded, shrank, in place, until they were squirrels. Yes, three squirrels: Cobweb the red squirrel, Moth the color of an eggshell, Peaseblossom light brown. They scampered away into the trees.

I stood, stunned. I dragged my coxcomb from my head in reverence, or perhaps bewilderment.

"You aren't alone, silly fool," Rumour had told me, pointing out the red squirrel above. Had he known? Of course he had known. I was glad the fairies had stolen his hat.

I was pulled from my reverie by the hee-hawing guffaws of Nick Bottom, who was nearly bent over in laughter, pointing at me.

"Haw, haw, maestro, it seems you have shagged a squirrel."

"I have not, thou rabbit-eared toss-toad, this is magic of the first order."

"Squirrel shagger, squirrel shagger, squirrel shagger."

"Did you not make the beast with two backs with Titania, also a fairy, just last night?"

Bottom smoothed back his ears. "I was an unwilling servant. Used and enchanted, and besides, I didn't know they turned into squirrels at dawn."

"I thought Peaseblossom told you."

"Only about the frolicking, not about the squirrel bit. Did she have a tail?"

"No she didn't have a bloody tail. You've seen them all naked, you nitwit."

"Oh, right."

"And *you* have a tail. And a long snout. And nostrils like teacups. You, sir, are an ass."

Bottom felt around to the rear of his trousers. "Oh," he said, and his lips described what approximated, for a donkey, a pout. He sat down on the spot, as if he'd suddenly been overtaken by fatigue, and cradled his great ears in his hands. "How shall I play Pyramus in the duke's play? The lads will be lost without me. You must help me, maestro."

"Really? That is your concern? The play?"

"The play's the thing, maestro."

"Bottom, you cannot do the play. You're an ass."

"But I must do the play, so people will look at me. So people will see me."

"But you're an ass."

"And they will see me!" He looked up, hope sparkling in his eye. "I could play it in a mask. So though I am an ass, I could play a proper man."

"It *has* been done before," said I, nodding as if giving the premise consideration. My anger at the ass-man was fading with the dew. With the Puck the author of the spell that transformed Bottom, the poor weaver might live out his years as an ass. Who was I, a wanton squirrel shagger, to shatter his dream of the stage? "Yes, a mask," I said.

"No, it won't work." Bottom began to weep again, in great hee-hawing sobs. "I am an ass."

"No, mate, I shall direct you. Your performance will be as honed as a barber's blade."

"No, I am hopeless. I have these great stupid ears and this ridiculous snout."

"And moods that swing like a bell clapper, but you *do* have a cracking huge knob." I grinned and did a dance step to cheer him.

"I am hopeless and my knob is huge."

"Bottom. Lad. Be of good cheer. We will go to the shadow king, who was the Puck's master, and he will reverse the spell."

"Oh, maestro, do you think so?"

"We shall see, good Bottom. We shall see. Now gather up the ladies' frocks and that hat of many tongues and let us be on our way to Oberon's castle." As I fitted on my own hat, I noticed that the knot on my forehead was gone, not even a scab where the gash had been. I examined my arms and legs. The scrapes and cuts from my tossing in the waves had healed, the rope burns on my wrist, from being carried on the pole to Theseus's dungeon,

gone, even the rash from my run-in with the nettles had disappeared. *Fucking fairies and their fucking frolicking.* I could smell her
on my arms, wildflower and moss, and stood there watching
Bottom gather up the fairies' fallen frocks and Cobweb's little
bowman's hat, grinning like a bloody loony.

"Bottom," I called cheerily. "If Oberon can't fix you, you can
always play the lion. You couldn't possibly do worse than Snug the
joiner. The show shall go on!"

Bottom snatched up Rumour's hat of many tongues and fitted it
over his ears, a sight that gave me a slight spasm of the willies up
my spine, as the tongues waggled with joy at finding a new home.

"I liked you better when you were sad," said Bottom.

CHAPTER XI

What Fools These Mortals Be

"How bloody far is it to Oberon's castle?" I inquired of Bottom, several weeks into our hike since dawn. "We've been on this trail for days. I think we're going in circles. This looks suspiciously like the trail near Athens. Are we headed back to Athens?"

"It hasn't been that long," said Bottom. "It's not even lunchtime."

"How do you know? How can you even tell? There are no bells to ring the watch, no sundials. This forest is bloody barbaric. Why didn't the fucking fairies give us horses? They have what passes for a civilization, if you don't mind sleeping in a pile of sticks, why don't they have horses?"

"Hard getting them in and out of the trees, I reckon," said Bottom.

"Ha," said I, with withering sarcasm. "Ha," I repeated, with no little scorn. "Ha," I reprised, dripping with venomous irony.

We trod on in silence for a bit, which allowed Bottom's malignant, amateur jest to dry up and die.

Then: "What do you suppose they were?" asked Bottom.

"What *what* were?" I replied.

"The three words that Puck would have us remember, according to that Rumour chap."

"Doesn't matter," said I. "They will not help in finding the Puck's killer."

"They might."

"Not unless they are 'BOTTOM KILLED ME' or some similar nonsense, which they aren't, because he said them before he was killed and so didn't know."

"Also, I did not kill him," said Bottom.

"Well reasoned, good Bottom," said I. I gentled my response to the once-weaver, for in the light of day, I could see that Bottom was becoming more donkey and less man as the hours passed. Dark, wiry hair had covered his hands and forearms already, and he had twice stopped along the path to graze, then had been quite stubborn about getting on with the journey afterward.

"So, who do you think killed the Puck?" asked Bottom.

"I've no idea. Every mortal in Athens is armed, it appears, but now we know it wasn't a fairy."

"Of course we do," said Bottom, snatching up a handful of grass from the side of the trail, on which he began munching. "How do we know that?"

"Because I was nearby when the Puck was murdered," I said, slapping the grass out of Bottom's hand, "and although it was early, it was broad daylight when Puck stopped the arrow. And I think we can say that a squirrel is very unlikely to have shot a crossbow, no matter how small the weapon."

"And you heard the horn then?"

"What horn?"

"This morning, just before dawn, there sounded a horn, like a hunter's horn, right before the fairies changed."

"I heard no such horn," said I. Although I remembered the horn sounding on that first day, on the beach where Cobweb had rescued Drool and me.

Bottom pulled off the hat of many tongues and pointed to his long ears. "Not just for show, these fellows." Then the weaver stopped, held a finger in the air. "Listen . . ."

I listened: wind through the trees, the occasional birdcall, an odd rustling of leaves, probably a hedgehog having a wank or snakes sneaking up on us, but nothing of note.

"A group of mortals. Men and women. Young," said Bottom. "Up ahead. I can hear them arguing. One is called Helena?"

"Oh fuckstockings," said I. "Perhaps we should go around, or stop for a wee rest."

"They need help," said Bottom. He began to gallop forward.

"I told you we were headed back to Athens," I called as I fell into a trot after him, surprised after a hundred yards or so that I was neither fatigued nor out of breath. Two years before the mast and being starved and shipwrecked hadn't taken the toll on my condition I'd expected. Even at a full run, as I caught up to Bottom, I found I still had the breath to complain.

"Why are you running? I know these Athenians and they're wildly annoying. The last time you came upon them you frightened them off, and how far ahead are they, anyway?"

We rounded a bend in the trail, the two of us pounding out steps like a chariot team, and ahead stood three of the Athenians, Helena, Hermia, and the dark-bearded Lysander, kneeling over the prostrate form of the piss-haired lad, Demetrius, an arrow protruding from the back of his neck just at the base of his skull.

"Did you see the killer?" said I, before I even reached the quartet.

Hermia shook her head.

"Which way?"

They all looked blank faced at me.

"From which direction did the bolt come?"

Hermia pointed off the trail into a thicket of berry bushes of some sort. I could see nothing but foliage. At that point their gazes all turned to Bottom and their eyes went wide. Helena stood, as if to run, but then began to whimper and wave her hands before her as if taken with a palsy.

"Fear not," said Bottom, "for it is I, Nick Bottom, the weaver, of Athens, here to assist you in your time of distress, except for that fellow on the ground, who may need help beyond my skills as weaver and actor." He bowed deeply, which helped not at all, for it gave them all a good look at his hat of many tongues, which were disturbingly agitated.

Helena's whimpers grew to panicked screams that escalated in frequency and volume until they sounded as if someone were pumping a bellows filled with owls. I grabbed the tall girl by the shoulders and shook her roughly, which served only to bat her bosoms into my face and calmed her not at all.

I stepped back. "Hit her," I instructed the petite Hermia.

"Beg pardon?" She was still enthralled by Bottom.

"Hit her!" I commanded. "To calm her. I am a gentleman and will not hit a lady, even an annoyingly tall one."

Without further consideration Hermia swung her fist in a wide and rapid arc, which landed smartly upon her friend's jaw, snapping the tall girl's head back and sending her folding to the forest floor, quite unconscious.

"Blimey," said Lysander.

"I meant *slap*," said I.

"Well you should have said 'slap,'" said Hermia.

"She *has* stopped screaming," said Bottom, ever the spirit of equine optimism, at which point the two remaining lovers turned to him and proceeded to stare in gape-jawed terror, or perhaps wonder, it is hard to say.

"This is Nick Bottom, a crude tradesman, as common as cat shit," said I. "Enchanted by the Puck to appear thus, and nothing to be afraid of." To Bottom, I said, "Sort this, I'm after the killer."

And off I ran in the direction in which Hermia had pointed, leaping over the berry bushes as if they were painted flat on the ground and drawing a dagger from the small of my back as I ran.

If Theseus wanted a murderer, I would bring him one, spitted like a roast pig, if it would help Drool's case. Running through the forest, off the path, required a rather indirect and serpentine movement, which is just as well, for as I made to jump over a cow-sized boulder, I decided at the last instant to zag around it, lest there be a snake or other unpleasantness waiting on the other side, and in that blink of movement, a crossbow bolt thunked into a tree behind the space my head had just occupied. I dove behind the boulder to pause and reflect upon my situation. Yes, now it appeared that dashing into an unfamiliar wood after a murderer with a ranged weapon was perhaps not the wisest path I had ever chosen. Then I remembered, while at the White Tower, upon a dare by the captain of the guard, I had devised a method to measure the time it took for a crossbowman to reload and fire—one that soldiers might use in the field when out of voice range of an officer. As it turned out, the time it took was precisely two stanzas of the romantic ballad "Milady Hath a Most Becoming Bottom."

And so I sang.

"Milady hath a most becoming bottom—"

I was around the boulder and dashing downfield with no thought of evading aim.

"She gave me crabs and I was glad I caught 'em."

As I ran I looked for any movement, any sign of where the murderer might be.

"The lads all say to leave her, I say rot 'em."

Was that a glint off the weapon in the sunlight ahead?

"Milady hath a most becoming bottom."

There was time; if the murderer was running, he wasn't reloading—

"Oh, milady hath the most ebullient bosoms—"

A bowstring twanged and my coxcomb was ripped off my head by the bolt passing through it.

"I still had the line about the Muslims and the bloody refrain before you were supposed to fire!" I shouted as I trod back after my poor punctured hat, which lay on the ground like a dead bird. "Shoddy bloody warcraft, that, not keeping time with the shooting song, ya bellend!"

I was singing the song in my head as I shouted, so as not to be surprised by the next bolt, when the niggling notion occurred to me that at the White Tower we had decided to table "Milady's Bottom" for a song less romantic and more suited to marching into war to kill and burn, and had settled upon the Irish hymn "When the Badgers Ate St. Bridget." I had been timing the bolts with entirely the wrong song. I was lucky not to be dead a third time in as many days. I quickly ducked behind a tree. "Sorry," I called.

As I waited for the next shot, and tried to remember the words to the hymn, there came a woman's scream from whence I had come. Had the killer circled back? Or worse, perhaps there were two of them? I shuffled straight back from my shielding tree for perhaps ten yards, then turned and dashed back the way I had come, zigging and zagging as I went, lest the killer still had me in his sights.

I came upon the trail to find Bottom standing over three bodies, Lysander on his knees holding the downed Hermia's hand.

"Oh for fuck's sake, Bottom, have you gotten another one killed?" I inquired.

The ass-man shook his great head. "No, no, she's just fainted. 'Twas Rumour appeared, trying to retrieve his hat."

"Bloke's face was just floating in air, like a mask," said Lysander. "Hermia saw him and over she went. Poor thing is at her wit's end. Exhausted and hungry."

"What did Rumour say?" I inquired of Bottom.

"Mostly he wanted his hat back, which I wouldn't give him, as it is Moth's, and he said something about the three words again, then he called me a tosser and was gone."

Helena began to make moaning noises and Bottom knelt beside her with his waterskin to attend her. I pushed him back and took his place. "Perhaps stand at a distance, mate, until she becomes accustomed to your handsome countenance." I took the waterskin from him. "There's a love," I said to Helena, helping her sit up. There was already a blue bruise blooming on her jaw where Hermia had smote her. "Have a little sip."

Helena pushed the waterskin away and looked first at Demetrius, then to Hermia.

"Oh good, the little bitch is dead," said Helena, having recovered from her grief rather quickly, I thought. "I suppose I shall have you, then, Lysander."

"She's not dead," said Lysander. "She's just fainted. There was a man, a thing, a strange thing here."

"I know, I saw it, a horrible man-donkey creature," said Helena.

Bottom, looking crestfallen, stepped behind the trunk of a large oak before Helena could turn to see him.

"No, worse than that," said Lysander. "A horrible thing, its face floating in the air like a mask. Moving like a ghost."

"There is nothing more horrible than that thing I saw, tongues all over its head," said Helena.

"That's just a hat!" brayed Bottom, from behind his tree. "Not even *my* hat."

Helena looked around, frightened. I offered her a drink. "Perhaps gentle your discourse, milady, Master Bottom is an actor and therefore is often fragile in his confidence. Apologies if his costume frightened you. He prepares for a play for the duke's wedding, and his method dictates he wear the aspect of his character to give an honest performance."

"Oh," said Helena as my balderdash took root in her mind. "Sorry," she called meekly to Bottom. "Do forgive me, but I had just seen my dear Demetrius slain." Then she was off, throwing herself upon the dead fellow and wailing. "Oh, curse the gods, Demetrius is slain. My beloved Demetrius is slain!"

As I handed the waterskin to Lysander so he might minister to Hermia, I said, "She didn't even like him the last time I saw her, and he didn't like her the time before that."

"The course of true love never did run smooth," said Lysander.

"Aye, blithe idiot, such is the path of all love stories: love is but tragedy's happy feint before a bolt to the heart. Or in this case, the back of the neck." I sighed. "But why would anyone want to kill Demetrius other than he was a massive bellend? That arrow was meant for you, was it not?"

"It was," said Helena, pushing up from her newly becorpsed lover. "They were arguing over Hermia. *Again*. Lysander was standing there, and Demetrius was on one knee pleading with Hermia to take him back, as if she had ever taken him in the first place. And Lysander called him a name."

"A wally," Lysander provided.

"Well spoken," said the puppet Jones, from his spot down my back.

Helena waved for the puppet to shush. "And when Demetrius rose to confront Lysander—*again*—the bolt hit him in the back of the neck."

"Came through to the front," said Lysander, "the point blooming from his throat. He seemed rather surprised. I suppose the bolt was meant for me."

"It was my father," said Hermia. And we all started a bit, as she hadn't even opened her eyes.

"Theseus's simpering toady?" I inquired. "The logic plays. He did try to hire me to do the same."

"That's how a respectable father shows his love," said Helena. "Not all the pretty praise and sweet embraces. Proper possession and control. Hermia's father so loved her he threatened death on her, unless she married Demetrius. None of that prattle of being the apple of Daddy's eye that I heard from my own father, great bag of rags that he is."

"Oh thou sad, broken thing," said I. "Since I landed here I have seen many wondrous and annoying things, but the glory of your wrong-thinking outshines them all."

"She's quite mad," said Hermia.

"Maestro," called Bottom from his spot behind the oak. "The watch approaches." He nodded his muzzle rather furiously down the trail.

I stood. "Grab the fairy frocks, Bottom, we are away."

"But what if it was the watch that killed Demetrius?" asked Hermia. "My father might have sent them, he is often in the company of Blacktooth and Burke at court."

"It wasn't the watch," said I. "Probably. Let them lead you back to Athens, before you all perish from the elements and stupidity. And say nothing about our presence here."

"But why?" asked Lysander, but I was already running down the trail with the ass-man clomping along behind me.

CHAPTER XII

The Squirrel is Strong with This One

THE FAIRIES dropped naked out of the trees, at dusk, and Cobweb immediately leapt into my arms and snogged me mercilessly, breathing her nutty breath on me, her skin redolent of bark and leaves from her squirrelly day out and about. I pushed her away after mere minutes.

"You're a squirrel!"

"Well, you stink of cheese!"

"But you're a squirrel!"

"Not all the time."

"Enough of the time that you might have mentioned it before shagging me. Common courtesy, innit?"

Cobweb, wrist to forehead as if she might faint any second, said, "Oh, didst thou shag me? Methought me fanny was lightly brushed in the night by a foraging hummingbird. Could it have been . . . ?"

Moth and Peaseblossom snickered. Bottom honked.

Sarcasm does not wear well on the naked. "We should go. Blacktooth and Burke are behind us."

"Not to worry, they are miles back, and not even following you."

"How do you know?"

"Fine view from atop the trees."

"Oh right. *Squirrel.* So, shall we gallantly bugger on, or do you need to gather some nuts first?"

"Why, haven't you eaten? Are you hungry?"

Sarcasm is oft lost on the recently unsquirreled. "Grab your kit, sprite, night's swift dragons cut the clouds full fast."

Cobweb and the others retrieved their frocks and hats from Bottom, who, with Peaseblossom and Moth on his flanks, led us through the darkening forest toward the Night Palace. Time passed with just the crunch of leaves underfoot and we trod the first thousand or so miles before we spoke.

"Were you with us through the day?" I asked.

"No, we had duties to perform for the queen."

"Even when you are a . . ."

"Daytime is the *best* time for gathering. We are always slaves, bound forever to serve."

An immortal slave? My breath caught in my chest at the thought of it. I had been a slave. I knew the singular succor that was hope of freedom, even if promised after the grave, and yet I had forgotten what it was to not only have nothing, but *be* property. And as the all-licensed fool I'd had more privilege than most slaves. Yet, I had received Cobweb's kindness and complained. Shame fell upon me like a hot shadow, and for the first time I found myself without words. I squinted and rubbed dust from my eyes and we walked for a long time before I spoke again, lest my voice break and she think me a wally.

When my shame settled, I said, "We encountered the young Athenian lovers again. One was murdered."

"One of the shoe whores? Well, what do they expect, strutting about the forest all tarted up with their smooth hair and their shoes. A wonder they lasted this long."

"It was the one you stabbed in the chin with the crossbow quarrel."

"The yellow-haired geezer?"

"Demetrius," I provided.

"Well, he *was* annoyingly tall. Did the pointy-bearded one do it? He had the look of a scoundrel."

"He was the target of the bolt that killed Demetrius. The same kind as killed the Puck."

"You reckon it was the same killer ended the Puck?"

"I don't know. I can't figure the *why* of it. Hermia's father, Egeus, propositioned me to kill Lysander—"

"Pointy Beard?"

"Aye, but why would he kill the Puck?"

"The Puck could be a right shit," said Cobweb. She bowed her head. "May his memory shine like the stars 'til the end of days."

"Right," said I. "But Egeus is just a toady in Theseus's court. There's no reason for it."

"Well, it wasn't a fairy what did it."

"Obviously, the sun was up when the Puck was killed, so that leaves out you lot. Wait, if the sun was out when he was shot and the Puck was a fairy, that means he wasn't a squirrel?"

"The Puck could be anything at any time. Take any form. A shape-shifter of the first order was the Puck. There was no one like him."

"But still, it couldn't have been a fairy because you are all squirrels in daylight, right?"

"Yes, but also it wasn't a fairy because we're shit at killing each other, aren't we? We live a long time but few of us are born, so if we were good murderers there wouldn't be any of us at all."

"But—and I don't belabor this to be difficult—during the day you are fucking squirrels."

"Not Titania."

I stopped. "The queen of the bloody night does not change shapes like the rest of you?"

She stopped. "She's different."

"Obviously so."

"She's taller."

"She's not bloody taller. She's a bit better kept, but she's the same size as the rest of you. More of a nutter, I suppose."

"Among my people, calling someone a nutter is a compliment. Moth is a smashing nutter."

"I am," said Moth.

"The squirrel is strong with this one," said Cobweb.

"I don't mean it that way," said I.

"I am simple," said Peaseblossom.

"We know, love," said Cobweb. "It means someone who is good at remembering where they've hidden their nuts."

"Fine," said I. "She's a nutter of the first rate. Do you think she killed the Puck?"

"I don't know, I wasn't tending her that day."

"Squirrels— Your people, I mean, tend her during the day? As squirrels?"

"Aye. She's a goddess, isn't she?"

"So we could just go back and ask the fairies who were with her on the morning the Puck was killed if they saw the murder?"

"Aye, if you want."

"Then let's do that," said I.

"Pocket, you daft dog pizzle, she's probably already killed one fool, do you want to give her another go at a second one? Fine, but I have become trifling fond of you and I shan't watch you slain."

"Perhaps not," I said, thinking she might have a point. But once again, what was the *why* of it? I said, "Why would Titania wish to harm the Puck? Especially that morning when he was on his way to Theseus on an errand for her?"

Cobweb shrugged. "It makes as much sense as Oberon killing his own jester, yet we are on our way to his castle to ask him."

"Do you imagine he'll confess?"

"Oh my, yes, and then he will change Bottom back into a man, and give you the love potion for Theseus, and I shan't be surprised if he lays a banquet for us, has his goblins bathe you in rosewater, and personally wanks you off in thanks." She nodded at me, her wide eyes doubly wide to show just how bloody earnest she was.

"Sarcasm will make your tail fall off," said I.

She feigned alarm and lifted her frock as if to check for a tail, then wagged her bottom at me. "Oh, blast! You're right. Oh woe!" She bumped her naked hip against me, then scampered ahead to walk with the others.

"Squirrel!" I called, but was paid no mind.

I trod on a bit behind the others, and as I watched Peaseblossom twiddling the tongues on Moth's hat of many tongues, I recalled Rumour's parting chorus: *"The passion of the Puck lies with the prince."*

"The boy!" I called to Cobweb. "The Indian boy in Titania's charge, does he change into a squirrel at daylight?"

"No, he is mortal."

But his ears were pointed. I'd seen them up close. Had Titania killed the Puck to protect the boy for some reason, perhaps from Oberon? The shadow king had banished her from the castle over the boy. If she had sent the killer, it would make sense she would blame Oberon for the Puck's murder as misdirection.

I hurried to Cobweb's side. "Were you with Titania when she fetched the boy from India?"

"No, none of us were. We don't leave the forest except to steal from the mortals."

"So no one knew this boy's mother? No one was there for her death, nor the travels Titania says she had with her?"

"Only the Puck. When they traveled far it was always with the Puck."

"They?"

"When Titania and Oberon travel the skies, of all the fairy and goblin people, only the Puck is—*was*—allowed in their company."

"So no ships? No carriages, horses, elephants?"

"Maybe elephants," said Cobweb.

"She traveled to India on a cracking huge gray animal, taller than a house, with great fan ears, tusks, and a long nose made for grasping?"

"Oh, no. No elephants either, then. Just she and the Puck."

"Oh, bollocks. I should have never left Puck in the grotto that morning," said I. "I would have seen he had been followed."

"I do not think I care for elephants," said Cobweb. "Wait, which grotto?"

"I don't know, a great tree and rock hole, with a great stone in the stream shaped like a turtle."

"Turtle Grotto?" said Cobweb.

"That would seem an entirely appropriate name for such a place."

"That's where Titania would meet Theseus," said Peaseblossom.

"What?" said I, and verily "What" was repeated among our merry band as we stopped and turned our attention to the simple fairy.

"That's where the night queen bonked the day duke," said Peaseblossom. "Watched from a tree. I will say, a mortal will take his time in the day, when he's a mind to. Not like a fairy bloke, quick poke under the tail and they're off to the next tree without so much as a by-your-leave."

"Titania was also shagging Theseus?" I asked.

The fairies all nodded.

"Can't blame her, really," said Moth. "After you two last night, thinking of giving a human mortal a go myself."

"Me too," said Peaseblossom.

"In all this time, you two have never shagged a mortal?" I said.

"Mortal *man*," said Moth.

"All what time?" asked Peaseblossom.

"Well, all of your hundreds of years—how old are *you*, anyway?"

"Seven," said Peaseblossom, not sounding entirely sure of her answer.

"Seven? Seven?" I turned to Cobweb. "You're nine hundred years old and your mate is seven?"

"We are not good at counting," said Moth.

"Nine hundred was an estimate," said Cobweb.

"The point," said I, "despite your appalling aptitude with figures, is Theseus and Titania were meeting at the very place where the Puck was killed. It could have been either of them, or both of them in concert."

"Except that Theseus sent you to find the killer, did he not?" asked Cobweb.

"Yes. No. Oh balls. So did Titania. Let us bugger on to the bloody Night Palace and ask the bloody shadow king to transform bloody Bottom back into a man, fetch us the bloody love potion flower, and confess to the killing of his bloody jester. Should be a piece of piss."

"You seem bothered," said Cobweb. "Shall I build a nest and we'll have a bit of a rest before going on?" She leaned in and whispered in my ear breathily and with no stealth whatsoever, "A wee nap to rejuvenate the humors."

"And to bonk his boots off," said Peaseblossom, deftly reading the subtext through her intrepid thickness.

"I am sorely tempted to nap, but I think it best we get to the Night Palace, then rest." Truth be told I was knackered from the day's marching and I was not ambivalent about the fairy's charms.

Cobweb said, "If you and Bottom need to get to Oberon tonight, then to Athens before Theseus hangs your friend, you'll need to travel all night tonight and all day tomorrow. We fairies will be fine, but you two will need to rest."

"You sleep during the day, then?"

"No, safer to sleep at night, like this. Less chance of being eaten by a cat."

"Right, hadn't thought of that."

"Fancy a frolic, then?" asked Peaseblossom.

Cobweb put her arm around my waist. I allowed it. "It will sustain you, you being a living thing. You felt it last night, didn't you?"

I had. The strength and speed I'd felt while chasing Demetrius's killer—of course, the dance. I didn't know *they* had known. "I thought you were forbidden to dance. Isn't that Titania's grievance with Oberon?"

"It is. And we *are* forbidden. But the Puck told us to dance as we please as long as Titania and Oberon do not see us."

"It feels ever so naughty when it's forbidden," said Moth.

"A frolic it is, then," said I. And without any ceremony or prelude, the three fairies shed their frocks and began to dance.

✢   ✢   ✢

BOTTOM AND I walked light after the frolic, this one in close proximity, washed us with an uncanny vigor. I felt again like I could run the rest of the way to the Night Palace, with a fairy or two on my back. I was barely able to resist adding a dance step to my cadence as we marched along the trail and I even taught the fairies the chorus to that alehouse standard "I Give Your Sweet Mum a Spot o' the Pox."

"She bonked me right proper, out of my sox," sang the fairies as we went.

"She's a friend indeed, to a thousand cocks," sang Bottom, because the fairies weren't good at counting.

And I filled my bellows to belt out, *"Oh, I give your sweet mum—"*

Which is when the monkey swung down from a rather twisted cedar tree and snatched the hat of many tongues off of Moth's head, then scampered to higher branches, where he screeched down at us.

"Jeff!" I called. "You cheeky monkey, you!"

"Why does that monkey have the same outfit as you, Pocket?" asked Cobweb.

"Do you turn into a monkey in the daytime?" asked Pease-blossom.

"No, why would you ask that?"

"Because it would be smashing," she said.

"Also, because she is simple," said Cobweb.

"That's true," said Peaseblossom.

"I love that hat," said Moth. "That is my first and only hat." She shook her fist at Jeff, who shook his little fist back at her, as is the way of his people. "If it were daytime I'd run that rascal down and get it back," said Moth.

"Sorry, love," said I, "but I'm afraid there will be monkey spunk in the millinery before you see it again."

Alas, I would have tried to call Jeff back, but at that very moment the ground began to undulate around us, lumps of forest floor growing like great blisters of leaves and pine straw to erupt into creatures, six of them, manlike, as black as tar, great heads low on their shoulders, with ears like bat wings and yellow eyes as big as a duck's eggs, each brandishing a short sword curved like a sickle.

Cobweb screamed and scurried up a tree as two of the creatures broke for her. Moth and Peaseblossom similarly shinnied up trees out of reach.

"Run," I shouted at Bottom as I drew a dagger from the small of my back and flung it overhand at the attacker who stormed at me, screeching, sword swinging over his head. The dagger caught the creature high on the chest, and stuck, but did not sink to the hilt as it would have in a man, but penetrated only to the depth of the first joint of your finger. It stopped the creature for only a tick. He yanked my dagger out of his chest and cast it aside, while I drew my second dagger and dodged behind a fir tree. The thing hissed and bared a mouthful of jagged teeth like I'd seen in sharks we'd caught at sea, his mouth fully twice as wide as that of any human I'd ever seen.

The single beast that pursued me swung his sword and I dove and rolled away. His blade caromed off the bark of the tree. I risked a look back. Three of the creatures were clawing at trees, trying to get the fairies, another two had taken off after Nick Bottom, who, no doubt fortified by the fairy frolic, was outrunning them easily.

I backflipped away from my attacker and rolled to put another tree between us. I dared not throw another knife and have the same result as the first. The fiend was covered in plates, as smooth as polished onyx, each approximating where there might be a muscle underneath, and although there was space between the plates, there was no way to know if a blade would even penetrate at those points, and before I could flip the blade to throw it, he was on me.

He hacked away at me with his sword as he advanced. By backing away and leaping I was able to avoid losing an arm. He was a shit fighter, really, signaling every slash with a great windup, so as long as I had a clear path to retreat to, I could avoid his blows. But even an agile warrior with only a knife cannot long hold off a stronger opponent with a sword, and when my heel caught on a downed branch and I fell backward, he was on me. I drew the puppet Jones from down my back and used his oak stick to parry a blow, then quickly riposted, hoping to lock his curved blade with the puppet, then slide under to plant my dagger beneath his breastplate.

But the puppet stick snapped.

"Oh, fuckstockings," said I, regarding the splintered stem of my puppety friend.

I should perhaps add here that I, too, am a shit fighter. Oh, I am nimble footed, and I can perform many acrobatic tricks, but they are not suited so much for fighting as for entertainment, so my base battle strategy is, generally, to jump around like a lunatic until my adversary is thoroughly confused, then stab him in the eye.

The creature made a quick recovery and swung straight down at my face. I parried the blow with my dagger and made to roll away, but my jerkin caught on whatever branch had caught my heel and I lay open to the next blow.

"Oi! Goblin!" Cobweb, behind my attacker perhaps four yards, stood with my first dagger, blade in hand, ready to fling. The goblin (for now I knew what the creature was) paused in his attack and looked under his raised sword arm to the attacking fairy.

"In the eye, lass," I called as I freed my jerkin and rolled away. Cobweb let fly with my knife.

A thrown knife is a fussy weapon. Not only must it be thrown with enough force to pierce an enemy, but it must arrive at its target point-first and perpendicular or you may as well have flung a stick for all the damage it will do. Thus is required an assessment of the blade's balance and weight, as well as the rate at which it will spin and how far the weapon will travel with each spin. With practice, and a matched set of throwing knives, one becomes able to instantly calculate the distance, time the rotation, adjust the force and attitude of the throw to match the circumstances, and, if truly aimed, drive a dagger into a soft target to the hilt. All this calculation, of course, depends on the ability to count, at which fairies are complete shit.

The dagger slapped flat against the goblin's back and fell to the ground, at which point I heard, for the first time, the sound of goblin laughing. The other goblins stopped trying to get after Peaseblossom and Moth and turned to see what was so funny.

"We're sent by the night queen, you gormless bloody git," said Cobweb. "Show him the passport, Pocket."

I hadn't thought about the blossom I'd put in my hat since we'd left Titania's leafy cathedral. I pulled off my coxcomb and reached in, to see my finger emerge from the hole the crossbow bolt had made when I pursued Demetrius's killer in the morning. There was some damp, plantlike pulp but little more. "The passport is ruined, but I've some of its essence. Here, smell my finger," I said as I held out my damp digit for sniffing.

He turned, made as if to sniff my finger, but with a closer look at his great maw of ragged teeth I withdrew the offer.

"Take my word for it," said I. "We are sent, to see the shadow king. Take us to him immediately."

The goblin regarded me, his cohort stopped worrying the trees and looked over.

"Do you have any silver?" he said, his voice a rat scratching in a tin bucket. I could see now that the shiny plates I had thought to be armor were, indeed, part of the goblin's body, like the shell of a turtle, only segmented and articulated. Other than a small silver ring in his ear, the goblin wore only a ragged loincloth and a thin dusting of the loamy earth from which he'd emerged.

"I do, I do, I do," called Nick Bottom, who had circled back at full gallop, leaving his two pursuers a hundred yards behind.

"Silver!" said the goblin with the earring. I assumed he was in charge, because when he held up his hand, thin fingers tipped with thick claws, the two chasing Bottom slowed to a limping walk, which was the way all of them seemed to ambulate—bit of a sideways crab stride, as if they had suffered some injury.

Nick Bottom had unbuttoned his fine waistcoat and was coming forward holding one lapel out. "This button is silver. It's sulfured black, but that will polish off."

I strode to the weaver, my dagger still in hand, the ranking goblin like a shadow behind me. I snipped the button from Bottom's vest and held it away from the goblin, who had become as single-minded as a begging dog with the scent of roast beef in his nose.

"No," said I. I polished the button against my jerkin and held it for the goblin to see the shining relief of a woven Celtic knot standing out silver against the black patina. His great yellow eyes rolled back in his head as he looked, and he reached for the button as if reaching for a dream. I pulled it away. "When we see Oberon."

The head goblin looked at the others. "We take them to the shadow king."

And so they did. Peaseblossom and Moth came down from their trees. Nick Bottom fell in behind them, muttering something like, "So this is why we weren't to go into the forest at night. I knew it wasn't the bloody fairies." I walked side by side with Cobweb, the silver button tucked into my belt, and the goblins formed a stutter-stepping formation around us, the one with the silver earring leading.

"You lived among these goblins when Titania lived at the Night Palace?" I asked Cobweb.

"We tended her in the forest. She came to us. We only went into the Night Palace for ceremonies, and never during the day. Except for Puck and the one hundred."

"The one hundred?"

"Oberon's concubines. They are locked in a chamber in the palace all day and night."

The head goblin began to drift back in the column until he marched at my side.

"I am Gritch," he said.

"I am Pocket of Dog Snogging, all-licensed fool and onetime king of Britain."

"Fool? Like the Puck?" said Gritch.

"Yes, like the Puck," said Cobweb. "So mind your bloody manners, you scuttling dung beetle, or you'll feel the fool's wrath."

We walked for a bit, the forest faded away to rocky scrubland, the foothills to mountains that rose like jagged fangs against the night. I carved a new stick for Jones from a green branch as we walked, Cobweb watching as if I were performing alchemy rather than whittling.

"So, love," I whispered to Cobweb. "Not looking for a warm welcome back to the palace, then?"

Before she could answer, Gritch sidled up to me and said, "Suck your dick for silver?" with all the subtlety of a fishmonger calling out freshly caught cod.

"No, piss off," said I.

"Fine," he said. And he scuttled across the column and came up on Cobweb's side. "Suck your dick for silver?"

"I don't have any silver," said Cobweb.

"Fine," said Gritch. As we made our way up the mountain, he went to each member of our troop, offering the same service to each for the same price, pausing next to Peaseblossom, who appeared to be haggling.

"She knows she doesn't have a dick, right?" I asked Cobweb.

"Doesn't have any silver neither. Pease is simple as sand, but she's the mongrel's dongles at bargaining."

When Gritch got to Bottom, the weaver looked at Gritch's saw-toothed maw and audibly yelped with dismay before declining, as his only silver had been the button on his waistcoat. Gritch sulked and fell in beside me again.

"Gritch, mate, do you have any idea what you are offering?"

"I am told that if you say that to mortals, sometimes they will give you silver."

"But you asked the fairies. Females."

"They can have silver," he reasoned.

"Quite right," said I. "Carry on."

CHAPTER XIII

In the Night Palace

THE PALACE rose into the night sky like a great pointed crown, nine ridiculously tall, angular towers constructed, it seemed, of the same smooth, black glass plates that armored the goblins. No man nor creature of forest had constructed this edifice, for there was no sign of joints nor mortar, nor even the mark of a stonecutter. It was a castle made by a demented jeweler, from pieces of polished night, which reflected every star in spectral brilliance and shone streaks of moonlight down its sides as if painted in molten silver.

Gritch led us through a gate of polished stone, down a tunnel, and out into an open courtyard, or bailey, as wide as some of the old Roman amphitheaters I'd seen in Tuscany and Provence. The interior was lit only by dim lamps up the high walls and the odd torch carried here and there by ambling goblins. The goblins and fairies had no problem seeing by the dim light, but Bottom and I were nearly tripping over ourselves until Gritch retrieved a torch from a rack by a brazier glowing with coals and lit it from the same. He held it high so we mortals could see our way.

A goblin carrying a sword with a silver earring somewhat smaller than Gritch's approached him and the two exchanged what seemed to me to be low grunts and growls.

Nick Bottom stepped up behind me and whispered, "He's

telling the other to tell Oberon we are here, sent by Titania." Bottom pointed to his long ears by way of explanation.

The soldier goblin hurried off, no doubt to deliver his message, and Gritch said, "Gathering is soon. Shadow king will bring down the moon. He will see you after the moon."

There was a raised stage at the far side of the courtyard, and goblins were beginning to gather below it, spraying out from gates at the base of each of the towers that made up the crown of the palace.

"Where is their market?" I asked Cobweb. "Where are the horses? The oxen? How do they feed a walled city without farms?"

"They eat things from under the ground," she said. "Farm things under the ground."

"And do they turn into gophers during the day?"

"No, they hide under the ground," she said, ignoring my snark. "They can go about in the day, but only for a short time, wearing a cloak. They can't see well and the sun burns them."

"So, one might shoot the wrong mortal simply because the daylight was too bright?"

She shrugged, nodded toward a set of steps that led to a platform just below the stage. Two goblins with crossed halberds guarded the stairs and made way as they saw Gritch coming. A silver earring carried a lot of authority in the castle, evidently, for beyond that, nothing distinguished Gritch from the other armed goblins.

As we passed by the guard he whispered, "Suck your dick for silver?" to Moth.

"Fancy a frolic?" she replied. Cobweb and Peaseblossom laughed and the goblin growled at them.

Once on the platform, the lower stage, our heads were level with the upper stage, but we were a man's height above the groundlings, which is how I thought of the goblins who were filling the courtyard. There was some sort of caste system at play here; the warriors carried all manner of weapons, were heavier of limb, and were perhaps a head taller than another group with spindlier arms and thick claws on their large toes. Workers, I suppose? If they were of different sexes, I could not tell, for there was no evidence of a difference in attire or body shape. They were a sea of shining black, like boiling pitch or swarming ants, perhaps. The flash of a weapon or the occasional silver ring in the ear was the only thing that distinguished one from another. Then just below the stage I spotted a flash among the black, on a warrior carrying a crossbow and a short quiver of bolts slung from a belt at his waist. On his right arm he wore a silver armlet cast with the image of the head of a Gorgon. I turned to Gritch to demand he bring the goblin to us, but before I could speak, trumpets sounded from balconies near the ceiling of the chamber, and all the goblins dropped to their knees in a single motion.

"Trumpets?" I said to Cobweb. "How are they playing trumpets? They don't even have bloody lips."

"Oi, Gritch," said Cobweb, "you got goblins with lips?"

Gritch looked confused, and I had no doubt that if he'd had eyebrows, he would have raised one quizzically. "Lips?" he asked.

Cobweb blew a raspberry at him to illustrate her question, just as the doors at the back of the stage swung open and Oberon walked out. The hall trembled and went quiet except for the dying echo of the horns.

Oberon looked like a man built of night sky. He was black, head to toe, but spotted everywhere but his face with silver and gold stars that shone their own light—I could see it playing in patterns on the doors behind him. He wore a cape made of night, too, that billowed out behind him, although I could feel no wind. His face was black, like the goblins', but he had handsome human features, like an Egyptian statue carved from onyx. Atop his head he wore a tall, nine-pointed black crown, the model for, or modeled from, the very palace in which we stood. He wore wicked silver claws on his fingertips that looked as if they would draw blood with even a delicate touch.

He raised his arms straight over his head and the trumpets blew again. There was an earth-trembling sound of machinery, like a dozen heavy mill wheels being turned at once, and as Oberon brought his arms down to cruciform, the ceiling of the great hall opened. Every goblin eye turned skyward as the arches of the ceiling pulled back into the towers, revealing a shining moon above.

Gasps of awe and ecstasy filled the hall as thousands of yellow eyes in a sea of black were illuminated by the full summer moon. I looked around. Even the fairies were on their knees, staring in wonder. Oberon and I were the only ones standing and not looking up. I looked at him, he at me.

"Oh for fuck's sake," said I. "He didn't create the bloody moon, you nitwits, he just opened a fucking window. You could have seen the same moon by walking outside."

There were a few cries of distress around the arena, as if I'd interrupted someone's especially somber moon wank, but most of the goblins were drooling at the moon like starved men at an apple.

Oberon floated, or seemed to float, to the edge of the stage and looked down on us. Gritch's feet began to make frantic scratching motions, like a dog having his belly rubbed, his heavy talons scoring the stone. If he'd been on soft earth he'd have dug his way under it and I realized that was exactly what his body was trying to do. Cobweb, Moth, and Peaseblossom were curled into tight balls, hoping not to be noticed, I guessed. I could see Cobweb trembling and I bent and patted her back before approaching Oberon, who seemed somewhat nonplussed that I was not overwhelmed with his sparkly fucking grandeur.

I reached into the small of my back and drew the bolt that killed the Puck. "The Puck is dead. Killed by this." I tossed the bolt onto the stage and it rattled at his feet.

"I am invisible," said Oberon. The shadow king whipped his cape into the air as if trying to form wings, and while it did send an impressive wave of silk across the stage, he remained quite visible.

Cobweb sneaked a peek from under her arm, first at Oberon, then at me. "He's not invisible," she said.

"No," said I. "He's not."

"Your Grace, I am Pocket of Dog Snogging, freelance fool. Queen Titania has sent me with a message, in addition to that bolt, which is from a goblin weapon, so the Puck's killer can be found. She bids you do me a favor as recompense for bringing you this message."

"I am invisible," repeated Oberon, but this time he didn't do the grand wave of his cape.

Gritch now looked at me under *his* arm, then dared to raise an eye toward the stage, where he spotted the shadow king being decidedly visible. Gaudily so, truth be told.

"I am now visible," said Oberon, with the cape wave.

"Much to my relief," said I. "For surely, when you disappeared, we thought you might have been slain by the same fiend who murdered the Puck."

"The Puck is slain, you say?" said Oberon, a quaver in his voice, as genuine in his grief as he had been in his invisibility. "He was my fool. My slave. My property. How happened this? Who would do such a thing?"

"Well," said I, walking to the edge of the stage until I stood directly above the goblin with the silver armlet. "Offhand I would say it was that crossbow what killed him, fired by this tosser."

Here and there around the hall, goblins were tearing their gaze away from the moon to see what manner of cheeky monkey was speaking to the shadow king in such a way.

Oberon picked up the bolt and leapt off the upper stage, trailing a wave of shimmering night cape behind him. He moved as if mountains might be humbled and slide away at his will. I stepped aside and reached to the small of my back, ready to draw a dagger, lest the shadow king decide it was his royal privilege to stab me in the head with the arrow. Bloody sloppy protocol, anyway, to let a complete stranger in jester togs trailing three fairies and a donkey-headed bloke within stabbing distance of your king. The guards with the halberds were as helpless with awe as the rest of the goblins. Irresponsible, it was.

"This tosser?" asked Oberon, pointing with a silver talon to the armleted tosser, who cowered under his king's attention.

"Aye," said I. Up close Oberon was as hard edged and dark as had Titania been pale and soft.

"Draw and cock your crossbow and give it me," said Oberon, crouching over the goblin soldier. "Do not load a bolt." Silver Armlet did as he was told and held the cocked crossbow over his head with both hands, his eyes averted to the ground, as if making an offering to a god, which I suppose, in his mind, he was. Oberon took the weapon, inspected it, and grinned down at me (yes, he was two heads taller than I, four with the ridiculous crown), his grin a cold crescent moon where lived no mirth. "This bolt killed my beloved Puck?" he said.

"Aye," said I. I fought the urge to take the piss, add a colorful sobriquet—"grandiose wankpuffin" came to mind. I had seen mad kings before,

The shadow king fitted the bolt into the arrow groove of the crossbow and inspected it, nodded to me. "Yes, it appears to be from a weapon exactly like this." He held the crossbow so I could see that the black finish on the stock was the same as on the bolt.

I nodded.

Oberon lowered the crossbow and fired it into Silver Armlet's chest. The bolt easily pierced the goblin's chest plate with a thunk and buried itself to the fletching. The goblin reeled and fell on his side, a look of surprise and betrayal in his yellow eyes, green goo oozed out of the wound. The goblins about the courtyard had all stopped looking at the moon as a thousand yellow eyes turned to their king.

"There," said Oberon, holding the crossbow out to me. "Puck avenged." The shadow king giggled, a high, mad giggle, then turned and leapt back up the six feet onto the upper stage with a single bound. As if calling to the sky itself, he shouted, "Take back the moon!"

The ground shook, the great gears began to grind, and the ceiling began to close. "Away!" Oberon gestured to the crowd and they swarmed to the exits as if running before a flood.

Oberon looked down on me. "I must go grieve. Tell Titania that justice is done. Tell her I will have the Indian boy now, and only then may her fairies dance again. This is the will of Oberon, ruler of all of the night, king of shadows, master of the moon and tides, giver of the planets and stars." Oberon turned, wound his long cape around his arm and cast it out behind him, then strode away toward the exit.

"Oi, king of the night!" said Cobweb. She snatched up the shadow king's cape and gave a good yank, causing Oberon to slip and barely catch himself before falling on his arse. The black crown tumbled off his head to the stones. As it turned out, one *could* get the attention of Oberon's guards, it simply required yanking the king back by his cape like a fast dog finding the end of a short leash. Four spearmen, two from either side of the lower stage, came up the stairs looking quite determined to ventilate Cobweb. She jumped up, caught the edge of the upper stage, and swung up to her feet above the guards. Oberon was kneeling, having retrieved his crown, he rubbed his throat as one does after being suddenly and violently choked. Four more spearmen came out of the door at the back of the stage. I quickly measured the damage I might do with my two daggers and a volley of cutting insults against a platoon of leather-skinned spearmen, and I determined that it might be time to take a hostage.

I leapt to the upper stage with a single bound. (There was more than trifling magic in a fucking frolic, and I felt it boiling in my limbs.) I made to draw one of my daggers, thinking the point to the shadow king's throat might persuade his guards to hold. Then, like a shooting star across a night sky of my mind, an idea . . .

"I have silver!" said I, pulling Bottom's silver button from my belt and holding it aloft.

And the guards stopped in place, every yellow eye trained on the button. I looked over at the still-kneeling Oberon. "Really?"

"That is mine," Gritch called.

I flipped the button in the air, caught it, showed it to them all, then made it appear to disappear. If they'd had lips, the goblins would have pouted. I made the button reappear from behind Cobweb's ear. The goblins' saw-toothed gobs fell open in wonder.

"You missed the part about him being a fool," Cobweb said to Oberon, but the shadow king was following my antics with the button, as rapt as his guards.

"Oi! Shadow king," said Cobweb, shouting in Oberon's face. "He's a bloody jester. Like the Puck. LIKE. THE. PUCK. He knows the Puck's three words."

Oberon's attention seemed to return to the scene at hand, even as I was popping the button from foot to foot to elbow to forehead.

He stood. "Enough!" Oberon waved off the guards. I caught the button and tucked it into my belt.

The shadow king was furious but seemed to have no idea how to vent his wrath. He did not know who I was, but he suspected *what* I was, and I could see there was doubt, if not fear, in his eyes.

"There ye be," said Cobweb.

Oberon appeared to see the fairy for the first time, standing in front of him, defiant and not a little angry herself.

"You have sticks and leaves in your hair," he said.

"Your queen has sticks and leaves in her hair," said Cobweb. "You live in this shining palace made of shards of midnight while your queen lives up a fucking tree in the forest. So pardon the bloody sticks in my hair, but that is the royal way, where we live."

"Aye," said Moth, running to the edge of the upper stage, then backing up so she could see Cobweb.

"Aye," said Peaseblossom, who ran to the edge of the upper stage and stayed below sight, no doubt wondering where everyone had gone.

Oberon looked to me, as if I might provide some guidance in how to deal with this situation. "She's got you there, mate, the bitch does, indeed, live up a tree."

"And she has to shag the donkey-donged chap while you have a harem of one hundred fairies," added Cobweb, bringing Bottom reluctantly into the scene.

That seemed to yank Oberon's attention back to the fore. He looked over the courtyard. Some of the goblins had stopped running for the towers and were watching, drifting back toward the stage. "Take the fairies to the harem. Have them washed and deloused."

The guards moved toward Cobweb and she ran and threw herself into my arms. "Oh, save me, good Pocket!" She buried her face in my neck and whispered frantically, "Play him. Then lose him. Bring the dead goblin to the harem before dawn. Do not tell Oberon the three words."

"I don't know the three words," I whispered back.

"Well don't let *him* know that, you git," she said as two of the guards pulled her away.

The guards dragged her off. Moth and Peaseblossom climbed up on the stage and followed along behind, chatting and cheerily negotiating with the guards, as they went, how much silver they would give to have their dicks sucked.

"Bottom," I called. "With me." I pulled the ass-man up on the stage and introduced him. "This is Nick Bottom, Majesty. He was a weaver, a mortal, before a magical misadventure with the Puck. Now he is my valet and he wears the head of an ass."

"*Enchanté*," said Bottom with a bow.

"Go keep an eye on our fairies," I told Bottom, once I was sure Oberon had gotten a good look at him. Let the shadow king stew in jealousy's emerald bile at the thought of his queen taking her time with the long-eared weaver. Bottom hurried out the door after Cobweb and her co-squirrels.

✦   ✦   ✦

"YOU MAY watch me dine," said Oberon, sitting at the head of a long table that could have seated a hundred yet had only two chairs, one at each end, high-backed, thronelike rascals, upholstered in blood-red velvet, one of the few nonblack things I'd seen at the Night Palace. "Stand there," said the shadow king, pointing a silver-tipped finger at a spot beside him from where goblins were serving some sort of roasted bird.

I set the puppet Jones on the table to mark my place, then made my way to the chair at the far end of the table and proceeded to drag it along behind me to Oberon's end. The chair was heavy and squeaked horribly as I dragged it, filling the hall with a sound akin to that of a tortured baby elephant. Each time I would pause to get a grip on the chair, Oberon would begin to speak, and I would resume the dragging and drowning him out, until, by the time I pushed the chair under the table at his right hand, he was quite annoyed.

"There," said I, climbing into the chair. "That's better. A long journey in the forest wears on one."

"You put your dirty puppet next to my supper," said the king.

"You're a dirty puppet!" said the puppet Jones (with my help). From the look on Oberon's face, he had never encountered ventriloquism before either.

My chair was so low that my shoulders were just above the table. The petite Titania must have sat on cushions or stood to dine here. I tore a leg from the roasted bird, a duck methinks, and had a taste of the greasy flesh, sans plate, settings, or goblet.

"Oh, scrumptious. Well done," said I. "Do you have any wine?"

The shadow king nodded to a serving goblin, who scooted off to fetch a goblet, as there was already a pitcher of wine on the table. "And a cushion or two as well, love," I called after. To Oberon, I said, "I can barely get my elbows on the table—must be a bother to Titania. Delicious little fuckbubble, by the way. Well done, there. Mad as a barrel of rats, though. Pity. Did you notice her tits go pink when she's lying? Oh, of course you did. I'll wager they look smashing against all this broody black and silver. Never mind. Sorry, I do go on. What did you wish to speak about?"

Oberon drained his pewter goblet, then slammed it down on the table. "I could send you to the most distant freezing shores of Neptune. Have you torn apart by dragons. You dare—"

"Aye, do that then," said I. "Send me to Neptune, Your Darkness. Banish me to night's plutonian shore, if you must." I paused, waited, bounced my eyebrows in anticipation. "No? It's customary to threaten a fool with hanging, beheading, and dismemberment."

Oberon stood. "I shall—"

"Hot poker up the bum? Torture and kill my family? Sorry, orphan—everyone is quite dead. Among the more genteel, my company is considered torture, although when I was king, it was agreed throughout the land that I was a fucking delight. Are those

turnips?" I drew one of my daggers and speared a roast turnip. A
server goblin started at the sight of my knife, which would have
been completely unnecessary if they'd brought me a place setting.
He ran off to fetch a guard or soldier. "Mate, bring back a *serviette,
s'il vous plaît*," I called in perfect fucking French. "I'm in duck fat up
to my elbows." Back to Oberon: "Sorry, do go on."

"I am—"

"Being the king of the night, does that mean that you just fuck
off during the day? Turn into a squirrel and run about demanding
everyone's nuts?"

ENTER RUMOUR, PAINTED FULL OF TONGUES

"Oh fuckstockings," said I. There he was, his coat of many
tongues wagging.

*"Majesty, this rogue, this wretch, this scoundrel, this blackguard,
this villain, this canker blossom, this twisted, disgusting, perverted little
worm of a creature, writhing in his own bilious moral filth, seeks nothing
but his own destruction, he craves your wrath to relieve him of his own
fetid company."*

"Bit harsh," said I, around a bite of turnip, which had been
roasted in the pan with the duck and so had picked up some delightful flavor from the drippings.

"You took my hat, vile hedge wag."

"I did not," said I. "I did not take his hat," I explained to
Oberon, who was still standing and seemed quite taken aback by
the appearance of the narrator.

"He doesn't even have a head," said the shadow king. "He's just
a floaty face."

"One of the many elementals under my command," said I.
"This one an unruly sprite, conjured for finding a lost hat. Pardon
his shit manners."

"I am the narrator, the teller of tales, the shaper of plots. I command the elements of substance and style."

"Back, sprite!" I commanded. "I forbid thee to harm the noble shadow king. Away, I say!"

"I will have my hat of many tongues or this story will turn on you."

"A fairy took your hat, sprite. I will inquire where she put it after I confer with the king and he finishes torturing me and sending me to Nepenthe."

"Neptune," Oberon corrected.

"Right, Neptune. Now, away, sprite, or I shall start trimming the tips from the tongues on your cloak and it shall become a cloak of many lisps. Bloody humiliating, really."

I feigned an exaggerated lunge at Rumour with my dagger and in an instant he was at the door of the chamber, standing behind two of the servants. *"You do not command me, hateful scalawag, I will have my hat and I shall recapture this narrative, and you, in it, shall not fare well, fool."*

I vaulted over the table toward Rumour and took but three running steps at him before he was gone with a whoosh, calling, *"Three words, fool!"* behind him.

"Beg pardon, Your Grace," I said to Oberon as I returned to my seat.

Oberon sat. "You command many sprites like that?"

"Sprites, demons, pixies, spirits, a firkin full of fucking ghosts. There's always a bloody ghost. But, yes."

Oberon sipped his wine, as if he was not trying to steady his hand. "With the Puck gone, I am in need of a fool."

"Oh?" said I, thinking I should give thanks to Rumour, for I could not have laid down a better testament to my magical powers if I had actually had them. "I am in the service of another at present, but when I finish my current task, I would consider it. I am no slave, though, good king, I will require payment, and favors in advance as my retainer."

"What payment?"

"There is a flower, I know not where it grows, but the liquor from it, when dropped into the eyes, will cause a sleeper to fall in love with the next thing he sees. I will require such a flower."

"I know of such a flower. For this you would serve me?"

"That, and my valet, Bottom, has been transformed by the Puck into a donkey, and I would have him changed back. This spell is not among my powers."

"I thought you did that when he displeased you," said the shadow king.

"The Puck did it on my request. Professional courtesy, innit?"

Oberon removed his great crown and set it upon the table, then rubbed his temples so I thought he might gouge out his own eyes with the sharp silver fingertips he wore.

"Alas, these things are not in my power. 'Twas the Puck who fetched the purple flower that enchants a lover, and I never thought I would have need to find it myself. It is the same with the spell on your valet. What other price would you ask for your services, for even by these requests you see I am in need of a jester? Silver, gold, the sweetest perfumes. I command the moon and the tides, the goblins and fairies do my bidding and could as well do yours. Name your price, fool, and I shall list the tasks I require of you."

"A night in your harem," said I. "Unattended and unrestrained, to do as I wish."

Oberon grinned like a child at the prospect of a spoonful of honey. "Done," he said.

"And when I leave, I bring with me the retainers who accompanied me. The fairies. I require them for my work."

"They are nothing, take them. But when you finish your task, you will bring me the Indian boy from Titania's camp. Deliver him, and she should not know where he has gone."

I scratched my chin as if I were considering it. "This I can do."

"And I would have you spy on her, in the manner of the Puck, so she knows not that she is observed. I would know if Titania has taken a mortal lover."

I measured my answer here, tempted as I was to wax poetic over what an obvious and egregious slut was the queen of the night, it appeared that this information had value to Oberon. "This I will do," said I. "She shall not so much as smile at a passing hedgehog that you will not know of it in an hour."

"And I shall need you to convey me to the Duke of Athens's wedding tomorrow night."

"That, I cannot do, Your Grace, for my task at hand is to perform at the very same wedding."

"You are in service of Theseus?"

"Among others. But when you see me, let us pretend we are strangers."

"Agreed."

"And, Your Grace, see to the security of your castle. For having so many goblins at arms, your fortress is as porous as a sieve."

"I have no fear. I am immortal."

"So was the Puck, Your Grace."

CHAPTER XIV

The King's Dread Pleasures

I PRETENDED TO drink, and regaled Oberon with lies of my travels and magical exploits well into the wide posterior of the night, when finally, the shadow king staggered off to slumber and a goblin servant led me to the harem as the king had instructed. Two guards with halberds stood outside the double doors, and between them, on the floor, lay the dead goblin that Oberon had shot with the crossbow. Over him crouched Gritch, his bat-wing ears drooping like wilted leaves. Nick Bottom sat leaning against the double doors, snoring quite loudly.

"Ring the bell," Gritch commanded a guard, and the goblin turned and pulled a cord strung through the wall over his head. Somewhere on the other side of the door a bell chimed.

"Gritch, you needed only to bring the dead goblin here. You didn't have to stay."

"Was my mate," said the goblin, stroking the dead goblin's brow.

"This monster was your wife?"

"My friend," said the goblin.

"Oh, quite right. Condolences." I reached into my belt and retrieved the button from Bottom's waistcoat and handed it to Gritch, who took it and stared mournfully at the silver Celtic knot pattern.

The two guards each bent over and regarded the button as if

it were a holy relic. Gritch growled at them and they returned to attention.

A small brass portal in the door opened and a painted face filled it. "What?" she said. The face was tarted up, but from the white hair around it I could tell it was Moth.

"It's Pocket, love. Let us in."

"What's the magic words?"

I looked to Gritch. "Magic words?"

The goblin shrugged.

"I don't know the magic words," said I.

"Do piss off, then." She snapped the little brass door shut.

I pulled the bell cord again and gently kicked Bottom awake. "Bottom, why are you locked out?"

The ass-man sputtered and looked around, realizing with some disappointment, it seemed, where he was. "They won't let us in. No goblins, they said."

The little brass portal opened. "Pocket!" said Peaseblossom, rather tarted up in her own right. "They painted us and shaved our bits. I hope that goes away at dawn. Methinks climbing trees will be rough with my bits shaved."

"Let us in, love. We've brought the dead goblin Cobweb asked me to bring." I pointed to the dead goblin, who was still wearing the silver armlet.

"No goblins," said Peaseblossom. "Eaters of squirrels. Do piss off." And she snapped shut the little brass door.

"Oh for fuck's sake," I said. "Gritch, do you eat squirrels?"

"Squirrels are delicious," said the goblin, with enthusiasm I'd thought they reserved for silver. The guards on either side of the door nodded in agreement. "Uh, I am told," Gritch added, rolling his large yellow eyes. The guards shook their heads, evidently having just remembered that they, too, had never tasted squirrel.

"Ring the fucking bell," I snapped at the guard beside the cord.

To Gritch, I said, "How is it that no one nicked that silver armlet from your mate? May he rest in peace. There must have been a thousand goblins horny for silver in that courtyard."

"To take silver is forbidden," said Gritch. "Silver must be given."

"Do you know who gave that armlet to your mate?"

"A human mortal," said Gritch. "I don't know which."

The little brass door opened. This time it was Cobweb. "What?"

"Cobweb, stop messing about and let us in," I said.

"That the dead one?"

"This one with the crossbow bolt in his heart and tongue lolling out of the side of his mouth? Why, you know, it could be."

"Sarcasm will make your willy fall off."

"Open the door, please, we need to be on our way before dawn."

"What are the magic words?"

"Oh, do piss off, Cobweb."

"Correct!" She snapped the portal shut and I heard the iron bolt thrown. The heavy doors opened a crack and Cobweb peeked out. "Just you and the dead goblin. Everyone in here is a bit fragile, it seems. Not sure the sight of Bottom might not send them round the bend. Sorry, mate."

"Do you have anything to eat?" asked Bottom. "Some dried peas or oats would be lovely."

"I'll have Moth bring you something," said Cobweb. "Now, drag him in."

I dragged the dead goblin in by the arms and Cobweb closed the door behind me. She was painted up like the others, wide blue brows and shadows around her eyes that almost described a mask, her lips painted lavender, lined in black. She wore a simple, hooded robe of black satin that hung to her knees and she was, of course, barefoot. We had not entered a chamber, but simply an antechamber with another set of heavy doors.

As soon as she bolted the door she turned, jumped into my arms, and ferociously snogged me. "Did you see?" she said, pounding my chest with one hand while keeping the other wrapped around my neck. "Did you see me take the piss out of Oberon? You're right, Pocket, it was bloody glorious. 'You live in this palace made of midnight while your queen lives up a fucking tree,' I told him. Felt finer than a frolic, it did."

The doors opened behind us and I let Cobweb slide to her feet. Peaseblossom and Moth were manning the double doors and had opened them into an expansive boudoir done up in draperies and cushions of black and gold. The floor, at least, was covered in woven wool rugs of red, yellow, and green amid the black, in the patterns of the Persians. Except for my three traveling companions, I saw no fairies at all.

"I know you're shit at counting, but I expected—"

"Come on then," Cobweb called to the empty room. "Come on, he won't hurt you." She turned to me and whispered, "I think it's your black and silver kit has them scared. Give them a bit."

"Why are we here, Cobweb?"

"Finding the Puck's killer, I reckon," said Cobweb. "Make your puppet stick talk. They'll love that."

Why not? I thought. Since, apparently, I had relinquished authority to a sometime squirrel. I pulled the puppet Jones from down my back. "Nick of time," said the puppet Jones. "This newt wouldn't know magic words if they smacked him on the bum."

Peaseblossom and Moth—actual magical creatures themselves— giggled, clapped their hands, and jumped with joy at my trifling trick.

I had Jones launch into a solemn hymn from my days at the nunnery, "Sister Lilly Oft Yanks Me Willy":

"Oh, she's pious as a vicar's nose."

The draperies, cushions, and covers began to move, nude and nearly-so fairies emerging from beneath and behind.

"All through vespers, she buffs me hose."

They gathered around, wide eyed—disturbingly wide eyed—as the puppet sang.

"To fancy a nun, just might seem silly."

There were, it seemed, a hundred of them, both male and female.

"But I'd give my all, to Sister Lilly."

I danced a step or two, tossed the puppet Jones in the air and caught him behind my back, then bowed with a great flourish. The fairies clapped and cheered. Upon my second bow I noticed hair-thin scars on some of the fairies' legs. Some were like white threads, some pink, as if fresher, none more visible than the scratch of a kitten, but each fairy was covered, head to toe, with a lattice of scars. Even amid the face paint I could see the white threads, and one or two of them had one eye that was clouded. Not unseeing, but bright blue or green iris paired with a clouded gray one.

I took Cobweb by the shoulder and pulled her aside. "What is this? What are these scars?"

"The marks of Oberon's pleasure," she said. "A frolic stops the bleeding. Two or three will bring an eye back, but the new eye doesn't always match."

I felt my supper sour in my stomach and rise in my throat. I swallowed hard to force it back down. "I would have never let Oberon send you here if I'd known."

"I knew," she said. "Well, I had heard. Moth has a brother here. She's right troubled about him."

Moth was touching foreheads with a male fairy with eggshell hair like her own.

"We are leaving, then," said I. "Oberon has given me passage on condition I become his fool."

"Ha! He fears you," said Cobweb. "The Puck trick worked. The shadow king fears my little fool."

"I am not your fool," said I. "And things did not go well with

Oberon. He doesn't have the flower I need to take to Theseus to secure Drool's release, and he doesn't know how to change Bottom back into normal."

"We're not done yet," said Cobweb. "Help me drag this dead one to the middle of the room." I did as I was told, since it appeared that Cobweb had settled into her role as my mistress whether I cared for it or not.

"Have a sit by him," Cobweb demanded. She yanked the bolt out of the goblin's chest with a grunt and handed it, dripping green with gore, to me. "This will be a cracking frolic with so many. You might be leaping over rivers by morning from the overspill."

And so she gathered the frightened, painted fairies, who seemed to have no will left of their own, and the frolic began, just as it had with the three of them in the forest before. But now a hundred fairies plus three dropped their robes and danced around me and the dead goblin—light firing in the air like exploding fireflies among them and the fairies rising from the floor until they were a whirlwind of color and life and power. Each hummed a high song that would have been barely audible had there been only one, but now it sounded like a hive of melodious bees, a hundred notes creating an all-enveloping harmony. My muscles and mind sang with the power of it, the life of it. *These* creatures turned the tides, made the trees blossom, the mare foal, clouds grow fat with rain, lightning crack the sky—*these* creatures, more than men, together made a god, brought the glory of nature to the now. But still, fucking squirrels at dawn.

And the dead goblin sat up. "What?"

"Ahhh!" said I, somewhat surprised.

The fairies ceased their dancing and gathered round the undead goblin.

"He going to eat us?" asked one wan fellow with a milky eye, a still-healing scar running from his nose to his ear, the point of which had been clipped off by the slash that took his eye.

"Not today," said Cobweb, pushing her way through. "Oi, goblin, did you kill the Puck?"

The goblin looked around at the fairies gathered round him and even with his fearsome teeth and eyes, it was clear he was terrified—his wits set to go wobbly any second.

"Fetch Gritch," I told Moth. "He's outside."

"No goblins," said a woman fairy, dark of hair, bright scars across her ribs that might have been gills if she were a sea creature, or the lines made by fingers tipped with blades.

I lifted my jerkin and pointed to my knives. "He'll not hurt you. I'll see to it."

Moth returned, dragging Gritch by a long ear, the goblin submitting completely for the chance to see his dead friend.

A goblin smile is not a pretty thing to see, yet those two, in a pair, nearly brought water to my eyes. Gritch embraced his friend and marveled at the healed wound in his chest. They shared grunts and whispers, and, still holding his friend, Gritch turned to me. I shook my head and pointed to Cobweb.

"Ask your mate if he killed the Puck," she said gently.

Gritch whispered to his friend, then said, "Yes."

"For silver," the reborn goblin said.

"Who gave you the silver?" I asked.

"A human mortal. A little one."

"A little one? A woman?"

"No, a man. A short man in black. In the forest. He gave silver to kill the Puck. I didn't want to, but silver." He touched the silver armlet.

"Did the mortal carry a crossbow?"

"Yes."

I looked to Cobweb. "Burke, the duke's watchman. Blacktooth's leftenant."

"Those wicked fucks," said Cobweb.

"Aye," said Moth. "Wicked."

"Aye," said Peaseblossom. "Fucks." She scratched herself. "Who?"

"They shaved our bits," explained Moth. She'd put on her black gown. She patted the sash. "I kept the razor. Never had a razor before."

The resurrected goblin looked around again at all the fairies staring down at him with a mix of dread and scorn. "I don't want it," said the goblin. He took the armlet off and held it out, beckoning for someone to take it from him. "The Puck were a shit, but he were good to me. Silver." He began to weep.

"Did you kill the young Athenian in the forest yesterday?" I asked.

"No." He shook his head. "No Athenian. Take the silver."

Cobweb pulled me aside, whispered in my ear, "He won't last long. Maybe an hour. Maybe less. He was really quite dead."

"Give it to your friend," I said. "Give it to Gritch."

Gritch took the heavy silver armlet but didn't put it on, only held it in his talon, as gently as if it were a baby bird. I called to him and gestured for him to come away from his friend for a moment. He did. "We need to go, mate. I need to get the fairies out of the castle, off this mountain, before the sun comes up. Will you help?"

He looked back at his friend, who looked the very picture of the goblin forlorn.

"Cobweb says he won't stay alive long," I said. "You should say goodbye."

Gritch nodded. "I will help."

"Gritch," I said, grabbing the silver ring in his ear and tugging at it gently with each word. "*All* the sodding fairies."

"They are the shadow king's fairies," said the goblin.

I held up the crossbow bolt still dripping with his friend's blood. *"All* the sodding fairies, Gritch."

"Talos, my friend, comes too?"

"Of course," said I.

"All the sodding fairies," said Gritch.

ACT III

Well, God give them wisdom that have it; and those
that are fools, let them use their talents.

—FESTE,
Twelfth Night, 1:5

CHAPTER XV

Of Perspective and Squirrels

"THERE'S THE horn," said Cobweb. We sat at the edge of the forest watching Gritch watch his friend Talos die for a second time that night.

"I don't hear it," said I. "Do you hear it?" I asked Bottom.

"I do," said the weaver, listlessly waving to his long ears. He was pouting, and rightly so, for Oberon had not transformed him back to a man before we left the castle, and I hadn't the heart to tell him that it would not happen. Although I held some hope for his recovery, as being near the massive fairy frolic in the harem seemed to have restored him somewhat. His hands were no longer covered with coarse hair and his voice was less of a bray than it had become.

"Do you need to go to Titania?" I asked Cobweb.

"I think not. Not today."

"Will she not visit some wrath on you?"

"I've had enough of the night queen and shadow king and their bloody wrath. We'll stay with you. Get your mate out of jail. Won't we, mates?" she called to the other fairies.

"Aye," said Moth, "she sent my brother and our other mates there."

"What?" said Peaseblossom. Since reaching the forest, the simple fairy had been fascinated with her newly shaven bits and was resolving a furious wank by an oak tree, her back turned for privacy. "Right. Me too," she said. "We should find Moth's hat with the tongues. I quite fancied that hat."

"Why wouldn't they come?" Cobweb said, cradling her head in her hands. "They only had to run a little bit and they would have been free."

Gritch and Talos, both some sort of officers among the goblin soldiers, had cleared a path out of the Night Palace, ordered the guards on duty to stand down and let us pass. Cobweb bade the harem fairies to follow her, but when we threw open the doors they cowered by the walls, backing away from the door as if a monster might come through it any second.

"Come on, then," Cobweb begged, but the harem fairies hid among the cushions and draperies, as they had when I'd first come into the harem. "The goblins won't hurt you, go on."

But they had stayed, terrified to leave, more afraid of the unknown than the familiar horror.

"Cobweb," I called. "We have to go, love. Perhaps they'll follow at dawn when they change."

She strode over to me like she was facing down an enemy, tears of frustration, perhaps anger, in her eyes. "They can't come out of here after they change. They couldn't run into a goblin city with no one to lead them, even if they did leave here." She turned. "Come on, you cowards, come be free of the shadow king's blades forever. Come to the forest where you belong."

I put my arm around her shoulders and she shook me off. "Help me with the doors," she barked. Inside, one brave fairy, the bloke with the clouded eye and clipped ear, peeked out from behind an arras.

"Bolt the doors behind us," Cobweb called to him, pushing her door shut.

As we ran down the hall after Moth and Peaseblossom, I said, "They all can't take the piss out of the shadow king to find their power like you did."

"What do you know?" she had screeched. "You know nothing. You are not a slave."

Now, in the forest, the dawn was nearly upon us, and Cobweb still wore the anguished mask she had put on upon closing the harem door.

"I *was* a slave," I said.

"You were?" A light in her eye. "How did you get free?"

"My enormous apprentice crushed my master to death."

"Well I don't have an apprentice."

"Then we shall have to find a different way for you."

"How? And how do we find a way for the hundred in there?" She waved in the direction of the Night Palace.

"You may have to learn to be selfish in this instance."

"Maybe you should be selfish and just fuck off to lands un-known."

"I can't. I have to save Drool."

"No you don't. Be selfish. How long would he live anyway? Another thirty to forty years. He's nearly dead already. Be doing him a favor, really. You mortals are as fleeting as dew under morning sun. Why not just fuck off and leave him to his fate? Like I should have when I found you."

I stood, paused, feeling, perhaps, as if a new perspective had opened upon the world. I said, "Why *have* you been watching over me? Saving me? Feeding me? Taking care of me?"

"I loved a man once. A mortal. And when I saw you wash up in the surf, you reminded me of him."

"I was limp and dead in the sea."

"He drowned."

"Sorry."

"So I saved you."

"Lovely of you."

"I know. It is the first time I have ever tried being lovely. And I quite like it."

"So you were a cranky little bitch for nine hundred years?"

"Not all the time."

"Why didn't you frolic then, on the beach, to heal my wounds?"

"We can't do it alone. I would have had to bring another to frolic, and you were mine."

I sat down in the leaves next to her.

"What now?" said I.

"We need to rescue your mate, don't we?"

"I don't have the flower for Theseus."

"You said it before. Rumour can fetch it. He said he taught the Puck to circle the world in forty minutes, didn't he?"

"He won't do that. He quite hates me. Showed up when I was dining with Oberon, looking for his hat of many tongues. Accused me of taking the piss out of the royals just because I thrive under the threat of death."

"True, innit?"

"He won't help. Although his appearance upon the scene did convince Oberon of my mysterious yet completely rubbish powers."

"He will if you trade him his hat."

"But Jeff—"

"Oi, Moth, Pease, after the change, you tarts think you can find that monkey and get that hat back by sundown?"

"Oh, that would be lovely," said Peaseblossom, well into her fourth wank of the morning, judging by her ascending scale of yips.

Moth came over, faced us, knock-kneed and coy. "Would you carry my new frock and my razor, Pocket?"

"My pleasure," said I.

"Piece of piss, then," said Moth. "I rather fancy that Jeff bloke, anyway."

"He's a monkey!" said I.

"Not all the time," said Moth.

"Yes, all the bloody time."

"Still," she said, shrugging off her robe and throwing the folded razor on top of it.

"If you get the hat, find us on the trail," said Cobweb, counting out the events on the same two fingers. "If you can't find us, meet us on the north trail into Athens at sundown. The wedding isn't until midnight. Rumour will have to find us, then retrieve the flower, then Theseus will release your mate."

"It seems there are very high odds against all of that lining up," said I.

"What are odds?" asked Moth.

"Well, it is the likelihood of all of those things happening, as measured against the likelihood of all of those things not happening, and happening by the time we need them to happen."

"So counting?" said Cobweb.

"Never mind," said I.

"We will do this," said Cobweb. "The north trail, outside of Athens, at dusk. Don't watch me change."

"What?" I said.

"Don't watch me change," she said. "And if after I'm changed, I'm still shaved, don't look." She stood and shrugged off her black robe. "Bring that. That cloth feels lovely. And Bottom still has my hat. Bring that. And don't let him eat us."

I looked to Gritch just as he stood over his dead friend and fit the silver armlet onto his arm. "He is gone," he said.

"Blimey," said Bottom. "That's strange."

I turned to see a horned-eared red squirrel standing on her hind legs in a puddle of black satin, looking at me with squirrelly recrimination.

"That's what's strange? After all we've seen and done, *that* you find strange?"

"The world is a wonder, isn't it?" said Bottom, musing philosophical. "Two days ago I was a weaver who had never been more than two miles from his house, practicing a play for a wedding, and today I am a transformed half man escaping from a goblin castle pondering shaved squirrel snatch."

"I'm not looking!" I said to the red squirrel, but she chittered angrily anyway.

The brown and white squirrels that were Moth and Peaseblossom were already away into the trees. Cobweb ran up a tree and perched on a limb high above us.

"We should be off, Bottom. Gather up those robes if you would. What of you, Gritch?"

The goblin looked back at his friend. "I will bury Talos and then flee the sun. We will be at the duke's wedding tonight."

"We?"

"Many goblins."

"Find us at the head of the trail, north of the city, then, as soon after dark as you can get there."

The goblin nodded. "What about the three words? The fairy said you know the Puck's three words. Puck said he would tell us."

"I thought they were 'do piss off.'"

"No," said Bottom. "That was just the fairies having you on before letting you in the harem."

To Gritch, "Sorry, mate, I haven't the slightest. But once I find out you'll be the first to know."

Gritch nodded as his skin began to smoke by the dawn's early light. He turned and ran away, scooping up his dead friend's body as he went and throwing it over his shoulder.

"I'll bet the lads are wondering why I haven't been to rehearsal," said Bottom.

CHAPTER XVI

Preview in the Forest

WE HAD been walking for hours, the red squirrel bounding through the trees above us all the way, chattering down at us if we dared to stop to rest or have a wee.

"So, if the goblin didn't kill that young Athenian, who do you think it was?" asked Bottom.

He was munching a handful of clover as he went and I let him. As I had not had the heart to tell him I had secured no remedy for his donkey form, I could not deprive him of that small green pleasure.

"Blacktooth and Burke were quickly on the spot, weren't they? Perhaps they decided to do their own killing and take the reward this time. Although my blood was high with the frolic when I gave chase, and I think if it had been a mortal I would have caught him, or at least caught a glimpse of him."

"Could be. A silver armlet like the goblin had would fetch enough in Athens to buy a small farm. I've no idea the value in goblin coin."

"The goblins don't give a tick's willy what you can *buy* with silver," said I. "They love it for the color, the beauty, and the feeling of it. Methinks a goblin would have the same passion over the reflection of the moon in the water. In fact, if you could convince him that you put it there, he would be your slave, I'll wager."

"And so did Oberon convince them thus," said Bottom. Then

he tossed away his bouquet of clover, raised his arms, and commenced to orate as if upon the stage. "Here are the moon and the stars, I have made them, only this Tuesday, and now I give them unto you, so that you might build me a great palace of night and pay me tribute with your sweat and your blood. All good things flow from me and it is only by my grace that you take breath, which I, the shadow king, will snatch from you on a whim." He ended his speech with a great flourish, as if winding up his cape of night and tossing it behind him.

I applauded his performance, as a measure more of pity than of appreciation, and Cobweb chirped from her perch in the tree above. "Good Bottom, thou hast righteously traded your bundle of clover to chew the scenery to a tattered motif. Bravo! Bravo! Bravo!"

"Thank you," said Bottom, bowing to me, to Cobweb, to the odd shrubbery as he went. "You are too kind. Too kind." He laughed, a hee-haw of satisfaction with himself, and danced a little jig. "I do hope I am transformed back in time to perform Pyramus for the duke. I would not want to let the Mechanicals down over a mere misadventure with a fairy queen. Wouldn't be brotherly, for surely, he who treads the boards with me this night shall be my brother, no matter how dimwitted he may be, and all the men abed in Athens shall hold their manhood cheap, that they were not on the stage with Bottom upon the duke's wedding day!"

And off he charged toward Athens, even though, for all I knew, we were miles from town. Cobweb ran down a fir tree until she was eye level with me, then tapped her paw and barked harshly at me, which I took to mean, "You had better tell him, you blistering fuckweasel!" (She had a very eloquent bark.)

"I was getting to it," I said to the squirrel. The bloody barking ginger squirrel did not relent. "Fine!" said I. "Fine, I shall dash the hapless weaver's last hopes posthaste."

I ran after the ass-man and caught up to him just as . . .

ENTER RUMOUR, PAINTED FULL OF TONGUES

"Zounds!" cried Bottom, going from a full gallop to backing up the trail away from the peculiar narrator as if he wore a cloak of vipers rather than tongues. I caught the ass-man by the shoulders and steadied him.

"And so, the ne'er-do-well English fool, devoid of principles or any sense of decency—nay, humanity—betrayed his own traveling companion by keeping secret—"

"Rumour!" I called, with great jocularity and joy, as if I had encountered a long-lost uncle along the trail. "Just the gent I was hoping to see, for I have splendid tidings to share, which shall bring you great pleasure."

Rumour squinted at me as if he might gaze into my intentions if only he could see beyond the glare of my sunny disposition. His suspicion was betrayed by the waggling of the tongues on his cloak, all of which seemed to be performing a silent and disturbing ululation.

"What are you up to, fool? I know, of course, but I'm just checking to see if you're even capable of telling the truth."

"I would embrace you, but alas, you are a horrid, hollow creature and the idea rather shrivels my wedding tackle, but nevertheless, welcome to our band of jolly travelers. What delicious trifle of narrative do you bring to us today?"

"Are you having me on?"

"Yes."

"Well it doesn't work if you just tell me you're having me on."

I made as if to put my arm around his shoulders, to take him into my confidence, but then, he *was* covered with tongues, so I merely mimed the gesture, allowing my arm to hover a handbreadth above his shoulders. Nevertheless, his cloak tried to lick me.

"You see, good Rumour, we have found your hat of many tongues, and you need only meet us at the head of this trail in Athens, at dusk, with a blossom from a purple love potion flower in hand, and we shall return it to you. You know of this flower, I presume, as you know everything twice more than everyone?"

"I'm not going to do that. Oh, I will have my hat, but I will not bring you your flower."

"Why not? Why would you not fetch a simple flower that would save my apprentice, who is a good-hearted if profoundly thick lad—an innocent in this heinous fuckery?"

"Because you are complete rubbish at following clues."

"I don't follow," said I.

"Exactly. I told you the key was the lovers. Nothing. I told you about the Puck's three words, you still know nothing. I told you the key to his passion lies with the prince. Nothing. Methinks you are a fool, fool."

"That is not true, I know the meaning of all of those clues, I simply have not had opportunity to reveal them."

"Oh," said Rumour.

"So help me release my mate."

"No, but the key to your revelation is the play. The play's the thing, wherein you'll catch the conscience of the king."

"That doesn't mean anything. 'The play's the thing'?"

"Aye, there's the rub," he said, and with a whoosh he was off again.

"Well that's a soggy sack of squirrel spooge," said I.

"But now how will you get your friend out of the dungeon without the flower?" asked Bottom.

"I suspect we are going to have to craft a plan for his escape. First, I will shave Cobweb's tail and rub ashes on her, so rather than a red squirrel, she appears to be a large rat. Then—"

At that point Cobweb ran down the tree I stood by, stopped at eye level, scratched, tapped her paw, twitched her tail violently, and let loose a rather angry fusillade of barks, screeches, and several noises I was not aware a squirrel could make.

"I don't think she's keen on the bit about having her tail shaved."

Cobweb made several barks of affirmation and tried to bite one of the tentacles of my hat.

"But you can sneak in by the guards as a rat, then at dusk, you will return to your most fit and comely woman form, not that you are not the loveliest of squirrels, to be sure, but then you can free Drool from his cell and perhaps provide him with a weapon."

At which point Cobweb leapt from her tree onto my head, relieved me of my hat, and began to remove my scalp in squirrel-bite-sized patches, until I snatched her by her tail and flung her affectionately back into the tree from whence she came.

"Fuck's sake, sprite!" said I.

"You keep making her cross, she's never going to shag you again," said Bottom.

"It was just an idea," said I.

Cobweb chittered angrily from the tree.

"She says that plan will not do," said Bottom. "The play's the thing. We must hurry and find my mates."

"Just because you are covered with fur, it doesn't mean you are suddenly able to translate from the squirrel," I replied, but he had galloped away.

* * *

"TWO HOUSEHOLDS, *both alike in dignity,*" read Peter Quince, the gray-haired carpenter, from his scroll. "*Two families, equal in stature—*"

"Oh, well done," called Bottom as we emerged from the wood into the clearing where the Mechanicals were rehearsing. "Well done!"

"Bottom!" cried Tom Snout, the tinker, who was still annoy-ingly tall and still wore the stupid bunny-eared doeskin hat. "You have returned, and in fancy dress too."

"What has happened to you?" said Peter Quince. "You have the voice and clothing of my friend Nick Bottom, but what is this mask?"

"He is enchanted," said I.

"And you have with you the elf!" said Robin Starveling, the bald-ing, bad-mannered wankpuffin who seemed eager to be beaten about the head with a puppet stick.

"Not an elf," I replied.

"Fear not," said Nick Bottom, his muzzle on a swivel as his friends gathered around him to examine the changes he had suffered. "This countenance is but a temporary spell, put upon me by the Puck, but soon to be lifted by Oberon, the king of the night and the goblins."

"Oh woe, oh woe, oh woe," said the young lad whom I had last seen playing Thisby, and who again wore the veil and spoke in falsetto. "Our Bottom has gone quite mad. He is ruined, a lunatic who must wander the forest, living upon rocks and tadpoles, oh woe, oh goodbye, sweet sanity! Farewell, sensibility! *Adieu! Adieu! Adieu!*" And he collapsed to the forest floor in a heap.

"The bitch is dead," pronounced Tom Snout gruffly.

The Mechanicals all turned to the fallen Francis Flute and clapped politely.

"Oh, brava," said Peter Quince. "I think you can see, Master Pocket, how Francis has taken your method to heart. He has played the brokenhearted maid since last we met. Was thrown out by his father and declared a simpering pooft by his sweetheart, yet the lad has not broken character. Although we have changed the name of Thisby to Juliet, and the wall is now a balcony, and oh, yes, the lovers die by poison, but there is a smashing swordfight and gobs of blood."

"All done with good taste, so as not to disturb the ladies," said Tom Snout.

"But am I to play Pyramus still?" asked Bottom.

"Now you shall be Romeo," said Quince. "Although the lines are nearly the same. And methinks you'll need a hat to cover those ears or there may be suspicions our play is not serious."

"Fear not," said Bottom. "By midnight I shall be myself again and with a spot of greasepaint I shall be a most passionate and pathetic Pyramus."

"Romeo," corrected Quince.

"I shall be the smoothest and most powerful of Romeos," said Bottom.

And Cobweb chittered angrily from a tree high above.

"Look! A squirrel!" said Robin Starveling.

"I cannot look, for I am tragically perished," wept Francis Flute, from his heap of femininity.

"Forget the squirrel," said I. "Bottom, I fear I have sad tidings. As fortune has it, Oberon said he would not change you back to your manly form. Sorry, mate." I waited then for the news to settle on the ass-man like a cloak of doom. His mates all watched with me, as if waiting for a prompt for their next line.

"But be of good cheer," I said. "You've got cracking great hearing, and your other gifts, I'm sure, will be much appreciated by Mrs. Bottom."

"If she will have me back," said Bottom, his crest beginning to fall.

"But you shan't be able to play Romeo," said Quince. "Even with superb makeup by Snout."

"I have been practicing on the wife," said the tall tinker with the stupid hat.

"My performance shall overcome my form," said Bottom, a finger thrust aloft as if balancing an idea. "I shall play Romeo as so dashing, so romantic, that all ladies in the audience will be in love with a man of prodigious ears and muzzle, and yearn to—"

"No," said Peter Quince. "If the duke finds displeasure in our play we shall all be hanged. We cannot risk it. I myself have learned the part of Romeo and shall perform it as well as the chorus."

"Hold," said I. "Didst thou say that if the duke finds displeasure with your play you will be hanged?"

Quince nodded gravely. "Oh yes, for offending his sensibilities upon his wedding day."

"It is part of the honor of being chosen," said Francis Flute, in his demure damsel falsetto.

"Bloody hanging you if your play is shit?" said I. "You? Tradesmen, ninnies at best, who have never before taken the stage, are going to perform with your lives in the balance?"

"After all, it is his right. Our lives and labor belong to the duke," said Robin Starveling.

I hit him then—spun the puppet Jones from out of the back of my jerkin and brought the green stick down on Starveling's bald crown with a crack. But it was not enough, and as the tailor yowled and rubbed his head I swung the puppet around in various directions, growling and hissing and doing a more-than-adequate impression of a madman with apoplexy. "That is as buggering a basket of badger bonk as I have ever heard! That is as slithering a satchel of snake spooge as has ever been spoken! Your lives are not the duke's." I waved Jones around a bit more until I began to tire and Robin Starveling ran and hid behind a tree.

"So we don't have to give him three-quarters of our labors?" said Quince.

"Three-quarters? You give him three-quarters? Of everything?"

"Not everything," said Bottom. "I was spared him having right of first night with the missus, as she is possessed of a birthmark on her throat everyone in the village thought the mark of a dark spirit."

"Shagged my Bess before me," said Snug, "but she is forbidden to talk about it."

"But Bess *is* a bit of a slut," said Starveling from behind his tree. "Respectfully."

"She was not always, not in those days. Robin Goodfellow turned her," said Snug.

"Which is why he had to murder the Puck," explained Quince.

"Yes," said Snug. "Couldn't be helped. It was my Bess's honor."

Which was when I hit Snug. I do not, generally, go about hitting people. I have traveled, lo these many years, with an oaf of profound dimness in my company, and had I hit him every time he did or said something stupid he would have been little more than large shoes piled with a tower of bruises. But no, other than being imprisoned and probably tortured, he was perfectly healthy. But this lot! This lot of ninnies, these Mechanicals, were a collective of such profound empty-headedness I was not sure that I was not becoming more stupid in their presence, my cleverness drained just by proximity, and thus I was frustrated and rather angry. I flailed around a bit with my puppet stick, cursing in various vernaculars, until the squirrel chirped at me.

"Look, it's the squirrel again," said Robin Starveling, who was wisely keeping a safe distance, although I could have speared him in the knee with a thrown dagger if I wished, the thought of which calmed me somewhat.

Cobweb ran down a nearby tree trunk to my eye level and barked at me again, evidently having appointed herself my conscience. The Mechanicals stared at her in wonder, and I almost set into another tirade before I remembered that only three days ago I had tried to talk Snug out of modeling his performance of a lion upon a chicken. So the fauna of the forest held more fascination for these fellows than most.

And Cobweb was right. It was not the Mechanicals with whom I was aggrieved, it was the circumstances in which I'd found them. The conditions under which they lived. Them, the fairies, the goblins, everyone in this godforsaken land. It was then that it occurred to me how to address the puzzle of the Puck and perhaps his three magic fucking words.

"Lads," said I. "The play's the thing."

"Aye," said Peter Quince. "Which is why we are here rehearsing."

"Yes, yes, yes," said I, waving him off. "First, Snug, you did not kill the Puck."

"I did," said Snug. "With a crossbow from my shop."

"You didn't," said I. "He was already dead and cooling in the duke's dungeon when I shared lunch with you and your wife and you thought him still alive at the time."

"I did. I avenged my Bess's honor. Shot that rascal right in the chest, I did."

"No, you didn't."

"In the neck. Put a bolt right in his throat."

"No, you didn't." I patted his shoulder, rubbing that spot where I had only recently smacked him with my puppet, hoping to bring him some comfort. "The Puck was shot in the back. By a goblin, who did it for silver."

"They'll kill anyone for silver," said Bottom. "But the goblin was only the weapon."

"There ain't no such thing as goblins," said Robin Starveling.

"I will kill you where you stand," said I to the tailor with a smile, one hand behind my back on the hilt of a throwing dagger. *Three words,* I said to calm myself.

"Around here, I mean," said Starveling meekly. "Maybe where you blokes have been . . ."

"Just so," said I. "Peter Quince, have you quill, ink, and parchment with you?"

"I do, Master Pocket."

"Then we shall write a new play, a variation on your themes, and we will rehearse it until sundown and you shall perform it for the duke at his wedding and be brilliant."

"Do you think . . . ," said Bottom. "Do you think you could write a part for me? A horse part, perhaps? I would be an excellent Pegasus, I think. No, a unicorn. Quince, write me a unicorn part and I shall be such a unicorn as will make the men weep and the ladies dampen their chairs with excitement."

I went to the bedonkeyed weaver and put my arm around his shoulders, for truly our fate had made us brothers in arms. "Oh, there will be a horse part for you, good Bottom. Such a horse part that before your hooves the world shall wither."

CHAPTER XVII

Maps for Squirrels

I CONFESS, A wall of worry rises for even the most confident fool when he realizes that his plot for saving the day lies with three squirrels, a troupe of earnest nitwits, a donkey-headed weaver, a silver-thirsty goblin, a notoriously unreliable narrator, and a hat-shagging monkey. And the narrator and goblins hadn't even arrived yet!

Therein, perhaps, lay the flaw in my quickly formulated plan to meet at the trailhead at dusk. For even with Rumour's hat retrieved—as Cobweb, Peaseblossom, and Moth had managed to somehow lure monkey Jeff and the hat of many tongues to the rendezvous, although they could not explain how, because they were still fucking squirrels—Rumour had not yet arrived at the trailhead, and even if he did, he had not agreed to retrieve the love potion flower to give to Theseus to secure Drool's release, and the backup plan, if he did not appear or agree, depended upon the fairies' still being fucking squirrels, which they would cease to be at dusk, the aforementioned meeting time. Therefore, I found myself drawing maps in the dirt for the squirrels, who, perched on Bottom's shoulders, looked on, along with a troupe of well-meaning ninnies, and monkey Jeff, who sat on a branch above, eating a fig and making lascivious eyes at the hat of many tongues, which Bottom was wearing.

"I will try to stay with you, but I suspect they may not let me in, so you'll need a plan." I pointed with a small stick. "This is the gate into the gendarmerie, which leads to the dungeon down this corridor." I drew a map of the corridor from memory, glad that I'd taken note of all the doors and passages on my way out. "You'll pass four heavy doors and you'll come to a passageway, where you will go left."

I looked up to make sure everyone was following along. "Nod if you understand. Wait, do squirrels nod?"

The white and red squirrels twitched their tails, while the brown squirrel stood motionless on Bottom's shoulder, as if trying to conceal herself from a hawk. Of course, Peaseblossom the squirrel was also simple.

"How many doors?" asked Snug the joiner.

"Never mind how many doors. There's no counting. My mistake. Just go until you run into the first junction of a passageway and go left. Left. Do you get that?" Three tails twitched.

I drew a plan of the rest of the dungeon, including the large central chamber that Drool's cell opened on. "There's a great iron key on a hook here." I pointed on the diagram to the spot. "Here there's a chair where I suspect the guard will be sitting, if there even is one. On the night of the duke's wedding, I suspect they'll either be on guard in the streets or making merry themselves.

"Next to the key is a rack of weapons, mostly poleaxes— halberds. One of you grab the key and run and hand it through the bars of Drool's cell. Cobweb, Drool knows you, so you go through the bars into his cell and be there when you turn. You open the lock for him and tell him to fight. One of you grab one of the poleaxes from the rack and give it to him as soon as the cell door opens, then get out of his way. If there are three or fewer guards, he will make quick work of them. Then you lead him out the way you came and bring him back here."

"But they'll be naked," said Bottom. "Even if they free your mate, people will notice three girls running naked through the city streets chased by a giant with a poleaxe."

"We'll have Drool drop the poleaxe," said I.

"Oh yes, that quite solves the problem," said Peter Quince. "No one will notice if he's not armed."

"Good Quince," said I. "I know you are new to the theater, so you have not learned its many secrets, but among professional thespians, anyone who uses sarcasm in that manner is thought to be a twat."

"I did not know," said Quince.

"I don't believe a word of it," said Robin Starveling. "The elf is lying again. These are just common squirrels, and that is a common monkey, and that a common hat covered with tongues which are wagging in a most common way. Pish-posh and balderdash."

"Just so," said I, having resolved to treat my cast with respect and a minimum of head bashing. "Which is why you lot will stay here and rehearse your lines while you wait for a tar-black goblin with a grin like a mill saw and a hollow man who moves like lightning and has a coat to match that very common hat."

*   *   *

"NO, SIR," said the spot-faced guard. "You may not enter the gendarmerie."

"But I have this passport, given me by the duke," said I, holding out the chip of wood with the duke's seal.

"Be that as it may, sir, I am on orders to report anything suspicious to the captain of the guard and your horse is suspicious."

"He is not," said I. "He's lovely." I was sitting on Bottom's back. The weaver was bent over, holding a pair of heavy, well-matched branches to serve as his front legs, and the Mechanicals had thrown a blanket over his back to complete the ensemble.

"No, sir, I must object. Your horse has suspicious front legs, what look very much like sticks, and he is wearing trousers, which are also suspicious."

"Well that is where you are wrong," said I. "My horse is, in fact, not a horse, but a donkey, and trousers are quite normal for donkeys. Which are sacred and unsuspicious creatures."

"No, sir, your mount is suspicious and shall be reported."

"Your mum's a suspicious mount," said I. Perhaps unwisely. Bottom snickered.

"Wait here while I fetch the captain," said Spot Face.

"But look at these ears," I said, holding Bottom's ears affectionately. "These are the very ears Jesus caressed upon his ride into the holy city. These are blessed fucking ears. Go ahead, touch them."

"I don't want him touching my ears," said Bottom.

"Well we're right fucked now," said I.

"Did that donkey just talk?" said Spot Face.

"No," said Bottom.

"No," said I.

"I must fetch the captain." He turned to run off.

"Fine!" said I. "Fine, fine, fine." I slid off Bottom's back to the ground. "I will go in to see the duke without my horse, now open the gate."

"Your horse wasn't going in either way. Horses aren't allowed. I'm simply saying he is suspicious."

"Agreed," said I. "The horse stays. Now let me in, please. I have been summoned by the duke."

"Then why ain't you going in the front door upstairs, like the other wedding guests?"

"Because I am the entertainment and entertainers must enter from the rear."

Bottom snickered again.

"Fine, but I'll have to check you for weapons. What's in that satchel?"

I had a leather shoulder bag loaned me by Francis Flute. "Simple squirrels." I flipped open the flap. A brown, a red, and a white squirrel all looked up, squinted into the late daylight.

"You've brought a satchel of squirrels to the duke's wedding?"

"Trained squirrels. For the show. Do something clever, girls."

The squirrels just blinked, looking very common and squirrelly.

"What's all that black cloth in the bottom?"

"Squirrel kit," said I. "Costumes."

"All that for three squirrels?" Spot Face reached into the satchel. "What's that? A razor?"

"Oh balls," said I.

And that's when Cobweb bit him.

"Ouch!" The guard jumped back, waved his one hand as if it were on fire while trying to bring his spear into a threatening position with the other.

"Run, girls," said I. The squirrels jumped out of the satchel and dashed through the heavy metal bars of the gate. "You only had to do something clever and this would have worked," I shouted after them.

"Hold!" said the guard.

"I am bloody holding," said I. "But they're getting away. Go get them. They're rabid. You don't want them getting to the duke's wedding party."

"You brought a satchel of rabid squirrels to the duke's wedding?" The guard was examining the bite on his finger, which was welling up with blood quite nicely.

"Yes, they were the only squirrels available on short notice. Now go!"

Spot Face took the heavy key from his belt and opened the gate, then started through after our team. "Wait," said I.

"What?" said Spotty.

"Take this," I said, handing him my satchel. "You'll need this to put them in when you catch them."

"Right," he said. He took the satchel and ran off down the passageway, leaving the gate swinging on its hinges.

"I don't think clever squirrel tricks were going to convince him if he wasn't moved by a talking horse," said Bottom.

"Quite right," said I. "But the door is open, the girls are in and have no doubt located Drool, and"—here I squinted at the sky—"I would say that the sun has safely set, so I pronounce the plan working, despite your somewhat weak performance as a horse."

"Does it seem strange that there was only one guard for the lower entrance to the castle on the night of a royal wedding?" Bottom asked. "This will be my first time inside, myself, but having seen Oberon's castle, and even Titania's castle of leaves, it seems rather sparse, don't you think?"

He had a point. While I expected the members of the watch to be patrolling the castle perimeter for the wedding, there had been at least six guards when I'd made my way out. "One guard does seem fortunate for us, but who are we to look a gift horse in the mouth? So to speak." I bowed and made way for my equine colleague to enter the gendarmerie, then followed. "Shall we?"

We were but twenty or so steps down the hall when a gruff and familiar voice shouted, "You there, stop!"

"Oh fuckstockings," said I.

"What?" said Bottom.

"Be a horse," I said, turning to face Blacktooth and Burke, who stood in the gateway where we had just entered.

"About time, thou smarmy lick-knobs," said I. "I've been looking for you. I have returned with the item the queen sent me to find. She told me to bring it directly here to you."

"Where is it?" said Blacktooth. "Show it to me."

"I would," said I, "but that pup of a guard you left at the gate took it from me and went off to give it to the duke himself. Hog the glory, methinks."

"See here, knave," said Blacktooth, "I will not have you expunge our integers."

I looked to Burke for some translation, but even the captain's personal catch-fart was baffled and merely shrugged.

"Well you had better catch him and stop him, hadn't you?" I said, pointing down the passageway. "Before he reveals your darker purpose to the duke?"

"Right," said Blacktooth, and off he went, lumbering after the young guard.

"Well go on," I said to Burke, who stood looking from me, to Bottom, to me.

"Why's your horse so funny looking?" he asked.

"Bad lighting in here," said I. "You need more torches. We'll have it sorted by the time your mum comes by to shag him."

"Burke!" called Blacktooth from around the corner.

"Off you go," said I.

And off he went, Bottom and I following ten or so yards back. We ran round the turn to the left, and I began shouting, "Foe! Foe! Friend! Friend! Foe! Foe! Friend! Friend!"

"What are you doing?" asked Bottom as he ran along beside me.

"You'll see," I said. Then, "Foe! Foe! Friend! Friend!" repeating the refrain until Blacktooth was rounding the turn leading to the vault and the cells, and the captain's head stopped in midair with a loud thunk, while his feet and torso continued on their way, somewhat airborne, until he tumbled into an unconscious pile in the dungeon.

Burke tried to stop but found himself sliding into the vault to see an enormous ninny holding a halberd with which he had just soundly brained the captain of the watch.

"Foe?" Drool asked as Bottom and I trotted up behind Burke.

"Aye, lad, but give us a moment."

"All right," said Drool, disappointed.

Burke reached back to feel the quite useless crossbow slung across his back, then glanced at the dagger at his belt, at which point I drew one of my own and Bottom brandished one of his ersatz leg sticks like a club.

"Consider, leftenant, before you draw your dagger, that my apprentice has dispatched your commander with the shaft end of that poleaxe, but had he used the blade end, Blacktooth's head would likely still be rolling free."

Drool, sweet lad, flipped the halberd so the blade was leveled at Burke's chest.

Burke did not move except to look at the unconscious forms of Blacktooth and the young, spot-faced guard lying next to him. I relieved him of his dagger and handed it, hilt first, back to Bottom.

"What do you want?" said Burke.

"For now, for you to stand completely still and refrain from shouting. Is there no one else here in the gendarmerie?"

"No, just that one." He nodded to the unconscious lad.

"Drool, are you hurt? Did they harm you?" The oaf looked as vital, huge, and filthy as usual.

"No, Pocket, I was real quiet and they left me alone."

"Except to feed you?"

"No, they didn't give me food nor water. I asked for some but the guards said they would cut off me willy if I asked again so I dinna ask. Cobweb give me some water just now. She's a love."

"Where is Cobweb?"

"She and her mates ran off when they heard you coming. Hiding, probably." He dropped his guard with the halberd a bit, then pretended to have a thought. "Hey, Pocket, did you know that Cobweb is a—"

"I know, lad. It's a secret, so let us not discuss it in front of this fucktoad. Later."

"Aye, Pocket." Drool nodded.

It was all I could do to not spear Burke's liver right then. Poor Drool had had nothing since eating the Mechanicals' lunch three days prior, while I had been dining with kings and being frolicked back to health. A quick thrust of my dagger and Burke would bleed out just slowly enough to know which particular of his cruelties had cost him his life. Instead, I reached over and tipped the quiver of bolts that hung at his waist until its contents rattled out onto the floor. There were six long oak bolts and a single, shorter, black, distinctly goblin-looking bolt.

"I didn't kill the Puck," Burke said, jumping ahead of my accusations.

"I know," said I. "But you paid the goblin who did."

"I did not. I swear."

"He told me such."

"Then he lied."

"Why were you at Turtle Grotto that morning then?"

"The duke sent us. To retrieve something the Puck was bringing him."

"But the young Athenian Demetrius fell to your goblin bolt, did he not?"

"Why no. I am an officer of the watch, I would never—"

"Kill him, Drool," said I.

The great ninny drew back the point of the halberd, deciding, for variety's sake I suppose, to skewer rather than bludgeon the watchman.

"Yes, yes, yes," said Burke. "It was I. I didn't mean to kill the yellow-haired one. 'Twas the other one I was aiming for."

"Why didn't you go back and kill Lysander as you'd been hired to do?"

"Well you'd seen me, hadn't you? Running like a loony after me in the forest. And I'd used all the goblin bolts I had with me. We'd have had to kill the whole lot. Egeus would have known it was us, and you were on task for the duke. Blacktooth thought it best to offer aid to the other youths and claim you'd been seeing things, or you were lying, if you lived to return to the duke."

"Then Blacktooth was in on it?"

"A half a mile back, yes. He moves like an ox crashing through the forest. I couldn't risk letting him come closer."

"And what are you up to tonight? Why is there only one guard down here?"

"The wedding. Half the watch is patrolling the crowd outside the castle and the other half is out in the streets getting pissed themselves."

"Will others come down later to relieve this lad?"

"Yes, any minute now."

"We had better kill you, then," said I.

"No," said Burke rather quickly. "He was to be on watch all night by himself."

"How do I get into the upper castle? Will there be more guards?"

"Straight ahead, left, then right, up a spiral staircase, gate at the top. No guards tonight. Hippolyta's Amazons perhaps—"

And that's when Nick Bottom brained Burke with one of his false horse legs. The watchman crumpled atop his colleagues and a rivulet of blood trickled out of his scalp.

"What'd you do that for?" I said.

"I thought you were going to kill him," said Bottom.

"I wasn't. I just needed him to think I would kill him."

"Well you had me convinced," said Bottom. "You are truly the master."

"Don't try to flatter your way out of this, Bottom. I had more questions for him."

"Pocket," said Drool. "Why is that donkey talking?"

"Oh, that's no donkey, lad. That's Nick Bottom the weaver. You ate his lunch in the forest. Remember his fine waistcoat?"

"No."

"Well he's been changed into an ass by magic."

"Smashing!" said Drool. "Magic is the mutt's nuts, innit?"

"Shall we find the fairies and carry on?" said Bottom.

"Fairies!" said Drool. "Smashing!"

"Cobweb is a fairy," I told the dolt. "As are her mates. And, Bottom, don't change the subject, I'm not finished being angry with you. You two, drag these three into Drool's old cell. Take their clothes and weapons and lock them in irons. I will look for the fairies."

"Aye aye, Pocket," said Drool. "Did we have any food?"

"I'll look, lad. The gendarmerie has to have a larder down here somewhere."

"Right," said Drool. He set his halberd on the floor, grabbed the unconscious spot-faced guard by the collar, and began dragging him.

Bottom was stripping Blacktooth and Burke of their weapons and tossing them into a pile. I headed deeper into the catacombs, calling softly for the fairies.

"Pocket!" Drool shouted, and I turned as to see him toss the young guard into the cell.

"Yes, lad?"

"Do we have any silver?" Drool asked.

"Fuckstockings," I hissed under my breath. Drool had been with me a dozen years in a score of cities and never had he asked me for coin. "What do you want silver for, lad?"

"Nothing," said the ninny.

"I found some, here," said Bottom. I trotted back to where I could see him. The ass-man knelt over Burke's prostrate form and was holding up a heavy silver armlet with the image of a Gorgon's head cast upon it.

"Keep that with you, Bottom. We may need it to buy our lives later."

CHAPTER XVIII

The Play's the Thing

WHY DIDN'T I, a shallow, callow fool, take my apprentice and my monkey and fuck off to who-knows-where, leaving the Athenians fuck-all for their trouble? Well for one, Cobweb and the other fairies had not returned to rendezvous at the edge of town, and I was the one who had sent them into the breach. Second, the Mechanicals were playing for their lives and had boneheadedly put their faith in me, willing ninnies that they were, and I could not let them perish. And finally, after my time as a diplomat, a spy, a pirate, a ghost, and a detector of crimes, I was, again, a fool, poised to take the piss out of power, and from the giddy delight I felt rising in my chest, this surely was my calling, and tonight I had been called.

The Mechanicals, Drool, and I were gathered in the anteroom off the great hall where I had first met Theseus, before he'd set me to the task of finding the Puck's killer and fetching the magic flower, which I had, of sorts. I'd given Egeus, the duke's toady, a morning glory blossom I'd plucked off a fencerow just outside the gendarmerie. From the vague way Theseus had told me to bring "what the Puck was fetching" he might not even have known it was supposed to be a magic flower, but one can't be too careful.

Upon leaving Egeus, among the many Amazon guards I had spotted the tall blond one who had laughed at my japes upon my first meeting the duke.

"Can you get a message to Hippolyta?" I asked her.

She merely nodded, not a word.

"Tell her that the Puck's potion, which I delivered to Theseus, is a fake. Tell her before the wedding."

"I will tell her, little one," she said.

"Little one? You would be pleasantly surprised at my oh-so-large talents, my butch and brawny lass."

She grinned, flipped one of the tentacles of my coxcomb. "I will see your talents well used before I take your nut sack for my coin purse."

"I shall keep your treasure trove safe until then, my leather rose," I said with a wink, missing having my codpiece to honk, which would generally accompany such a promise.

She scoffed, no doubt to hide her profound arousal, and marched off, her hobnail boots clacking a tattoo on the flagstones as she went.

Now, in the antechamber, with the Mechanicals fixing costumes, running lines, and generally fighting down their instincts to vomit, I opened the door to the great hall a crack and measured up our audience. The wedding couple, their ceremony finished, sat in high-backed chairs at the right, just below the stone dais that we would use as our stage. Hippolyta was in a simple white gown, now without her chain mail chemise, wearing a golden crown in the shape of a laurel wreath. Theseus wore a white robe trimmed in gold and a heavier crown of golden laurel. Right of the stage sat Oberon and Titania, with the Indian boy sitting between them. The petite fairy queen was draped in opalescent material that might have been woven of spider silk and unicorn spooge, as it shimmered blue-green even under the golden lamplight in the hall. Oberon was a great tower of onyx, his black robe and crown trimmed out in silver, and, of course, the wicked silver-bladed tips on his fingers. The Indian boy was dressed in finery, a long coat of jade silk and a gold silk turban with a red jewel pinned at the front. His countenance was vacant, as if he were drugged or just profoundly empty-headed.

Beside the wedding couple sat Hermia and Lysander, who had been married in a quick ceremony after Theseus and Hippolyta, the duke having relented on Egeus's insistence that his daughter be put to death or sent to a nunnery for not marrying Demetrius, since the piss-haired lothario had been rendered quite unsuitable for marriage by a crossbow bolt through the neck. Behind them sat foreign dignitaries, lords and ladies, ministers and magistrates, military commanders and merchants—perhaps two hundred in all, reclining on cushions or sitting on benches, all having feasted at the other end of the great hall before the entertainment began. Above them, in the six balconies that looked down on the hall, were those who had weaseled their way into the ceremony but had not been given a seat, hangers-on, sycophants, and lickspittles. At each of the six double-doored entrances stood four guards, two spearmen from Theseus's forces and two unarmed Amazons, who nevertheless seemed poised and painted for battle, unlike their Athenian counterparts, who just seemed bored and resentful that they weren't taking part in the revelry.

These would be our audience, the judges and jury and executioners if we did not please, and oh, I did not think our modest play would please. No I did not.

Egeus, still shaking with anger over Hermia's finding her way past his condemnation, as master of ceremonies, sat directly beside the wedding couple, and behind him, rather cruelly placed, I thought, sat Helena, who had served as a bridesmaid for her friend. We would enter stage right, from our little antechamber, but there were great tapestries, hung from a line behind the stage, that provided us a backstage, too, and most of the players would move there upon Peter Quince's reading of the prologue.

A troubadour playing a lute was finishing a sad ballad, then we would be introduced. Nick Bottom peeked over me into the room, looking around the crowd for a friendly, or at least allied, face.

"No sign of Gritch or Rumour?" he said.

"Not tooth nor tongue," said I. "Did you put Rumour's hat in a satchel to keep Jeff from it?"

"I did, but he's had a go at Snout's deerskin hat and was pulling on my ears for a bit before Drool restrained him."

"That little scamp has singular enthusiasm, doesn't he? Are you ready?"

"As I can be. But I'll be using the notes you had Quince make. Short notice."

I had Peter Quince write down each of the players' lines on strips of parchment that they carried. Bottom had had less time to study his lines than the others, as he had been with me, invading the gendarmerie. It had been four hours since we locked Blacktooth and Burke in the dungeon, yet no one seemed to miss them, which was suspicious in itself.

"You know, Bottom," said I, "your cause to return to a non-equine form may not be lost. When the fairies were frolicking, at the harem, I noticed the hair on your arms receded. They may be your hope for a cure when we finish here."

"Except we're going to be executed when we finish here."

"Either way, you won't have to face Mrs. Bottom looking like that," said I, ever the optimist.

"Oh joy," said Bottom. "Pocket, do you see those black robes in the back? Are those Cobweb and the girls?"

There were figures in the back of the hall, where the tables were still laid out from the feast, wearing hooded silk robes like those the fairies had taken from Oberon's harem. They were far away, and the light dim, but they seemed the right size. Then, one of them moved, and I knew it was not Cobweb nor her two friends, for even from the length of the great hall I could see it scuttling sideways, with none of the light-footed grace of the fairies. Looking around the crowd I noticed black-hooded figures manning the balconies and lurking by the entrances. I counted at least a dozen before I heard the troubadour pluck a final chord and polite applause signaled our cue.

"Places, everyone," I called to the room. "Quince, you're on."

Egeus rose from his seat and walked to the edge of the stage, unrolled a scroll, and, with a voice and manner only slightly less pompous than Rumour himself, read: "And now, for your pleasure or their pain, a group of tradesmen, hard-handed men who have until now never labored in their minds, rude mechanicals, shall present the most lachrymal and laughable tragicomedy of *Romeo and Juliet*, the original said to have been written by the Ninth Earl of Bumsex, upon his mistress's bare bottom."

"A tongue-in-cheek comedy, then?" said Lysander.

"Oh, both lachrymal and laughable," said the duke, laughing. "Good we've had plenty of drink to fuel our tears, be they of laughter or of tragedy."

"I loathe you with the heat of a thousand suns," said Hippolyta, staring a hole into the duke's head, she, evidently, not an aficionado of the theater, and not doing very well at pretending to have received the love potion.

Theseus said: "If it be horrid, we shall take sport in their mistakes and find amusement in their lowly skills—find in their paltry talents the couch of our superiority. Players, play on!"

And around the hall amid applause they echoed the call of "play on!"

As the rest of the company scrambled out of the antechamber,

Peter Quince took his place at the corner of the stage and unrolled his own scroll. "Gentles, welcome to our most grisly comedy and tragically romantic Grand Guignol."

"'At's fuckin' French, innit!" shouted Drool from behind the tapestry.

"Not to contradict our esteemed master of ceremony, but we shall not be performing *Romeo and Juliet,* but instead a most raucous and respectful adventure, called *A Fool in the Forest,* penned by our own *maître de drame* Pocket of Dog Snogging."

At which point I bounded out onto the stage, doffed my coxcomb, and took a deep bow to what should have been thunderous applause.

Egeus stood and waved his scroll. "Now, see here, this shall not stand! 'Twas *Pyramus and Thisby* you submitted for consideration, and by the grace of the duke, you were given permission to do *Romeo and Juliet* because you did not have a wall, but this change shall not be permitted."

In a single motion I drew a dagger from the small of my back and flung it underhand Egeus's way. The dagger sailed past his ear and buried itself with a thud in the high back of his chair, exactly where I had been aiming.

"Sit the fuck down and shut the fuck up, thou pompous toady," said I.

Egeus began to protest and I drew my second dagger. "Or don't," said I.

There were gasps throughout the audience. The guards were gobsmacked, while the duke and even Hippolyta seemed somewhat amused at Egeus's dismay. The powerful hold nothing but contempt for those who toady to them, all but the toadies know this.

Egeus sat, leaning to one side as if that were his preference and not because of my dagger by his ear.

"Proceed," said I to Quince, giving him a grand "by your leave" flourish.

"Fear not, ladies, do not be dismayed, for the dagger you have seen is but a stage dagger, a trick of the craft. Tonight we shall also present a lion, who, while fierce, is also false, and no more than Snug the joiner in costume, so cast because he cannot hold lines in his memory."

"RAWR!" roared Snug from backstage, and the audience tittered, because Snug's roar was still shit and really only his saying the word "rawr" rather loudly.

"Also," read Quince, "when you encounter the moon, do not be afraid, for it is not a real moon, but a stage moon."

"No one is afraid of the moon, Quince," said I.

"Fear not the moon," Quince continued, "nor by the many grisly deaths and gratuitous bonkings be dismayed, for they are but tricks of the stage. Be not afraid."

"No one is afraid," said the duke. "Methinks the players are afraid of the play themselves. Play on!"

"Aye, Your Grace," said Quince. Then, back to his scroll. "Upon a tossing sea tossed the handsome and clever hero Pocket of Dog Snogging."

The Mechanicals began to make storm noises. Drool, wearing a skirt made of barrel slats attached in the shape of a boat, came forth from behind the tapestries, with Jeff clinging to his head. "I present boat," said Drool, "and this, Jeff, presents Jeff." He swept me up in his great arms and held me like a babe as he rocked me to the rhythm of the imagined waves. Jeff climbed partially down Drool's face and grasped at my coxcomb as we pitched upon the waves.

"And when all was thought lost—" read Quince.

"Oh no," said I. "All is nearly lost. We shall have to eat the monkey."

"—Pocket was tossed upon the fair shores of Athens."

Before I could instruct otherwise, Drool tossed me onto the stone stage with much more enthusiasm than was required. I was not able to get my feet under me before coming down smartly upon one shoulder. I was able to roll to my feet, but I felt a crack in my chest upon impact and my breath left me in a great explosion. I turned back to shout at Drool but could find no air to push it.

"And so," read Quince, "the hapless fool found himself wandering in the enchanted forest."

Drool stood on the stage, well past when he was supposed to exit. Instead he pulled a strip of parchment from the front of his shirt and squinted at it, as did Jeff. "I forgetted me line," said the oaf to the audience with a curtsy.

"You don't know how to read, you ninny," I said, finding my breath at last.

Drool held the scrap of parchment up closer to Jeff.

"He can't read either."

Quince had had only enough time to write each actor's sides, the parchment scraps with each of their lines, so there was no master script from which to prompt Drool. Thus, Robin Starveling, carrying a lantern and a branch, drifted onto the stage.

"I present moonshine, or this lantern is the moon, and I am the man in the moon. Be not afraid."

"They're not afraid of the fucking moon," said I.

"Oh no, someone doth break character and ruin the illusion we have endeavored to create," improvised Starveling. Once beside Drool, he stretched so that he could read Drool's line, then whispered to the ninny.

"Alas," said Drool, in Robin Starveling's voice, which was twice as annoying coming out of a larger package. "Alas, I am carried out by the surf to be dashed to bits on the rocks." And with that, Drool backed off the stage, through the tapestry, and tossed out the barrel slats that made up his hull, which clattered on the stones. Robin Starveling found himself standing midstage, alone, lantern in one hand, branch in the other.

"And I, moonshine, am also dashed upon the rocks." And he backed offstage, between the tapestries, and threw the branch out to signify his dashing.

The audience howled. From backstage, Jeff screeched. He was a performing monkey, after all, and the audience's laughter meant he had done well.

I climbed to my feet and pantomimed looking around in a dark forest.

Peter Quince returned to the corner of the stage. "So the brave and handsome fool found himself lost in the forest, and soon he happened onto a young woman, who was weeping."

I don't know if Francis Flute was an excellent leaper or if Drool had flung him headlong through the tapestries, but Flute came to the stage airborne and landed center stage in a heap of limbs, wig, and veil, where he commenced to weep in the falsetto he had practiced as Thisby and briefly as Juliet.

"Dear child," said I. "What tragedy hath befallen thee?"

"Oh, good sir," said Francis, turning his wig around on his head so he could see. "I am heartbroken, for I have been used like the wanton tart that I appear to be by the yellow-haired tosser known as Demetrius. He now loves my friend Hermia, who only has eyes for Lysander, and the two of them have fucked off to the forest to be married in secret, and Demetrius has followed, for I grassed them out to the authorities."

"Why would the authorities care?"

"Hermia's father has put a sentence of death upon her unless she marries Demetrius, and he is a puff toad of great self-importance, so the authorities will bring her back, and likely arrest Lysander."

"So your friend will be forced to marry the fellow you are in love with, or she will be killed."

I was quite impressed with Flute's ability to deliver the lines I had written for him and was desperately trying not to break character by showing it.

"I suppose. Oh, I am miserable. I am lost. I shall die friendless and alone, a spinster. Oh woe! Oh despair!" Flute wailed and wept with great drama. I glanced into the audience to see Helena, the real Helena, also sobbing into her hands. Had the child no family to comfort her?

"Hold there, knave!" came a voice from offstage. Tom Snout the tall tinker entered wearing a wig made of yellow straw instead of his stupid doeskin hat. "It is I, Demetrius, the piss-haired tosser. What evil do you perpetrate on this maid?"

I stood, met the tinker nose to sternum, as, even in character, he was annoyingly tall. "I am but comforting her."

"Hold there, knave," came another voice from offstage, and Robin Starveling, wearing a dark wig over his bald pate that looked suspiciously as if it had been fashioned from the hair of a donkey tail, and a pointy beard drawn on with charcoal, stumbled onstage. "It is I, Lysander, the pointy-bearded tosser. Who makes this maid weep?" He checked his note. "Why, I shall box his ears."

"But wait," came a bad falsetto from offstage, and now Peter Quince entered, wearing a long gown, and, for some reason, a veil. "It is I, Hermia, the tiny tosset, who hath defied my father, the aforementioned puff toad of dubious motivations. Who vexes my friend Helena?"

"Oh my love," said Lysander (Starveling). "Snog me publicly so we may make everyone miserable."

And Starveling bent Peter Quince over backward and passionately stage-snogged him, hiding the fact that both of them were furiously whispering, "What's my next line? I don't know, what's my next line?" to each other. I shot a glance into the audience. Egeus was very displeased and agitated, but he did not dare stand or voice protest. The reminder of my knife-throwing skill was still buried in the back of his chair by his head.

There was a loud twang offstage and on cue Tom Snout screamed and bent over quickly, then stood holding a crossbow bolt, which he held as if it were stuck in his throat, while squeezing a sausage casing we had filled with beet juice. "Ahhhhh, I am slain, I am slain, I am truly fucking slain, ouch, ouch, ouch, squeeeeeeeeeeeeek!" Snout approximated his last breath's escaping the hole in his throat even as he sprayed beet juice all over the other players—all but me, that is, as I danced deftly out of range—and Francis Flute screamed a lovely aria of bloody murder. Snout (Demetrius) lowered himself to the floor, checked his line note, and said, "Thud." Which had been written as a stage direction, but on a stone floor, I suppose saying it worked by way of improvisation.

At which point Peter Quince broke character and walked to the edge of the stage. "Ladies, ladies, do not be dismayed, for that is not a real arrow, but only a stage prop, and that is not real blood, but only beet juice, which Tom Snout's wife poured into a sausage casing, and this fellow is not slain, and all is well, thank you." Then he skipped back to his mark and Starveling (Lysander) proceeded to stage-snog Quince (Hermia).

Francis/Helena fell to her knees over dead Demetrius and wailed, "Oh, my love, my Demetrius, who would do such a dread deed? Oh, I shall surely die of grief."

At which point Drool entered with Snug the joiner, both dressed in uniforms of the watch, both their uniforms comically too small. Snug carried a crossbow. "It was not us," said Snug.

"Not us," said Drool. "We are only wandering around the woods like ninnies."

"Like ninnies," said Snug. "And despite all appearances, me holding this crossbow with no bolt"—he checked his parchment—"and despite you lot being out here on the edge of nowhere, we just happened by."

"Aye," said Drool as Blacktooth, "and we was hired to kill the bloke with the pointy beard, so this fellow is colorful damage."

"Collateral damage," Snug corrected, the dim leading the dim. "'At's right. Egeus, royal puff toad hisself, hired us to kill that bloke over there snogging the carpenter."

There was a scream of rage in the audience and I thought, *There, there it is, Egeus, hearing his name evoked, has lost his mind.* But when I looked, in fact, the scream had come from Helena. She had pulled my dagger from the back of Egeus's chair and had quite smartly driven it through the top of his head. Helena released her two-handed grip on the blade and Egeus slumped over on the floor and commenced oozing fluids as he twitched. Two men in finery caught Helena by the arms, not sure if they were restraining her or holding her as she fainted.

As gasps and screams filled the hall, I stepped to the edge of the stage and said, "Oh well done, love. You're not the soggy Ophelia we all thought you to be." Which served to calm the audience not at all. As I considered my next improvisation, because I had diverged grievously from the script, Nick Bottom galloped onto and then around the stage, braying loudly and flapping his arms, affixed to which were wings that seemed fashioned from bits of watchman uniform and the barrel slats that had recently been my shipwrecked boat.

In a moment, everyone had stopped fretting about the murder and had turned their attention to the lunatic in the winged donkey outfit, at which point Nick Bottom strode to the edge of the stage and lifted his wings. "Gentle ladies, fear not. Gentle gentlemen, fear not. Fear not, for I am Pegasus, magical horse of mythology and mystery, and I am here to make all things right. This is not blood you see, but stage blood, and that knife but a prop knife."

I skipped over to Snug and Drool and whispered, "Grab the dead puff toad and drag him to the antechamber, now, and bow before you drag him in the door."

"And this good gentleman," continued Bottom, pointing to the quite dead Egeus, "to show his love and appreciation for the duke and his bride, agreed to be part of our romantic comical tragedy. He is playing the tragic victim part, because it didn't require a special costume."

Drool and Snug had seized Egeus's body by the arms and were dragging him past the duke and Hippolyta, leaving a red trail on the stone. When they reached the door, they dropped the body, bowed, then picked up the expired puff toad and dragged him in.

When the door closed I started applauding wildly while nodding at the audience members, who, afraid that they were not important enough to be let in on the joke, began to applaud with me. I applauded at the exiting watchmen, at the lovers onstage, at the newborn Pegasus, and even at Helena, who had come to her senses and smiled as I smiled and nodded to her. *Go with me here, love, your life is on it.* The two blokes holding her arms let her go and she took a bow and nodded her gratitude around the room.

"And that is act one," I announced. "There will be a brief intermission, then act two." Then I took my bow and ran offstage, dragging Bottom out of a flourish of bowing so effusive one of his wings had fallen off. I pulled him by one of his long ears until we were through the entry of the antechamber, where I slammed the heavy door and leaned my back against it.

Peter Quince, standing over the body of Egeus, said, "I have a few notes."

"That were smashing!" said Cobweb, bouncing on her toes in front of me like a child waiting for a sweet.

"Where have you been?" I asked.

"Having a wee frolic," she said.

"We were at wit's end. You were supposed to meet us in Drool's cell. It's been hours."

"It was a long frolic," said Peaseblossom. "We are not good at time."

CHAPTER XIX

Act 2

A KNOCK ON the antechamber door.

"They've come to take us to the gallows," said Peter Quince.

"And they've decided to knock first?" said I. "So as not to surprise us out of costume?"

"True," said Quince. He opened the door a crack. The girl Hermia stood outside.

"When is my father going to return?" she asked.

I stepped over her dead father to a spot where I could peek out the open door. "In a bit, love. Still cleaning the beet juice—stage blood—off of him. After act two, methinks."

"It looked so real," said Hermia.

"We are using the master's method," said Peter Quince. He shut the door and turned to grin at me.

"What creature of dark snark have I borne?" said I.

Before Quince could answer, another knock. He cracked the door. Looked out.

"Suck your dick for silver," came a gravelly voice.

Quince closed the door and looked back to me. "It's for you."

I looked around at my players, Drool, and the fairies, one of whom, Moth, was petting my monkey, and strangely, he was letting her. I said: "Drag Egeus further away from the door—put him in that corner. And someone get my dagger out of his melon, if you would be so kind. Mechanicals, do not be alarmed, but you are about to meet a goblin. If you scream I will dirk you in the gonads to give you good reason." (I looked at Robin Starveling then, who would likely have denied goblins existed even as one was gnawing off his knob.) "At our last meeting, this goblin was an ally, we shall assume he remains so. Drool, we do not have any silver. Give Jeff the tongue hat for a bit to keep him distracted."

With the company moving at my instruction, I opened the door just wide enough to accommodate a goblin, reached out, grabbed Gritch by the arm, and dragged him in.

The goblin was wearing one of the same black hooded robes that the fairies of the harem wore, and with the hood up, he looked like a short, shiny monk, if you didn't look too closely.

"Gritch, where were you?"

"Here," said the goblin. "I told you we were coming here."

"Then all those black robes on the periphery of the hall, your soldiers?"

"Yes."

"Blacktooth and Burke let you in through the gendarmerie, the dungeon?"

"Yes."

I looked to Nick Bottom. "That's why only the one young guard, and I'll wager he was sent off on an errand when the goblins came in."

"Yes," said Gritch.

"How many?"

"A hundred. Twenty in the hall. The rest around the doors and balconies."

"Goblins are very good at counting," said Peaseblossom in admiration.

The Mechanicals, except for Bottom, who was beyond being surprised, all stared at Gritch with various levels of curiosity and horror. I put my arm around Gritch's shoulders and walked him into the corner, where, yes, we were standing over Egeus's corpse, but also, there was some privacy.

"Gritch, mate, what's the plan here with your one hundred soldiers?"

"To take the castle."

"On Oberon's command?"

"No, on command from the warrior queen."

"Hippolyta?"

"Yes. She gave us silver."

"Bottom," I called. "Bring me that armlet."

Bottom brought me the Medusa armlet, the match to the one Gritch was already wearing. I took it and placed it in the goblin's hand. He almost went to his knees in ecstasy at its touch.

"Don't kill any of us," said I. I gestured to everyone in the room. "Can you do that?"

"Yes."

"Okay, carry on then. We've a show to do." I patted his shoulder, which was very much like patting a millstone.

Gritch started to head out the door, then stopped, turned, and looked to the three fairies, who now stood together against the wall, all wearing the same garment as the goblin. "We let them go," said Gritch.

"Pardon?" said Moth.

"We let the fairies go." Gritch looked back to me. "All the sodding fairies."

"Where are they?" asked Cobweb.

"At the castle of leaves with the other fairies."

"How did you get them out?" asked Cobweb. "They were too afraid to move. Did you hurt them?"

"Squirrels," said Gritch. "We caught them when they were squirrels and took them in cages to the castle of leaves. There was sun. We needed robes." He tugged at his black hood.

Moth's disturbingly large eyes filled with disturbingly large tears. She ran to Gritch, threw her arms around him, and snogged his disturbingly smooth forehead, making a disturbingly wet smacking sound. Gritch looked to me, as if I might rescue him from his pale attacker, which, of course, I did not.

Then Moth pushed away from him. "Wait. Squirrels? Did you eat my brother? Any of our friends?"

"No," said Gritch. "But they were afraid. They ran when we let them go."

Cobweb took Moth by the shoulders and walked her away from the goblin. "They'll be fine. The others would have found them at sundown. They'll take care of them." Cobweb looked past Moth to Gritch. "Thanks, mate."

"Yes," said Gritch. He went to the door, opened it a crack, peeked out. "They are waiting," he said. Then he pulled his hood down over his face and slipped out into the hall.

"Players, we shall need to improvise a bit. Cobweb, you will need to pretend to be Hippolyta, the Amazon queen. And Peaseblossom, you shall be Titania."

The fairy looked on the edge of panic. "I can't read."

"You shan't need to read, love, just prance around acting mad until I pretend to shag you, then make all manner of moaning and sounds of ecstasy."

"Like Cobweb did with you?"

"You mean you shagged this ginger fairy who was a squirrel but a few hours ago?" said Robin Starveling.

"Now you believe it?" said I.

"Well things have changed, haven't they? Fairies and goblins and squirrels running around willy-nilly. Anything could be possible. Elfs shagging squirrels, not such a stretch anymore, is it?"

"Not an elf," said Drool note for note in my voice. Then, in his own, "Pocket, you shagged a squirrel?"

"Drool," said I, "you and Snout shall again play the watch—wait, no, the part of the king requires reading. Tom Snout, you shall play Oberon. Snug shall play Burke."

"We have no part written for Oberon," said Peter Quince. "We have no costume for the fairy queen and none for Oberon."

"Grab your quill and ink, we shall write a short speech for Oberon, but the rest shall be improvised cruelty. Moth, give your black robe to Snout. Starveling, blacken all parts of Snout that show out of the robe with charcoal from the brazier, including his stupid hat. Peaseblossom, you shall play Titania *in flagrante*." I bounced my eyebrows at my masterful use of Latin.

"That means 'on fire,'" said Quince.

"No it doesn't, it means 'naked,'" said I.

"No, it means 'on fire,'" said Quince.

"Well I'm not going to do that," said Peaseblossom. "You can just pretend-shag yourself on fire."

"No, no, no," I said. "Just naked, as is Titania's way, anyway. And Cobweb, you shall play Hippolyta, the warrior queen."

"Why does Peaseblossom get to pretend to shag you?" said Cobweb. "It's because you want to set her on fire, isn't it? Is that what you like to do with your shoe whores? Put them in their shoes and spark them up?"

"No one is going to be set on fire." I thought for a second. It wasn't necessary to the plot, except it might evoke anger from Oberon, but there would be plenty to spur him without it. "Fine. You, lamb, shall pretend to shag me, while Peaseblossom will pretend to shag everyone else."

"As is my way," said Peaseblossom. "The queen's way, I mean."

"You will need a costume for Hippolyta," said Peter Quince.

He was right, of course. "Fine, Starveling, come here." I cracked the door and pointed out to the audience. "See that girl, the one sitting behind the duke? Go fetch her. Tell her I need her for the play."

"The one who stabbed that fellow in the head?"

"That's the one. Go get her."

"Why don't you go get her?"

"Because I am the lead and I must prepare for my role." I shoved the balding fuckwit out into the hall, where the audience was already clapping and calling for our return. While Starveling was gone I quickly dictated some lines to Quince, who wrote them on parchment, cut them with my dagger, and handed them to the appropriate players, as well as a few lines for Quince himself, the narrator. It was the same story, but now, knowing Gritch's orders, we needed to compress it, I thought.

There was a tap on the door. I let Starveling in and pulled Helena in after him, then shut the door behind her. She stood there, rather vacant-looking for a new murderer. I sized her up. For once her annoying height would be a help. (Robin Starveling's tailoring skills could make great use of all that fabric.)

She looked down at Egeus's body and began to breathe in short, yipping sobs of panic. "Calm down, love, he won't bother you."

"But Hermia will be so cross with me."

"No she won't. She knows he was a twat. Now, off with your frock, we need it."

She wore a white gown, not dissimilar to Hippolyta's and Hermia's, and a wreath of flowers in her hair. I snatched the flowers off her head and tossed them to Peaseblossom. "There, fairy queen, there's your kit."

Peaseblossom donned the wreath, then curtsied as Moth helped her weave it into her hair.

"Off with it," said I. "We've a play to do. No one is looking, we're all actors here."

Drool, the Mechanicals, the monkey, Bottom, and the fairies all stopped and waited for Helena to take off her dress.

"Why are those tiny women naked? And why is that fellow all

covered in coal? And why is there a monkey in here? And why does that fellow have the head of an ass? And why are those tiny women so tiny? Smaller even than Hermia. And so are you."

"Cobweb, would you trade gowns with Helena, please?" I said, with patience I was not feeling. "Everyone else, look at that tapestry on the back wall while the ladies change."

"But—" said Helena.

"Or we can murder you and take your gown," I said with a charming grin.

"Give it up, shoe whore," said Cobweb.

*   *   *

"AND SO," read Peter Quince, "we return to the fairy wood, where the shadow king, Oberon, meets with his jester, Robin Goodfellow."

Tom Snout and I jumped from behind the tapestry onto the stage. Snout was smeared head to toe in black, and wearing one of the black harem robes and his blackened, stupid, bunny-eared hat, and I wore only a loincloth, fashioned from a foot or so of Helena's skirt, and my daggers across my back, of course, because sod the fucking play, I was not going unarmed into a room full of scoundrels.

"Puck," said Snout, reading from a slip of parchment. "Fetch a magic flower, you know where they grow, and put a drop of its nectar in Titania's eye so that the next thing she lays eyes on is some horrible beast, with which she will fall madly in love. When she is thus engaged, I need you to spirit away her Indian boy and bring him to me."

"I'll put a girdle round the world in forty minutes, and she'll be snogging the beast before you can say Robin Goodfellow." Then I made a fairy fucking trilling noise and Snout stepped offstage. To the audience I said, "Oh, I shall fetch the flower and go to Titania, but the fairy queen has tastes which I am obliged to indulge."

And I ran around to the back of the stage even as Peaseblossom stepped out from behind a tapestry, quite naked except for the wreath of flowers in her hair. There were gasps and giggles from the audience. "Lo—" said Peaseblossom. She looked around, noticed, it seemed, that several hundred people were watching her. "Lo—" she said.

"I am Titania," whispered Snout, furiously, from behind the tapestry.

"I am Titania," said Peaseblossom. She looked around, looked out, looked down. Put her hand over her bits.

"Queen of the fairies," whispered Snout, loudly enough to be heard in the third row.

"I feel naked," whispered Peaseblossom, loudly enough to be heard in the fourth row.

"You *are* naked," whispered Snout.

"But I forgot they shaved my bits," whispered Peaseblossom.

"Say queen of the fucking fairies!" whispered Snout.

"Queen of the fucking fairies!" said Peaseblossom.

The hall filled with laughter. All the royals squirmed except Oberon, who sat forward on his chair and began to scissor the silver-tipped blades of his fingers together. I had expected a reaction from him, but not so soon.

I stepped back out onto the stage. "Milady, it is I, your servant, bringing the love potion that you anticipated." I held a blossom from Helena's wreath close to Peaseblossom and whispered her line to her.

"Have you brought me my pleasure?" she repeated.

"I have, milady." I reached behind a tapestry and pulled Bottom out onto the stage. "Here he is, milady. A man with the parts of the donkey."

"Give it me," said Peaseblossom.

I made as if I were squeezing the love potion flower into her eye. Once anointed, she looked at Bottom like a goblin at the silver moon. "Oh, sir, thou art fair indeed and methinks I do so love thee."

And she was on him, her arms around his neck, her legs around his hips, snogging his rough face and dry-humping him with great enthusiasm, while Bottom reciprocated by braying rhythmically and giving the fairy queen a galloping ride in a circle, to exit through the tapestries while the two of them made a rising caterwaul that ended in a screaming crescendo, followed by a short sigh. And Peaseblossom was pushed back onto the stage, her hair in her face, her flower garland fallen over one eye.

"Oh, well done," she said. "A true lover, not like that needle-dicked Oberon." She'd delivered the line without prompting and with no little venom. There was real hatred there, and she had captured Oberon's attention. "I am off to Turtle Grotto. Ta!"

And she skipped to center stage, where she was met by Robin Starveling, who was now made up to look like Theseus, which did not stop him from announcing, "I am Duke Theseus of Athens."

Drool and Snug in their Blacktooth and Burke togs were lurking at the edge of the stage as Peaseblossom fluffed her hair a bit and coyly tiptoed up to Starveling.

"Duke," she said, by way of greeting.

"Queen," said he, a bounce in his eyebrows.

And she was on him, approximating the same scene she'd played out with Bottom, only with less braying and more moaning, and they both disappeared behind the tapestries, did a bit of orgasmic screaming, then returned to the stage, massively out of breath. The audience loved it, cheered through the entire scene. Titania seemed bothered not at all, but patted the Indian boy's hand, as if to assure him that everything was fine. But the duke was aghast

and continued to glance sideways at Hippolyta, who seemed curious but not particularly concerned.

"I am troubled," said Starveling. "I am to be married in three
days and my wife loathes me."

"Have you tried a love potion?" asked Peaseblossom.

"Is there such a thing?"

"There is, and for your favor now and in the future, I shall send
you one. Put a drop of it in Hippolyta's eye when you are the next
thing she shall see and she will be yours. I shall send the Puck
here tomorrow morning with one. Have your agents meet him at
sunup."

They both ran offstage. Drool and Snug whispered between
themselves conspiratorially, then nodded and skulked off behind
the tapestries.

Peter Quince retook the stage.

"Ladies and gents, be not afraid of all the shagging going on,
for it is merely stage shagging and not actual shagging. Nor are
the betrayals real betrayals. Or the murders real murders. All is
staged for your delight and is completely suitable for ladies and
children.

"Now, we are taken to the chambers in the castle of the beautiful Amazon queen, Hippolyta."

Cobweb, wearing the remnants of Helena's dress, trimmed
down to her size, and the remnants of Helena's hair, woven into
her own short tresses so it hung in plaits like Hippolyta's, scampered out from behind the tapestries and whispered in Quince's
ear, then retreated to center stage.

"For the purposes of drama, the audience should imagine the
queen is wearing shoes," Peter Quince said, then exited.

Cobweb sighed heavily, which was my cue. I ran from the floor
stage left, leapt onto the stage, and did three cartwheels and a

backflip to land in her arms, my back bent, faux Hippolyta holding me up. I had some doubts about my tumbling ability, having been starved and shipwrecked, but it appeared the fairies' frolic was still sustaining me.

"Hello, Puck," said Cobweb.

"Your Grace," said I. "Fancy a bonk?"

"Perhaps. If you promise me a favor."

"I am your servant, ma'am," I said with a bow.

"I am to be married in three days, and before that time, I would like to meet with the goblin king. Can you arrange that?"

"A piece of piss, love. I'll have him here before dawn."

"Then lay on, Robin Goodfellow!" She was on me, and in the manner of the previously stated trysts, we raucously bounced through the tapestries, much to the delight of the audience. Once offstage she whispered, "You are a shit."

"*Moi?*" said I, in perfect fucking French.

She kissed me quickly and made for her mark onstage, where Drool and Snug were waiting as the watchmen.

"What do you tossers want?" asked Cobweb.

"Ma'am, to report, ma'am, that we witnessed something that would be of great interest to you and would be worth a reward to us."

"You shall have your reward. One of my silver armlets. What is your news?"

I peeked out to see Hippolyta rubbing her biceps where once she wore her silver armlets. Surely, this was not how it had happened, but it was close enough that the point was finally reaching her. She knew we knew. Theseus leaned forward on his chair and was paying close attention. The rest of the audience was watching a silly farce, but the royals were all watching an indictment.

"The duke is to receive a love potion from the fairies," said

Snug, reading slowly from a slip of parchment. "Which he intends to enchant you with upon your wedding day. We are to retrieve it from the Puck at Turtle Grotto at dawn tomorrow."

"Well that shall not happen. You shall stop him reaching Theseus with the potion," said Cobweb. "In any way you can."

"The Puck is very clever. The duke had us out searching for him all day."

"Do not let the duke receive that potion," said Cobweb. "Now be gone, I have a guest coming."

Drool and Snug exited.

"Oh, I need some air," said Cobweb. She went to the back of the stage and held aside one of the tapestries, through which I stepped, then bowed as Tom Snout in his Oberon togs skipped through.

"Away, Puck," said Snout as Oberon. "Come for me before dawn."

I exited through the arras but peeked out. This would be the scene where the show would shift to the audience. I checked my two remaining daggers and nodded to Peter Quince, who had two short scripts from which he might read, as well as a third option I'd alerted all the players to, which was to run for the antechamber if it came to it.

"Oh, my dark lord," said Cobweb. She moved to Snout and rubbed against him in a lascivious and seductive manner, accentuating their height difference, which, while ridiculous, was no more than that between Titania and Oberon. "Take me, use me, like the warrior tart that I am." Cobweb looked past Snout to catch my eye and made a silly grin, proud of her improvisation. What she couldn't see, and neither could the audience, was that much of the soot that we had used to blacken Tom Snout was now smeared on Cobweb's face and all over the front of her once-white gown.

I laughed. Cobweb saw her hand, blackened, then looked down her front.

"But no." She turned suddenly and went to the front of the stage, as actors do when changing their mind, so the audience may see the conflict in their visage. Or, in her case, the soot all over her. The audience burst into laughter, which energized Cobweb no little.

"First," she said, "you must help free me from the bonds of that putrid dongwhistle Theseus."

The players definitely had the attention of the royals now. Cobweb was doing smashingly improvising her lines with only the rough instructions we had come up with in the antechamber.

Snout moved up behind Cobweb and put his hands on her shoulders, leaving black prints wherever he touched.

"Anything, my warrior queen, if you will submit to my dread pleasures."

"You know I am a prisoner here," said Cobweb, "and even if I escape, there are scores of my soldiers who are hostages, for even as they walk free about the castle, they are allowed no weapons, and every one of my warriors is watched by one of Theseus's guards."

"A sad affair," said Snout.

"I am to marry, three days hence, and you and Titania are invited to the wedding. When you come, I want you to bring a cohort of your goblin soldiers, and when I give the signal, they must kill Theseus's guards and give arms to my warriors."

Before Snout could reply, before the audience could react to the idea of goblins, which they thought something made up to frighten children, a ferocious female war cry filled the hall, echoing up into the vaulted rafters, as Hippolyta pulled a dagger from under her gown and drove its point under Theseus's sternum. She continued to scream, even as she twisted the blade in his chest and his heart's blood poured out over her hand. "Now!" she screamed. "Now! Now! Now!"

"Go, go, go," said I to my cast. I shooed the players back toward the antechamber. Cobweb and Snout ran off the side of the stage after them.

In the hall the dark hoods were pulled back and goblins put blades to soldiers' throats at every door, disarming but not killing the soldiers. The audience screamed and rose to run, but each of the six double doors was slammed shut and bolted. Above, in the balconies, soldiers had been disarmed and yanked away, presumably held at sword point on the floor, while the balconies filled with goblins bearing crossbows, which they trained on the crowd below. Several of Hippolyta's warriors reached for the soldiers' weapons but were beaten back by the swipe of a sword or the aim of a crossbow.

"Now! Now! Now!" screeched Hippolyta, but her Amazon warriors could not respond to her call, all of them held harmless by armed goblins.

Hippolyta pulled the dagger from Theseus's chest and let him drop to the floor as she stood. She crouched and brandished the bloody dagger, ready for a fight. The audience members, including Hermia and Lysander, had moved away from her, leaving her alone with her dead duke. At the other side of the stage, Oberon was on his feet too, looking confused and furious. "Kill the guards!" he shouted, to no effect at all. He looked from balcony to balcony, and from each, a dozen crossbows were trained upon him.

I hopped on the stage and danced a jaunty jig to the edge, stage right, where Hippolyta waved her knife. At spirits, evidently.

"Everyone please take your seats," said I. "We are not finished here. I know this is unsettling, and several of you have probably soiled yourself, but be of good cheer, I assure you no one will be harmed."

"Yes they will," said Hippolyta, shaking the dagger at some goblin archers. "They will *all* be harmed."

I looked down on her, gave her my most beatific smile. "That knife is mine, love," said I. "If you don't mind." I held out my hand.

She turned as if to attack me and a crossbow bolt thunked into her empty chair, then another one right next to it. I looked to the first balcony, where a goblin wearing two silver armlets stared down, his crossbow ready to be reloaded. Gritch.

Hippolyta twirled the dagger and held it out, as if I would come get it.

"No, love, you bring it here. And do wipe it off." I gestured to my loincloth made from Helena's gown. "I'm wearing white."

CHAPTER XX

Act 3

"THE PROBLEM with act three," said I as I paced the stage, now back in my black and silver motley, my three throwing daggers home together across my back at last, the audience paying rapt attention, their concentration no doubt sharpened by the prospect of shiny black death raining down on them at a goblin's whim, "the problem is, we have prepared no act three. True, we could have just killed off all the sympathetic characters as we would have in *Pyramus and Thisby*, or in *Romeo and Juliet*, and sent you on your way grieving for lost love, but now we've rather written ourselves into a corner from which we must cleverly extricate ourselves with the use of guile, subterfuge, and, of course, the staple device of royals around the world: heinous fuckery most foul."

"Shoot him!" Oberon shouted to the goblin archers. "Kill the fool!"

I danced to Oberon's side of the stage. "But they won't, will they, oh king of shadows? Because you have no power but that they give you, and they seem not in a giving mood. Do sit down."

Oberon made as if to protest and I tsk-tsked at him. "All-licensed fool," I said, reminding him of what he still did not know—whether or not I had the powers of the Puck.

"You all will no doubt want to get to burying your duke, but first, let us meet the players and solve a mystery, shall we?" I waved my company onstage, all of them still in costume but for the fairies, who were back in their black robes. Helena had joined them and wore what was left of her torn, shortened, soot-stained gown.

"Ladies and gents, the Rude Mechanicals," I said with a wave of presentation. And there was terrified silence in the room. "Well clap, you wallies, if they weren't here you would be but a pile of bleeding corpses."

Tentative applause expanded to a full ovation, at which point I took my place at the center of the players and led them in a bow. The Mechanicals were veritably glowing with the attention, while the fairies looked a bit confused. Drool, wearing the hat of many tongues, well, drooled. Moth cradled monkey Jeff in her arms while I looked to the fairies and winked at Cobweb.

"Now, doubtless these three and Titania are the first fairies most of you have ever seen. But they have always been here, in the forest, where you are afraid to go at night. And you should know that only by their fertile magic are your lambs born, do your crops grow, are your milk pails filled, because this strange Athens of yours runs by forces not known in the rest of the world. These"—I waved to the balconies and around the edges of the hall—"these goblins, who graciously hold you hostage, while fierce, and frightening, and hideous—"

Gritch lowered his crossbow and waved to the crowd, displaying a smile you could grind your bones upon.

"—well, they are not entirely awful, but if you're afraid to go into the forest at night, they are a much better reason."

Gritch bowed.

I continued. "The one magical being you all know, by person or reputation, is, or was, Robin Goodfellow, the gentle Puck, who was murdered in the forest outside of Athens, and his killer is here tonight, and there he stands." And I pointed to Oberon, who seemed not at all surprised.

"I didn't kill the Puck," he said, less emphatic, I thought, than the situation called for.

"No, you did not fire the bolt that killed him, but you sent the goblin assassin."

"I did not," said the king of the night.

"Well why, then, did you kill Talos, the goblin who *did* fire the bolt? I saw it."

"Because *you* told me he killed the Puck, and the Puck was my faithful servant, and Titania wished justice. Or so *you* said."

"Aha!" said I. "Admit it, you met with Hippolyta, and she promised a silver armlet for the goblin Talos as pay to kill the Puck, then you arranged for him to be at Turtle Grotto at dawn to kill the Puck."

"How would I know where the Puck would be at dawn?" said Oberon. "I had sent him to enchant Titania, as in your little pantomime, and never saw him again."

"Twat," said Titania out of the corner of her mouth.

"Tart," retorted the shadow king.

The Indian boy studied the air before him, his visage as vacant as a cloudless sky.

"I see," said I, now walking back among my players.

"You're doing smashing," said Cobweb. "Tell them about Puck's three magic words, like Rumour told you."

I wheeled on Oberon. "But you were jealous of the Puck having dalliances with Titania, so you killed him."

"You're bloody barking, fool. You know well the Puck's talents, and their value to me, why would I kill him over this well-used slag?"

"Who killed the Puck?" shouted one of the goblins from the balcony.

Then a second goblin, from the floor. "Oi, who killed the Puck?"

Before I could get the crowd back a chant rose up, more voices each time, until two hundred or more voices were chanting, "Who killed the Puck? Who killed the Puck?"

I had really thought I had solved the murder, but this ungrateful rabble was not allowing me to formulate a second theory of the crime.

ENTER RUMOUR, PAINTED FULL OF TONGUES

He didn't blow in like a whirlwind, nor blink into existence like a shooting star, he came through the antechamber door and quite deliberately trudged to the stage, past Drool, from whom he snatched his hat of many tongues, which he pulled onto his non-head. Then came to stand next to me, center stage, where he glared for a moment while the crowd continued to chant.

"You're late," said I.

"*You are a disaster, a calamity, and an abject failure all rolled into one,*" said Rumour. "*I would say you were a disappointment, but with expectations below a worm's belly, that is not possible. You are a disappointment to disappointments.*"

"And you are ever a delight," said I. To the crowd, I shouted, "This is Rumour, a teller of tales." Which settled them not at all.

Rumour stepped forward, took off his hat, then pulled open his coat and turned, slowly, in place. And as he turned, the great hall went quiet as man and goblin took in the sight of a creature holding open a coat of waggling tongues, wherein there was no body, and above it floated a face with no head for a home.

"*I see you've killed the duke,*" said Rumour, his coat still open wide.

"I didn't kill him, the bloody queen of the Amazons killed him, and if you'd been here on time with the magic flower she'd be blissfully in love and the duke wouldn't be an expanding bloodstain on the pavers."

"*Well you've cocked it all up just the same.*"

"He's been bloody brilliant," said Cobweb. "Except for forgetting about the three magic words. Brilliant."

Rumour shook his head, turned to the audience, closed his coat of many tongues, and began.

"*Who killed the Puck? To know that, we must know why someone would want to kill the Puck.*"

"Because he was a shit," shouted Snug, rather out of nowhere. "'At's why I killed him."

"You didn't kill him," said Peter Quince.

"Well I wanted to."

"*Was it love? Was it greed? Or was it power? I submit, it was all three. The story starts a thousand years ago, when Theseus came to this land with an army, intent on conquering it as his kingdom. Well, the men who lived in this land submitted without a fight, for they were not warriors. But then Theseus's men ventured to the edge of the forest in search of new villages to tax, and when night fell, they were slaughtered by the hundreds by creatures that could barely be scratched by their bronze swords, the goblins. They knew no way to fight these men of stone, as they called them, so they explored to the south, where they encountered a race of tiny people we know as the fairies. Some they killed, some they enslaved, but most escaped deeper into the forest, and search as they might, Theseus's men could not find them by day. But that spring the grain did not sprout, the fruit trees did not blossom, the cows gave no milk, and even babies born to the women of the village were small and weak and soon perished. In hiding, the fairies did not dance, and in this land, there was no life but by the power of the fairies. Another season without their light and the mortals of Athens would be in famine, yet Theseus did not know the source of his misfortune and continued to send raiding parties into the fairy forest looking for fairy villages they might plunder.*

"*The queen of the fairies knew that her people could not long live in hiding and on the run, so she went to the black mountain in search of the*" *shadow king, the goblin king, Oberon, to ask him a favor. She knew the goblins were fierce warriors, and the mortals feared them, so she begged the shadow king to protect her people. So began a love story, for the fairy queen and the goblin king fell deeply in love. Oberon agreed he would pro-tect the fairies, send the goblins to the fairy forest to meet the mortals in battle and frighten them away, but he needed something beyond her love in return. Oberon's power over the goblins was tenuous, by birth only, and he was not one of them, but a hybrid creature of some other race. To satisfy his goblin soldiers he needed silver, and there was no more in the black mountain. The fairies had no silver, no possessions at all to speak of. Only Theseus, and the mortals, had silver to give, and while the gob-lins could slaughter the people of Athens and take their silver, they would then lose their source. The goblins were not sailors and could not go about in the day. But Theseus had an army, a navy, ships that could raid and trade and bring silver back to the goblin king.*

"A three-way bargain was made. Oberon would protect the fairies from the mortals, and in exchange, the fairies would dance and bring their fertile magic back to the mortals, and in addition, the fairies would do their dances just for Theseus, and from them, he would be-come immortal."

Well that explains how he could be so dogfuckingly old, I thought, and still walking about talking about his adventures.

"Under the arrangement, all the races prospered. Oberon, like Theseus, did not age or become ill, for he, too, was sustained by fairy magic. By and by, Titania had a child, a son, half fairy and half goblin, with more than the powers of either of the races. As he grew, his powers manifested.

"He was a shape-shifter, a spell-caster. He could travel great distances in an instant and return again as fast. But in his mind, he was as sim-ple and unassuming as a fairy, as dogged and steadfast and sturdy as a goblin. He took his parents to distant shores, planets even. He conjured skies full of art for their entertainment. Like his fairy brethren, he thought himself nothing but a servant, and as he grew more powerful, the king

and queen did nothing to disabuse him of the notion that he was merely a servant like the others, a slave to do their bidding."

"The Puck," said Cobweb loudly enough for it to echo in the high rafters.

"You were shagging your son?" I said to the fairy queen. "I know you poxy royals are inbred, but—"

"No," said Rumour. "Titania would use her son as a beast of burden, but she did not lie with him as a lover."

"On the day I first met him, Puck said he shagged two queens that day," said I.

"He said he'd 'seen two queens shagged,' that is not the same."

"Well, that's just unseemly," I said.

Rumour cleared his throat unnecessarily by way of dismissing me. *"As time passed, Oberon and Titania grew apart, indulged in dalliances with others, played out their jealousies, and, in the case of Oberon, his cruelties. Titania was banished from the Night Palace. She and her fairies went back to living in the forest. Oberon demanded Titania give him a harem of a hundred fairies to dance for him to keep him vital and alive, but his pleasures with them became much darker. He demanded the Puck stay with him and no longer serve Titania. By then, the Puck had grown into a young man, or a fairy-goblin version of a young man. Oberon found a spell that made the boy forget that the king and queen were his parents, and he thought himself only a servant, the goblin king the commander of all of his magic and powers. Yet the Puck still felt a bond to Titania, one he did not recognize, and although Oberon forbade it, he would sneak away and meet his mother and whisk her and an entourage off to distant lands, jeweled beaches and crystal mountains, where they could pass months at a time and return to Athens to find only a moment had passed. It was on one of these adventures that Titania found a tribe of feral fairies in India, wild creatures who lived among tigers and elephants. They were small like the fairies of Athens but dark skinned, with black hair, and they wore only leaves and the brown lace from coconut palms, or nothing at all. The Puck was smitten with one of the Indian fairies, and she with him, and in time she became pregnant with his child, although the Puck did not know it. Being a fickle youth, he moved on to other lovers and forgot his Indian love.*

"Oberon had become more cruel, and more jealous of the Puck's time away from the Night Palace, so the Puck would take Titania to a distant land, leave her with her entourage, and return to Oberon to quell his wrath, then retrieve his mother when time had passed. In such a way did Titania watch the Indian fairy grow big bellied with her grandchild, and the fairy queen was present with her servants when the girl gave birth. But alas, the Indian fairy perished giving birth to the child, and when the Puck came to retrieve his mother, she held a babe in her arms, which she brought back to Athens to raise in the fairy forest."

Every eye turned to the Indian boy, including Oberon's, whose face was a mask of fury. He loomed over the boy, glancing back quickly at the balcony, where Gritch still had a crossbow trained on him. Titania put her arm around the boy and pulled him close.

"He is still young, but already the boy shows signs he will have the powers of his father. Come, boy."

In an instant the Indian boy appeared next to Rumour on the stage, looking as bored and vacant as he had in his seat. The audience took a collective gasp.

"Go back to your seat."

The boy was back in his seat in a blink.

"I knew it!" said Oberon.

"You did not know," said Titania. "You are as dense as the stones you live among."

"At last Titania had her Puck, a protector more powerful than Oberon and his goblins or Theseus and his soldiers, so she set out to free herself from her bond."

"But," said I, "Talos, the goblin who killed the Puck, wore one of Hippolyta's silver armlets, given him by the watchman Burke. Surely—"

"I gave the watchman an armlet," said Hippolyta, "but it was pay to them for letting the goblins into the castle tonight. My other armlet I gave to the Puck."

"Which the Puck gave to the goblin Talos, as Titania instructed him."

"Talos described Burke as the one who gave him the bracelet," said I.

"As Titania wished. The Puck was a shape-shifter. She told him to deliver the silver to Talos in the form and uniform of a watchman. He did not know he was paying his own killer."

"I wanted only to stop Puck from delivering the love potion to Theseus," said Hippolyta. "I knew nothing of his murder."

"You killed our son!" said Oberon, and with that he reached over the Indian boy and seized Titania by the throat, lifting her completely out of her seat and throttling her as he roared, shaking her like a great onyx terrier worrying a rat, the silver blades of his fingertips digging into her neck. Oberon's motion caused his great crown to wobble precariously on his head, which was entirely too much hat for monkey Jeff to bear. He jumped from Moth's arms, leapt from the stage, and landed on Oberon's head, where he commenced to apply a rigorous monkey fuck to the shadow king's crown. In his enthusiasm, one of Jeff's back feet found purchase in the goblin king's eye and Oberon dropped the fairy queen and slashed at the monkey with his silver blades. Jeff screeched and slapped at the goblin king until his screams were drowned by a louder, angrier scream. Sensing something coming at my head, I ducked as Moth sailed over me, from the stage to the goblin king, where she caught him by the head as she flew by and raked her razor across his throat, swinging around as she went, sending Jeff tumbling to the floor and Oberon spraying green blood over her, the still-twitching Titania, and the Indian boy, who calmly looked down on Titania's supine form sprawled on the flagstones.

Moth, sitting now next to the two dying royals, held out her arms and Jeff jumped into them. She petted his head and whispered to him. She stood and walked away, letting the razor clatter to the floor.

I looked to Gritch in the balcony. "Mate?"

The goblin shrugged. "I didn't know who to shoot."

"Which leaves us," said Rumour, calling the horrified audience's attention back to center stage, "with the three words left us by the Puck. The three words that he wanted to be his legacy. The three words that, had the hapless English fool figured them out, might have saved us much of the carnage we have witnessed tonight."

"Oh, do fuck off," said I.

"Good guess, but no—"

"Oh, for fuck's sake," said Cobweb.

"Is that three?" asked Peaseblossom. "I feel as if that may not be three."

"Kill them all!" came a voice from the balcony, and everyone looked up to see Robin Goodfellow standing on the edge of the balcony.

"Kill them all!" said the Puck.

CHAPTER XXI

The Three Magic Words

"DON'T KILL them all," said I. "Don't kill anyone." I looked to Gritch to confirm my command. A nod from him so terse his great goblin ears flapped a bit.

The Puck looked around the hall. "I was going to kill them all. It was to be a surprise."

"No," said I. "No more."

"What about her?" said Puck, pointing to Hippolyta. "We should kill her. Kill all the powerful and corrupt."

"No," said I. "No more."

"But she killed me."

"No she didn't. A goblin killed you, on the order of Titania."

"Well that's hurtful," said the Puck. "I was going to kill her anyway, for sending the fairies to Oberon's harem, but Titania kill me? No."

"Yes. You paid the assassin yourself when you delivered the silver bracelet to the goblin Talos."

"She said that was for weapons for the Amazons, so I had to appear as a mortal to deflect blame."

"She lied."

"But I was her favorite."

"Not anymore. The Indian boy was her favorite in the end." I nodded to the boy, who now stood over the dead king and queen, studying them.

The Puck leapt from the balcony, but instead of falling he blinked to a spot by the Indian boy. He leaned in close to the boy, examined him, looked him top to bottom, then looked to Rumour, who was smiling in a self-satisfied way center stage. "Why does this sprout get a hat? I didn't get a hat."

"*The boy is your son, Puck,*" said Rumour.

"Bollocks," said the Puck. "Did he say that? Did you say that?"

The boy looked at his father like a dog watching a bee working a flower, intrigued by the movement, but relatively sure he was not good to eat.

"*Come here, boy,*" said Rumour. And the boy blinked to his side. "*Could anyone but the progeny of the Puck do that?*"

"Blimey," said the Puck. "A son. With a hat."

"Yes," said I. "Magical and a bit thick—the boy is yours. Not so his turban. Puck, mate, you are short of time and there are things you need to put right."

I jumped onto the stage and waved for the Puck to join Rumour at center stage, while I went to Cobweb. "This is why you were so late?"

"Took a massive fucking frolic to bring him back, dinnit?" she said. "He'd been dead three days."

"Does he know? Does he know he won't last?"

"I think he can feel it." She nodded at the Puck, who was leaning on Rumour as he coughed, which seemed to distress him more than finding he had a son.

I pulled my coxcomb from my head, went to the Puck, and fitted it on his noggin while I whispered in his ear, "This is yours, mate. You traded for it fair and square. Now we have to put this disaster in order. Your best magics, Robin Goodfellow, for this shall be your legacy."

I patted his back and pushed my way in front of Rumour. "You could have just told me," I said sotto voce. "Those were not magic fucking words."

"I didn't say they were. I said they were the key."

"You said the lovers were the key as well, and that was utter rubbish."

"Puck used his second flower on the lovers. There was no flower to give to Theseus to use on Hippolyta. He had no intention of delivering that potion. Had you not been so thick, you would have known he had gone to Turtle Grotto for another purpose. His intent, since hearing Hippolyta's plan with Oberon to bring the goblin soldiers to the wedding, was to gather the powerful and corrupt and kill them all."

"Your hat smells of monkey fuck," I replied. I turned to the audience and raised my hands for quiet.

"What you have seen here you shall remember only as a dream. When you wake, people of Athens, you shall go about your business, your farming and your trades, and give thanks to the forces of nature, and once a year, in the spring, take an offering of fabric, needle and thread, and simple tools, and leave them in the forest to the east. And four times a year, take a hundredweight of silver to the forest in the north, and for this the gods shall protect you from invaders. As now, you may never enter the forest at night, and never shall anyone do harm to a squirrel, for any reason, lest they bring bad harvests onto the city. You will remember goblins and fairies only as stories you tell to delight your children. Further, the working people of Athens shall keep the fruits of their labor, and only give so much of it to the city as is required to pay these offerings and protect the city, not to enrich their leaders or maintain a conquering army."

I looked at the Puck, who was now holding himself up by bracing himself on Rumour. "Can you enchant them thus?" He nodded. "And change Nick Bottom back to a man?" Again the nod.

"Hippolyta, you shall take your warriors and your ships and return home to your island, never to return to this land again, lest you meet the wrath of the goblins. Do you understand?"

"Can't we kill her?" said Puck.

"No, we can't kill her. She did not come here of her own will, she was as much a slave as you. Can you do the spell?"

"Yes. But they should give shoes and hats to the fairies as well."

"As you wish."

"Goblins, return to your castle of night, and remember that the stars and the moon are yours, always, and you owe no one obeisance for their silvery shine. Return to this city no more, and never harm your fairy brethren, for their magic sustains you too."

"And no eating fucking squirrels!" shouted Cobweb.

"Yes, that too," said I. I turned to the Puck. "The stage is yours."

The Puck struggled forward but gathered his strength, sucking in great breaths of air, and puffed his chest and prepared to speak. But there came a loud clacking noise before the stage.

Hippolyta looked up at me and shrugged. In front of her, Drool and Peaseblossom were bent over the body of Theseus, and the fairy was forcefully beating the dead duke in the face with an iron candlestick, which was where the racket was coming from.

"What are you doing?" I asked.

The two simpletons looked up with great satisfied grins. "Drool told me about tooth fairies," said Peaseblossom. "I shall become a tooth fairy."

"We've nearly a bagful," said Drool, holding up a coin purse that looked suspiciously like it had been fashioned from someone's scrotum.

"I'm going to get silver for them and give it to the goblins for saving our mates," said Peaseblossom, holding up a bloody molar.

"That is not how it works," said I. "That is not how it works at all."

Rumour cleared his throat loudly and hopped off the stage, deferring to the Puck.

"The magic is done," the Puck said to me. "They will not re-member." Then he moved to the edge of the stage, and to the audience, said:

"If we shadows have offended,
"Think but this, and all is mended,
"That you have but slumber'd here
"While these visions did appear.
"And this weak and idle theme,
"No more yielding but a dream,
"Gentles, do not reprehend:
"If you pardon, we will mend:
"And, as I am an honest Puck,
"If we have unearned luck
"Now to 'scape the serpent's tongue,
"We will make amends ere long;
"Else the Puck a liar call;
"So, good night unto you all.
"Give me your hands, if we be friends,
"And Robin shall restore amends."

Then the Puck took a great bow, another to the right, another to the left, and the audience, on their feet, applauded, even the Amazons and goblins. And the Puck dropped to one knee. Cob-web ran to him and caught him before he fell, lowering him to the floor. I hopped up on the stage and knelt over the Puck. Cobweb held his head, cradled in her lap, and the players gathered round and watched, heads bowed, as he died.

✣　✣　✣

TWO DAYS later, Drool and I stood at the edge of the city, kitted out for travel, faced down by Nick Bottom and the three fairies.

Bottom shook my hand. "You shall always be our master of the theater. Thank you."

I slapped his back. "You were a brave player and a good friend," said I. "I hope Mrs. Bottom forgives you your trespasses."

"Ah, I don't mind sleeping out with the animals for a bit. Finding my sense memory, don't you know. Her anger is waning. I'll be back in the house in no time."

"Good luck, then."

"Jeff is staying," said Moth, holding Jeff. "We are in love."

"But he's a monkey," said I.

"Not all the time," said Moth.

"Yes, all the fucking time."

"Well, in the daytime we play in the trees together and it's lovely."

Jeff, cheeky monkey that he was, nodded and nuzzled into her neck.

"He is his own man," said I. "Perhaps you could get a hat, to keep his interest when you're a fairy."

"She can have mine," said Cobweb. She removed her bycocket hat and fitted it over Moth's eggshell-colored hair.

"I bought *you* these," I said, pulling a pair of shoes from my satchel and handing them to Cobweb. "I think they'll fit."

She took them, turned them around in the air, examined them. "I am ruined now," she said.

"Yes," said I.

"And I have these," said Peaseblossom, holding up her nut-sack full of teeth. "For I am now a tooth fairy."

"Yes," said I. "How many do you think you have?"

"Don't be a twat, Pocket," said Cobweb. Then, as she eyed her shoes suspiciously, she said, "Where will you go?"

"We have no master but the road, love. We shall wander looking to bring laughter and joy to all we meet."

"We are fools," said Drool.

"Fancy a frolic before you go?" said Moth.

"Thank you, lamb, but I think not. We already waited until sundown so we could say goodbye."

We hugged them each, except Jeff, who is a shit and tried to bite Drool. Cobweb clung to my neck for a long time and, truth be told, I did not want to let her go when I did.

"Farewell then," said I, and I turned and headed down the road.

"Ta," said Drool.

I was determined I would not look back, and did not, until Drool said, "Pocket." He threw a thumb over his shoulder. Cobweb was following along behind us, taking awkward and tentative steps in her new shoes.

"What are you doing?" I called.

"I'm coming with you."

"We may never come back this way."

"I know. But I have never been anywhere but here. I would see other places."

"There probably won't be other fairies. You won't be able to frolic."

"I have frolicked before."

"But you're a squirrel."

"Not all the time."

"But a great crashing lot of the time. The time when it's not dark."

"In the day I shall ride on your shoulder and listen to you tell stories of wonder and adventure. Besides, you fancy me, Pocket of Dog Snogging."

"Fuckstockings," said I, defeated. "Come along, then."

AFTERWORD

A Fool in the Forest

I KNOW WHAT you're thinking. You're thinking, "*A Midsummer Night's Dream* is my favorite Shakespeare play—it's the only one I've ever made it all the way through without thinking about things I'm going to eat—and you, sir, have besmirched this delightful, spirited sex comedy with murder, goblins, and gratuitous squirrel shagging. You, sir, you cad, you dilettante, you scrofulous scribbler of unscrupulous satire, have made a sow's ear from a perfectly lovely silk purse. Why? Why, why, why?"

Okay, harsh, but fair.

Why?

I picked *A Midsummer Night's Dream* because it's my favorite too! It's everybody's favorite (except for Shakespeare scholars and people who still believe in love). It's the most performed of all of Shakespeare's plays, largely, I'd guess, because the plot is so silly and the setting so flexible. Sure, the script says "Athens," but it's no Athens anyone has ever seen. There's no historical period referenced at all, and most of the play is set in the fairy wood, which can be anywhere, really. Once we're into the wood (and we more or less have to accept that the fairy wood is "but a dream"), the possibilities bloom. I've seen productions of *MSND* where the motif was punk, glitter rock, punk-glitter-rock, Victorian country house, Bollywood London, and even one high school production where the fairy wood was the city dump and the fairies wore bin bags as costumes (clever cost-cutting move for wardrobe). In fact, it was the fungible nature of the fairy wood that made me want to send Pocket there in the first place. I found him in a false medieval Britain (*Fool*) and moved him to a historical thirteenth-century Venice (*The Serpent of Venice*), largely because I wanted to tell a story about a water monster in the canals, so I thought, how could I challenge my oh-so-articulate fool? It would be easy enough to get him from the last story to a thirteenth-century Athens, but then what? Since the fairy wood could be anywhere, why not, I thought, make it 1940s San Francisco? Golden Gate Park, to be specific. Have fairies and fools talking tough in the mean streets of Fog City, playing with the language and the extreme discomfort of Pocket dealing with cars and firearms and floozy fairy queens that would as soon stick a shiv in you as take your hat. So I send a rough outline off to my editor, like I do, to make sure we're all on the same page, and she comes back to my agent with, "Maybe not this next book. We'd like to see a one-off this time."

This is a first for me. So I call.

"So," I say, "I hear you guys would like something different?"

"Just right now," she says. "You can do a Shakespeare book after this if you want. What else do you have?"

Well, what I have is a giant bucket of nothing, but I *have* been researching the bejeezus out of 1940s San Francisco. So I say, "I could do a kind of noir thing set in San Francisco in the 1940s. Sort of a *Maltese Falcony* kind of thing. Or another whale book. Or, uh . . ."

"Yes, do that," she says.

"Do what?"

"The *Maltese Falcony* kind of thing."

"Okay," I say, having absolutely no idea what the hell I'm going to do.

And that is how big-time publishing is done.

I know you hear about screenwriters doing this all the time—pitching a Gothic horror novel set in Empire-era England, and the producer saying, "Great, can you set it in L.A. in the 1970s, and can it be about a dog?" And you go, "Sure thing." But in the book business, this was new for me. So I said, "Okay." Then I went off to write a book that I cleverly titled *Noir*, so you would know that what you were getting was not derived from a Shakespeare play. Which brings me back to a book set in the world of *A Midsummer Night's Dream*. Now that I've used up all my 1940s San Francisco research and tough-guy talk, and I'm left with a deadline and a dream, I think, *I'll just dive into the history of Shakespeare's source material and see what I can find.*

See, of Shakespeare's thirty-six plays, thirty-three of them are derived from other sources: Italian love stories, or history, or myth, or in some cases, just lifted from someone else's play (*King Lear*). Unfortunately for me, *A Midsummer Night's Dream* is not one of the thirty-three. Sure, Hippolyta is first mentioned in Greek mythology as the daughter of Ares, the god of war, and the queen of the Amazons, and is killed by Heracles for her girdle, killed by Theseus at her wedding, or killed by another Amazon fighting beside Theseus at her wedding, but generally, her role in mythology is to have a magic girdle, become a prisoner of war, and get killed at a wedding.

Theseus, on the other hand, is an epic hero, and appears in the *Odyssey,* where he slays the Minotaur; jilts Ariadne, who gave him the thread to get out of the Minotaur's maze; kidnaps Helen of Troy (whom they just called Helen when she was at home in Troy); and generally does a lot of fighting and questing stuff—so, a great backstory, but the Theseus of myth is clearly not the staid and formal character Shakespeare portrays in *MSND*. So he offers little help in expanding the story, except to serve as another noble from whom Pocket could "take the piss."

The fairies, I thought, *surely they will offer some unexplored gem of myth that I can festoon with knob jokes!* And while Oberon, it turns out, appears first in a thirteenth-century French heroic song, *Huon de Bordeaux,* as Auberon, a fairy king who helps Huon (the knight who kills Charlemagne's son) work off his crime with quests, about Oberon's character we are told almost nothing except he is the son of Julius Caesar and Morgan le Fay. Really? Ancient Britain? So the Oberon of myth is what we in literature call "a frog fart in a wind storm," and, although interesting, he isn't as interesting as Shakespeare's Oberon, who sets up his wife to shag a were-donkey over a little Indian boy with whom he is inexplicably obsessed.

And Titania doesn't show up in literature at all, it appears, until Shakespeare names her in the play in 1595, although the entire *MSND* play may have been inspired by the success of Spenser's epic poem *The Faerie Queene,* which was written for Queen Elizabeth five years before, and which met with great approval by the queen and other dignitaries in court who were mentioned in the poem. It might be noted, however, that while Spenser's fairy queen, Gloriana, is a chaste and virtuous virgin (the hero of book II, Guyon, is the leader of the Knights of the Maidenhead—I'm not making that up), which is why Elizabeth I loved her, Shakespeare's Titania is an egregious floozy, which is why audiences love *her.* So there *were* possibilities, but nothing quite as fun as what was already in the play. (It should be noted, though, that the first and second moons of the eighth planet are named for Titania and Oberon and even now they are chasing each other around Uranus.)

The other characters are numerous and almost indistinguishable from one another, and the lovers are mostly annoying, although the magic potion Puck puts in the boys' eyes was a fun device, a version of which I used in *Fool,* the first of Pocket's adventures. The lovers are made doubly annoying by a habit of Shakespeare's that we learn not to do on the very first day of Famous Novelist School, which is giving characters names that start with the same letter. It's so annoying and often confusing that I even found myself having to look back to the character list at the beginning of the play to keep Helena and Hermia straight. On the stage, where each character is represented by a different actor, not a big deal, but on the page, where they are but names, a huge pain in the ass. So I found no backstory to expand there.

So left with nothing to expand the story, I came back to where I started with the inspiration in *A Midsummer Night's Dream*: Puck, Bottom, and the Rude Mechanicals. See, Pocket himself, although he first appears in the context of *King Lear* in *Fool,* was born of Puck and Nick Bottom. His name, in fact, is a fusion of Puck and Bottom. Like the Puck, he is a rascal, a servant with more presence than his masters, a catalyst for the action, and, like Nick Bottom, he is rather inexplicably used and abused by powerful females, and not entirely against his will. The Mechanicals, the ragtag group of well-intentioned working-class dolts, are more or less the team that Pocket has to put together to accomplish his mission. His Seven Samurai, his Dirty Dozen, his Impossible Mission Force. With a monkey. The key, then, was to give them a mission to accomplish. So, as one does, I murdered the Puck.

He's everywhere, at warp speed, with unimaginable magical powers, yet beyond seducing the odd joiner's wife or shagging the odd marmot, he seems rather humble and subservient. It could not stand, and leaving Puck and Pocket too long in the same story is one rascal too many, so down goes Puck. So everyone has a mission: find the killer.

I am always drawn to Shakespeare's subservient characters: Emilia, Iago's wife in *Othello*; Nerissa, Portia's maid in *The Merchant of Venice*; Shylock's daughter, Jessica; even Kent, in *King Lear* (and Oswald in *Lear* makes for a terrific minor villain). They're more of- ten than not more clever and more noble than those they serve, and often, they are the only speakers of truth in a play, yet they function as foils, sometimes little more than placeholders. And there's no more interesting group of foils to me than the fairies in *A Midsummer Night's Dream*, so I brought them into Pocket's mis- sion force to sort of explore their own agendas.

I sense you thinking, "What about the squirrels?"

The squirrels are mine, not Shakespeare's. These days I do my writing at a small getaway hovel in the redwoods, about an hour and a half north of San Francisco, a place I affectionately call the Squirrel Ranch. The room where I write is three stories up and surrounded by redwood trees, so I quite literally work among the squirrels. I started feeding them a few years ago, so now at any given time there are one or two fluffy-tailed rodents out on the deck crunching away on peanuts or walnuts or sometimes pizza, pretending they don't see me or the other squirrel sitting right there. (Gray squirrels are solitary feeders, but they know a good deal when they see it, so even if it's against their nature, they'll put up with each other if there's a free lunch. Authors are like that as well.) I guess they sort of worked their way into the story, because it occurred to me that there would be some fun possibilities if the fairies changed into squirrels during the day. So there you have it. The elements that went into making *Shakespeare for Squirrels*.

In addition to the characters from *A Midsummer Night's Dream*, I also modelled Blacktooth and Burke on Dogberry and Verges, the men of the watch from *Much Ado About Nothing*, but upon rereading *Much Ado* in preparation, I found I quite liked Dog- berry, and although a nitwit, he endeavored to be virtuous, so I changed the names to allow Blacktooth and Burke to fall on the more villainous side of the fence. Rumour, Painted Full of

Tongues, the narrator, is drawn from *Henry IV, Part 2,* where he is, indeed, described as being "painted full of tongues" but exhibits none of the supernatural powers nor hubris with which I have endowed him. There have been lines and phrases drawn from the other plays as well, but as I forgot to make note of them, you may bask in your own cleverness if you recognized a line.

Acknowledgments

Thanks to Austin Tichenor, intrepid leader of the Reduced Shakespeare Company, who read the manuscript and gave helpful notes, despite being more than somewhat over the charm of *A Midsummer Night's Dream*. Also, thanks, as always, to my editor, Jennifer Brehl, for her cool head and composure in the face of so much heinous fuckery, and of course, thanks to my wife, Charlee, for putting up with it all.

About the Author

CHRISTOPHER MOORE is the author of sixteen previous novels, including *Noir, Secondhand Souls, Sacré Bleu, Fool,* and *Lamb*. He lives in San Francisco, California.